THE
CRYSTAL
DOVE

THE
CRYSTAL
DOVE

MOLLIE HARDWICK

St. Martin's Press
New York

Library of Congress Cataloging-in-Publication Data

Hardwick, Mollie.
  The crystal dove.

  I. Title.
PR6058.A6732C7   1986   823′.914   85-25154
ISBN 0-312-17823-9
First published in Great Britain under the title *Girl with a Crystal Dove* by Methuen London Ltd.

First U.S. Edition

10 9 8 7 6 5 4 3 2 1

FOR HERMIONE,
*when she's old enough
to enjoy magic and marvels*

AUTHOR'S NOTE

I have explained the workings of some stage 'magic' tricks in this book – but only those already given away by Victorian magicians. Modern practitioners need have no fear.

CONTENTS

BOOK I: ELEANORE

BOOK II: NELDA

... yet shall ye be as the wings of a dove
                              covered with silver
And her feathers like yellow gold.

THE PSALMS OF DAVID

BOOK ONE
ELEANORE

Young girl, fleeing her position as a
governess, finds love and fame as a
magician's assistant on the streets
of nineteenth century London.

'You shan't eat it, Mamma!'

'Eleanore – my dear – please ... '

But Eleanore Carey's strong young hands had picked up the dish and tipped its contents on to the carpet. It was a threadbare carpet, and would be still more threadbare by the time the congealed mess of fish, fats, onion and flour and curry powder had been scraped off it. Eleanore regarded the horrid sight with satisfaction, her mother and small brother Harry with shock, and in Harry's case, regret. His dark eyes filled with tears.

'It would have been *something* to eat, Nell,' he gulped. 'Better than nothing.'

She turned on him. 'Curried cod? Made without cream, and the fat rancid? *I* know, I've seen what they do in that kitchen. Well, it's not good enough for you, either of you. Look at you – skin and bone, not enough on you to feed a sparrow.'

They were certainly no advertisement for the cook. Amy Carey was small-boned and fragile, her once-pretty auburn hair faded to a cindery nondescript hue, her fair delicate skin, withered and wrink-led from the suns of India, sallow against the unrelieved mourning she wore for a husband six years dead, killed at Lucknow. The bell of her skirts was unfashionably narrow, like a servant's, since material cost money – her half-sisters' money. The only relics of the Captain's Lady she had been were the small diamond earrings that she would never give up, for they had been a wedding present from her bridegroom.

Harry, ten years old, would be tall one day if he were properly fed, but now he was thin and stunted. The face of a starved cherub was

11

crowned by the family hair, the red hair of the Bromes, but of a paler shade than the lioness's mane that streamed about his sister's shoulders.

Something more than food had nourished Eleanore through her eighteen years; pride, will-power, joy in life, an animal quality which her spinster aunts, Eudora and Minerva, thought deplorable. Fatherless, dependent on their charity, the girl should have been humble and thankful, careful of their money, polite and submissive. Whereas she had never been any of these things, since she had come to their house, five years ago in 1858, wearing the airs of a memsahib, with her widowed mother and small Harry. Sternly and repeatedly she had been told that in England one does not clap one's hands to summon a servant, bark commands in a foreign language, or expect constant personal attendance and the picking up of objects fallen on the floor. Slowly, disbelievingly at first, Eleanore had learned the new rules. They seemed to her very silly. What were servants for, after all? And there had been great affection and respect between the Indian servants and her family, whereas Aunts Eudora and Minerva spoke to their English ones as though they were pariah dogs.

Eleanore now felt sorry that she had tipped their supper on to the carpet. After all, it would be the wretched maid, Patty, who would have the job of scraping it up. She would offer to help. Her mother's eyes followed hers to the unpleasant mess.

'They'll be *so* angry,' she said. 'And it won't do any good.'

'It might just make them realise that we don't want to live like paupers, Mamma. Their own relations! They ought to be ashamed.'

'But they are only my half-sisters, dear – it isn't quite the same ...'

'So half-sisters and their children only rate half-rations, is that it?'

Amy sighed. Eleanore was always battling for her and Harry, which was very noble and commendable of her, but her mother often wished she would not, since it caused so much rancour and coldness. It was sad enough to have lost a dear soldier husband and to be reduced to the charity of relatives without having to go through unpleasant scenes. But there was no quelling Eleanore, who seemed to have inherited her father's fighting spirit as well as his height and strength. How incongruous she looked now, in her badly-cut skirt

12

and bodice, with its prim round collar and neat row of buttons down the front threatening to fly off, impelled by the swell of her full young bosom. Long ago, before she was grown to womanhood, she had looked enchanting in a native sari, its folds of silk gauze sheeny and brilliant as a butterfly's wings, and embroidered with jewels, wound gracefully round her body, a circlet of coins about her brow and bright hair. They had sometimes dressed her as a boy, a young princeling, in trousers and jacket of cloth of gold, the hair hidden under a majestic turban of golden gauze. The child had burning ambitions to be a temple dancer, one of those lithe maidens whose sinuous limbs could weave and twist into seemingly impossible postures, whose wrists and ankles and toes tinkled with the chime of tiny silver bells. Their perfume was as of many flowers, their kohl-darkened eyes were as huge and lustrous as the eyes of does, and their bodies were like Eleanore's body, full-breasted and full-hipped, with hand-span waists and long lovely legs.

But a memsahib could never become a temple dancer, her *ayah* gently told her, for it was not permitted. Yet the child Eleanore danced at home as she had seen Siva's and Parvati's acolytes dance, with supple snake-like writhings that translated bone and muscle into a fluid ripple of movement.

Perhaps she had breathed in all that was beautiful of India with her earliest breath, drawn when her father's regiment was in the Punjab, fighting in the First Sikh War, and her romantic young mother lay under a mosquito-net in their bungalow, nursing her daughter and languidly reading the early poems of Tennyson, from which came the baby's name.

> Thy dark eyes open'd not
> Not first reveal'd themselves to English air ...
> The oriental fairy brought,
> At the moment of thy birth ...
> The choicest wealth of all the earth,
> Jewel or shell, or starry ore,
> To deck thy cradle, Eleänore.

Eleanore, as she grew, disliked her name increasingly. The original of the poem seemed useless for anything but drooping about smiling a deep ambrosial smile, or sitting, in a shadowy saloon, on silken cushions half-reclined, while her idiotic lover drooped even more uselessly, with a languid fire creeping through his veins, losing his colour, losing his breath, and drinking the cup of a costly death. It all seemed even sillier in this cold, foggy England, where in the dark house in Bloomsbury two unmarried women led their dessicated lives without joy.

The cushions in this house were not silken, but coarse hessian covered with knobbly needlework; the languid fire burned in only three grates, those of the aunts' drawing-room, the kitchen and the upstairs sitting-room shared by the three Careys, while drinking the cup of a costly death might have been pleasanter (depending on how it tasted) than drinking tea, coffee and cocoa which were invariably cold by the time they had been carried upstairs to the drab room, once a bedchamber, with its dully patterned walls stained with patches of damp, furniture not wanted elsewhere, and pictures which Eleanore thought of as Views of Nothing and Nobody.

A turn-up bedstead, which by day became a mere blank panel against the walls, and had to be pulled down and re-made every night, was Amy's. A low passage led off the room – so low that even Harry could not stand in it upright – to two tiny antechambers where the children slept. The servants themselves had no worse, possibly better, if one had explored their attic floor. Harry was frightened of the passage, running through it bent double to his own cubby-hole with its fly-blown print of the Infant Samuel and the battered, beloved remains of a toy elephant made for Eleanore by a *syce* who had adored her. Now its grey cotton skin hung away from its stuffing, the imitation gems that had decked its saddle and headdress were gone, its *howdah* shapeless and flattened. But Harry loved it: his papa had given it to him, he said, and had been smacked by his Aunt Eudora for saying so.

Nobody ever smacked him again after Eleanore heard him weeping desolately over the elephant, which Aunt had not been able to remove from his clutching arms. Fourteen years old, a fire-haired Fury in a

14

flannel nightgown, she had marched into her startled aunt's bedroom.

'You beat my baby brother, I hear?'

'I chastised him for telling lies. What are you doing here, Eleanore? Go back to bed at once.'

Eudora pulled the bed-clothes up to her chin as she sat up, unable to believe she was hearing aright, though her nightcap was only a cotton one, and loose-fitting. Her hand hovered near the bell-rope.

'If you knew any history,' continued her niece, 'which I don't suppose you do, you'd know that little King Edward, the boy-king who died, was never beaten, ever, whatever he did wrong. His friend Barnaby Fitzpatrick was beaten instead, because he was Edward's whipping-boy. He was big and strong, and Edward was little and weak, which is just like me and Harry, so if you're going to beat anybody, it will be me. Here – get on with it!'

Before the shocked eyes of her aunt, Eleanore jerked open the top buttons of her nightdress and dragged it down, exposing a lily-stem throat and tender breasts which would have stayed the hand of an executioner. But not Aunt Eudora's. With a smile of grim enjoyment she clambered down from the high bed and reached for her cane, kept conveniently close to assist her rheumatic steps.

'If that's what you want, my girl, you shall have it. Kneel.' She pushed Eleanore to her knees facing the bed, and began to lash the bare shoulders. Faint gasps escaped Eleanore, but no cry. Her aunt punctuated the blows with words.

'Shameless – wicked – wretched – heathen – brat! Not fit – to – live – in a Christian house.' Thus she worked off the hatred she had always felt for Eleanore's mother, the pretty petted youngest child of their father's second wife, the one whose birth had put hers and Minerva's noses out of joint, the object of their spite and jealousy. Amy had married when they had not, Amy had borne children, Amy had come home to foist herself and her orphaned offspring, the puling boy and the brazen girl, on the half-sisters she had wronged by her very existence.

When the beating was over, the arm exhausted, Eleanore got to her feet and pulled the nightdress up, agonizingly chafing her back

15

and shoulders. She had not known it would hurt so much; it was the worst pain she had ever suffered in her life. She managed to say haughtily, 'There, that's how it's to be in future,' before stalking out. Barnaby Fitzpatrick would not have allowed himself to cry within his floggers' hearing, nor would she. Only when she reached her own room did she allow the tears of pain, shame and anger to gush out.

The scene had been repeated, though never again so violently, whenever Harry committed some innocent misdeed, and Amy's hair grew greyer with grief for her children. Then, quite suddenly, the slight girl matured into a young woman, slim but strong, taller than either of her aunts; and it did not need saying that a hand laid on her would be repaid doubly and the menacing cane snapped in two. Barnaby Fitzpatrick's occupation was gone.

A timid knock preceded the entrance of Patty. Under-sized for her twelve years, clad in a parody of a uniform, consisting of a tattered and dirty bib and apron over a too-short black dress, a wisp of material which might once have been somebody else's cap attached to her straggling hair, the charity-girl from the Union workhouse paused aghast at the door, staring at the overturned dish and its contents.

'Oh, miss!' There was no doubt in her mind that Miss Eleanore was responsible, after all the threats she had muttered about bad food. Unhappy thoughts chased themselves through Patty's mind: what a cruel shame to waste good food that she would have eaten with thankfulness, what a mess the carpet was in, and what terrible hot water she would get into, for they would certainly blame her. Her childish mouth trembled and turned down, and Eleanore was instantly remorseful.

'It's all right, Patty – it was my fault, I'll clear it up. Just smuggle a dishcloth and some water upstairs, will you? Then nothing will be said about it.'

'But – miss, you won't get no supper.'

Amy said, 'I see you have brought us a pudding, and that will do. Go along, now.'

When the child had gone, still big-eyed with apprehension, Amy

16

turned to Eleanore. 'My dear, I know you meant well. But you see where your impetuous behaviour has got you. Now my sisters will not learn that you rejected their food, so it will have been in vain, and that poor creature will be blamed in the end – just you see. Harry, eat your pudding, dear.'

It was a bread pudding, cheap to make, especially if the smallest quantity of sugar and only one egg were used in it, but Harry ate it gladly. Amy pecked at her portion, and Eleanore's was soured by remorse and dread, for mutiny in this house would surely be followed by retribution.

Indeed it was. Two sets of footsteps on the winding staircase announced its arrival. The Misses Cordwell stood in judgment over their prisoners.

Eudora and Minerva were respectively fifty-one and forty-seven years old, and with no pretensions to looking any younger. Eudora was the taller, wrinkled of face and scraggy of throat, her mouth a hard line of disappointment with life and determination to make the lives of others as disagreeable as possible. Minerva, short and plump, was lymphatic of countenance, her cheeks fat cushions squeezing into slits her small chilly eyes, masked by steel-rimmed spectacles, and her three chins irked the high collar of her bodice. Both ladies were encased from waist to boots in fashionable crinoline, making them perfect moulds for large-sized dinner-bells, and their sloping shoulders were encased in coarse-knit lace shawls, long enough to sit on and known as Yaks, since they were supposed to be made from the hair of that animal. Their own grey hair was pulled into net snoods. Amy's one constant source of gratitude was the fact that her half-sisters took after their mother.

'Well, Amy!' Eudora generally took the lead in any campaign. 'What's this I hear?'

'I don't know, Eudora,' said Amy innocently, while Harry quaked and Eleanore put down her spoon and prepared for battle.

'Don't know? We have just encountered Patty on her way upstairs with cleaning materials, and a tale of some kind of accident in your room.'

Minerva's eyes encountered the 'accident', and she pointed

17

accusingly to it. 'There's your answer, sister.'

'So it is, so it is. May I have an explanation of this extreme carelessness?'

Amy was about to speak when Eleanore saw a chance to state her case. 'It wasn't an accident, Aunt Eudora. I threw the dish down because I was so angry and – and disgusted with the food.'

'Angry and disgusted – I see. May we know why?'

'Yes. The fish was the cheapest kind, and not fresh – I daresay that poor skinny cat in the kitchen had turned it down already. And the fat was stale too. If the dish had not been curried, Cook wouldn't have dared to send it upstairs – but I expect she was drunk as usual.'

Eudora had gone pale, Minerva purple. They struggled for words, but Eleanore continued relentlessly. 'It isn't for myself I mind, you know. I'm strong and healthy, but poor Mamma and Harry need good food and ought to get it. It isn't as if you were poor …'

Eudora stepped forward and struck her niece across the cheek. 'Be quiet, you insolent, low girl. How dare you speak to me like that! I thought you at least a young lady … '

> 'There was a young lady of Deal,' recited Eleanore wildly,
> 'Who ate up five platefuls of veal,
>> A sausage, a ham,
>> And some raspberry jam,
> And said "I have made a good meal."'

Harry giggled uncontrollably, but Amy's hand went to her heart, which always began to pound when a domestic scene threatened. If she were lucky she might faint and distract attention from her daughter.

'The severest punishment, I think, sister?' Minerva suggested, and Eudora nodded.

'If you think you can whip me you may think again,' said Eleanore, her eyes flashing. 'I could take you both on with one hand, as the boys say. Well?'

'No, you are a little too old for chastisement. But a night in the cellar should cool your evil temper – yes, sister?'

18

'By all means.'

Eleanore felt her blood run chill. She had twice endured confinement in the room beneath the kitchen, so damp that little could be stored in it but coal. Black beetles swarmed there (though they swarmed even more thickly at night in the warmth of the kitchen fire), the stench of household rubbish piled in the area for the dustcart to collect seemed to have soaked into the very stones of the walls and floor, and rats skittered in and out of holes and through the narrow grating. It was a place of terror and extreme loathsomeness.

Very briefly Eleanore contemplated resistance. She was more than a match for her aunts, but besides them there was stout Cook and bony Eliza-Ann the housemaid; between them they could haul her ignominiously down the stairs, and that was not a scene she cared to picture. Minerva saw her hesitation, and said slyly: 'Perhaps Harry should accompany you.'

'No! It's all right, Harry, you shan't go. Don't cry, Mamma, I shall do very well.' And with head high she stalked out of the room and down the stairs to her dungeon.

Harry, not looking at his aunts, said with great bravery for his gentle nature, 'Mamma, I wish we didn't live here. I don't like it, and Nell don't either.'

Eudora, about to follow Minerva downstairs, turned in the doorway and bestowed on Harry a slow, thoughtful smile.

Eleanore was sitting on a packing-case, moving as little as possible, for the big crooked nails which studded it waited to tear her skirts and her hands. The cellar itself was pitch dark, only faint darts of light filtering in now and then from the street above through the rusted iron bars of the grating; the rays of a policeman's bull's eye lantern, the thin glow from a gas street-lamp, the lights of a carriage going by. There was no moon on this cold night of early spring, for which the prisoner was thankful – moonbeams would have shown her things she preferred not to see, such as the rat cleaning its whiskers in the corner.

Since that first experience of the cellar, when she had cried and screamed, she had found that the only defence against its horrors lay

19

in the use of her imagination. Again she retired inside it, seeing mental pictures behind her closed eyelids.

First she took herself on a tour of the house, starting with the kitchen and scullery, where the servants worked, ate and gossipped, and Cook drank porter with her soldier friend, who dropped in most evenings. Nothing worth lingering for there – a few wool-work texts on the walls, crude figurines of the Queen and the late Prince Consort, a fire always burning and a kettle always on the hob, piles of dirty dishes, which diminished by night and grew again in the morning. She could hear their clatter now, faintly, and the clink of patterns as somebody crossed the brick floor.

Upstairs went her fancy, to the ground floor, a narrow passage, two doors leading to a room whose front half was an austere dining-room, the back a cold little parlour looking out on a sour-earthed, cat-haunted garden. If there had been a man of the house it would have been called his study, or den, or library; as it was, nobody used it much. Eleanore was sorry for it; mentally she furnished it with chairs and a sofa upholstered in bright chintz, pretty lampshades, and some charming little chairs of black wood inlaid with mother-of-pearl.

Upstairs again to the sisters' drawing-room and bedroom, where the furnishings were old-fashioned because they dated from the days of the sisters' father's first marriage. When Amy sat with them she would look wistfully at this piece and that, and remember it in her childhood, so happy with lovely young Mamma and kind elderly Papa, only darkened by the shadow of her half-sisters. Eleanore knew this, and longed to move those particular things upstairs to their own parlour, when Amy could enjoy them. But much hope of that ... Their furniture was utilitarian and cottagey. Only a few dear prized things made that room their own: Roderick Carey's sword, brought home by a fellow-officer, was one. Nothing else had been retrieved after the mutineer's rifle-fire had killed him – his comrades defending the Cawnpore battery post had no choice, in that perilously exposed position, but to drag away the bodies of the fallen for swift burial. (And there had been no possessions of his of any value in the officers' quarters, which might have been sold for his widow's benefit; the sale of his commission was all the compensation she got.)

His photograph, framed below the sword, was fading now to a yellowish tinge, the handsome dark features blurring, the splendid uniform disappearing into the background of artificial palms and balustrade the photographer had set behind him. But Eleanore would never forget him. Tears pricked her eyes, and she hastily switched her mental vision to the other picture in their parlour.

It was a portrait, not more than a foot square, in a black-painted frame, showing the head and shoulders of a woman. Age had darkened and cracked the oil paint, making detail hard to see, but the character of the sitter had been stronger than the medium. A firm-featured, high-nosed face, not very young but with beauty still lingering in the fine dark eyes and shapely mouth, framed by waves of dark hair on either side of a widow's peak, and above the hair a heart-shaped cap or bonnet edged with pearls and coloured gems. The head was set firmly in the centre of a wide mill-wheel ruff, elaborately starched and goffered, as in later portraits of Queen Elizabeth.

Eleanore longed to know what the dress had been like, but Amy thought that the head had been cut out of a much larger picture, now vanished. What was arresting about the lady was a look most unusual in stiff Elizabethan portrait subjects: a look of controlled mischief, of merriment that lurked around the eyes and in dimples at the corners of the mouth. The face was not like Eleanore's in detail, yet in a strange way she saw herself in it. Not surprising, said Amy, for she was Eleanore's ancestress.

'What was her name?'

'Jacquette – the Lady Jacquette Brome. She was wife to Sir Harry Brome, a knight of Berkshire in Elizabeth's day, but there was a story in the family that she was not as well-born as he – that she had been a singer, or dancer, something of that sort.'

'Even a witch?' The tale had often been told, but Eleanore never tired of hearing it.

Amy smiled. 'Something like that was hinted at. But your papa said any witchcraft she used must have been in her eyes and her smile. He was very taken with her – I was quite jealous. The other story was that the family had royal blood and were distantly related to Queen Elizabeth.'

21

'The red hair?' Eleanore prompted.

'That was her husband's, Sir Harry's. My mamma, who of course was a Brome herself, told me that the husband's and wife's colouring had come down in the family in a strange way – always dark eyes like hers and red hair like his.'

'Like mine.'

'Yes, and my own and Harry's. Our Harry's. That was another tradition – the eldest Brome son was always called Harry.'

'But none of the girls Jacquette?'

'No. I suppose the name went out of fashion.'

'What happened to her – to them?'

'Nothing very remarkable, I believe. They managed not to get into much trouble, having suffered religious persecution under that terrible Queen Mary, and kept well clear of the law. Only Sir Harry was rather extravagant, like his family before him, and so were all the eldest sons, right up to Sir George a hundred years ago, who gambled away most of his inheritance.'

'He wasn't really the heir, Mamma, or he would have been Sir Harry.'

'Quite true – his elder brother was killed while hunting. So all the money and estates went, and no sons were left. My father took his wife's surname, you see, to keep the name alive, so I was born a Brome. Once I went to the place we had once lived in, Brome Hall in Berkshire, but it was all gone, turned into cottages and many of the bricks taken away for building. Nobody knew anything about Lady Jacquette, except one very old man who called her "the French-woman". I wonder if she was?'

'I wonder.' Eleanore sought the almost-smiling dark eyes for an answer, and got none. 'But I think she knew secrets, Mamma.'

'What kind of secrets?'

From pondering on the secrets, and what they might have been, Eleanore's thoughts strayed far away from the cellar, from the house in Gower Street, through other streets that lay around it: London the rich and rare, which she was free to roam without maid or other escort. Only, sometimes, she called upon a relative whom the aunts despised and hardly acknowledged – Uncle Gil, their blood brother

22

but 'nothing to them', as Eudora put it. He was quite old, but white hair had come upon him prematurely, and his face was dark red and flaccid with drink. He had never married, and lived alone in two poky rooms above a bookseller's shop in Great Russell Street.

There Eleanore found a refuge, for Uncle Gil was a gentle soul much like her grandfather and not in the least like his fearsome sisters. With him as a willing guide she explored the dazzling treasure-house of the British Museum, the dirty thoroughfares which had been Hogarth's Beer Street and Gin Lane, the strange Museum of Sir John Soane in Lincoln's Inn Fields. Here Eleanore was fascinated by an Egyptian sarcophagus which was quite solid yet so transparent that when the guide shone a light just inside it one could see a full-length figure of the Goddess Isis lying there enclosed, like a corpse.

There was no end to the wonders and excitements poor lonely Uncle Gil showed her, and when he was 'a little lushed', which was a polite phrase for his having been too dead drunk the night before to get up the following morning, she adventured on her own.

The museum exhibits and spectacles like the Diorama and the waxworks were wonderful, but what Eleanore liked best were the outdoor entertainments. Of course it wasn't possible for her to enter a theatre or music hall, but what richness there was on the streets! The German bands, players of the hurdy-gurdy, eccentric dancers and mimes, Punch, Judy, the Baby and the Policeman, dwarfs and giants and monstrosities filling in time before the next Fair, acrobats and conjurors luring the idle with the cup-and-ball trick − this last intrigued Eleanore very much, not because she thought it easy for the conjuror to fool his customers, but because it must be possible to be one jump ahead of him. Why should he always win?

One day, in a little court off Covent Garden, she had stopped to watch credulous strollers being taken in by the swift interchange of the coloured cups that covered the desired ball. When her turn came to risk the precious sixpence she had to spend a curious thing happened. It seemed to her that her wrist, extended to point out the cup she fancied, grew heavier as a quite firm grasp descended on it, though nobody stood by her. Without her volition, her finger switched to point to the red cup, not the blue one. The conjuror started.

'Burst me! Nobody never pulled that 'un before.' Honest within his limits, he removed the cup; there lay the ball beneath. 'You a pro, young tiddler?'

Eleanore had been fourteen, and still very close in spirit to India. Yet she had no notion why she answered, 'It was not me, but the *burra memsahib*.'

'The *wot*? Ere, gerroff. Take yer tanner and scarper.' He tossed the sixpence back to her, and she ran before he could change his mind.

Half-dreaming now in the dark cellar, too cold to think clearly, her mind wandered back to that day. She saw her own extended arm, and upon it a hand, pretty and shining-nailed yet very strong in appearance, and above it a lace cuff of the most delicate intricate workmanship, through which black velvet could be seen. The hand of a *burra memsahib*, a great lady? But who, and how, and why ...?

Now her grasshopper mind was away again, to another great lady, the beautiful Princess Alexandra of Denmark, flying across the sea in a flurry of bridal lace, like a great swan, to marry the Prince of Wales, but then unaccountably turning into a white marble statue in the middle of springing fountains which shed a foam of bright bubbles around it, and they in turn became the billowing steam in the wash-house on a Monday morning when Eleanore took the family linen downstairs for the laundress ...

And then a bell was clanging loudly, not far away, and hoarse shouts were encouraging domestics to 'Bring out your dust'. It was morning; the dust-cart was trundling up the street, and grey light filled the cellar. Eleanore stirred her stiff, cold limbs, tore her wrist on a nail of the packing-case, swore briefly in Hindi, and got to her feet with difficulty. The night was over, and her punishment. With luck last night's episode would soon be forgotten.

But she had not seen her Aunt Eudora's parting smile at Harry.

II

A Penniless Usher

'The girl is getting out of hand, sister,' remarked Eudora, biting off a thread. She was embroidering in Berlin-work a chair-seat, which would never be directly sat on, but covered by a linen protector.

'True, sister.' Minerva pulled irritably at the large mourning brooch enclosing a lock of her dead mother's hair, which was pressing against her third chin. 'Last night's behaviour was unpardonable. She has no manners and no graces. I fear the money we spent on her education was wasted, every penny of it.'

Eleanore's education had consisted of attendance at a small day-school in Alfred Place, a short distance from the house. Seven or eight children usually made up the number of the pupils, and were of various ages. The teacher was a retired governess, who had suffered so much from the tormentings of her charges that she had settled for her own premises, two rooms on the first floor of a tall thin house. She had a smattering of knowledge of several subjects, enough to pass muster with parents who cared to test their children at home, though her French did not go beyond the confines of the textbook or her simple arithmetic embrace anything beyond addition, division and multiplication.

But she was a natural story-teller, who could hold a child's attention by her recital of tales from history – respectable history, uncomplicated by too many tedious treaties or shocking battles. From her came accounts of Noted Children in History (Edward and Barnaby Fitzpatrick were among them), strongly flavoured by Miss Sutton's own preferences and prejudices. Thus, little Lady Jane Grey was a paragon of learning and already a martyred angel in the sight of Heaven, and so was the weak young prince who would become

25

Charles I, while the infant Mary Tudor can only have been a stubborn and cruel child with nasty foreign ways, and Oliver Cromwell a great coarse bully. It was all entertaining and harmless, and cost the sisters only two shillings a week.

Harry's had cost nothing at all, since there was no local establishment for boys. His mother had taught him as well as she could, and now Eleanore was passing on some of Miss Sutton's lore to him. She no longer went to school, and Miss Sutton had intimated, very gently, that perhaps Eleanore was not quite suited to being an assistant teacher.

'It is time she was put to work,' said Eudora.

'High time. But to what? Miss Sutton was quite clear that she would make a very poor governess. She is too much of a romp, too obstinate, too ... '

'Fleshly?'

'Exactly. The other day I saw a Man looking at her ... '

They exchanged a wordless glance of understanding. The time had been when Men had looked at the young Amy, never at them.

'No use to ask advice of the pastor,' sighed Eudora, 'since they attend that other place.' Amy, in a nonconformist household, had remained obstinately Anglican, taking the children every Sunday to the church of St Pancras in the New Road, a fine classical building whose west front was held up by six strapping caryatids. Her sisters were members of the congregation of Bethesda, a nonconformist chapel in the Tottenham Court Road. Eleanore had been allowed to attend a service there once and sit on a seat of extreme slippery hardness with her aunts sitting on either side of her, like warders. In the free seats behind sat the poorer people, studiously ignored by the Misses Cordwell entering and leaving, their peculiar aroma drifting into the more privileged pews. The sermon, delivered in alternate shouts and hoarse whispers by a gentleman in lay clothes, did not edify Eleanore apart from giving her food for thought about the possible life-history of the Worm that Dieth Not, and the music was not pretty as it was in church.

No, the pastor would not be much help.

'She might serve in a shop – a respectable shop,' suggested Minerva.

'*Our* niece? Most unsuitable. Better to become a companion to some widowed lady ...' As far off as possible, both silently thought.

'I fear there will be nasty tantrums, when she is forced to leave her mother and brother. You know her temper, sister.'

'Too well,' Eudora brooded. Then her face brightened.

'I have had an excellent thought. If the boy were not here, she would not wish so much to stay. How can we ... ?'

They conferred, heads together, as though the three upstairs might be clustered outside the door to listen.

But they were not. Harry was at his lessons with his mother. Eleanore had gone to visit Uncle Gil, who was comparatively sober, in funds and good spirits. He took her for midday dinner to a chop-house near St Paul's.

'Let's treat this as your birthday, my love, though it an't. 'T'wouldn't do to buy you any pretties in the shops; those two hags would have 'em off your back. Lord, that I should be cursed with a couple of sisters like that! What a confounded borin' family to belong to.'

'Never mind, Uncle, you're nice.'

'Yes, I am, an't I, when I'm not bosky from Blue Ruin. Don't you ever take to it, gal - cheers you up, then pulls you down. Why, I've been known to blub like a babby, a feller of my age. Don't you ever touch the gin-bottle, niece – there's murder in Old Tom.'

'No, I won't, it smells horrible. I'll take ...' She studied the neatly handwritten menu. 'I'll take a half-pint of porter, a dozen oysters, pease pudding ... no, I won't, for it comes with trotters. I'll have a steak and kidney and potatoes in jackets. If all that's not too expensive, that is?'

Uncle Gil shook his head, gazing on her with admiration. 'Not for you, Nell. Nothing's too good for my little Nell. What a spanker of a wench you are, to be sure!'

Eleanore turned pink with pleasure, tossing her mane under its little pork-pie hat. 'You're very kind, Uncle, and I'm glad you call me Nell, for I hate my proper name. Only you and Harry don't use it. But I say, not *little* Nell, if you please, for it reminds me so of that awful droopy creature in *The Old Curiosity Shop*, that Miss Sutton was always reading to us, and I can't abide her. A regular muff, if you ask me ... oh, oysters, how splendid, and bread-and-butter too.' She abandoned conversation to the enjoyment of her meal. Gil Cordwell, who also liked food, though not so much as drink, watched her with the keenest pleasure. He had never seen a young person eat so much, yet she'd a waist like a bed-post.

The meal over, he voiced a notion that he had been turning over in his mind. 'I suppose you wouldn't – seeing it's your birthday, or as good as – you wouldn't like to look in at the Oxford tonight?'

Eleanore's mouth fell open. The Oxford Music Hall, an elaborate new building at the corner of Tottenham Court Road and Oxford Street, was familiar to her, sitting on its island opposite Meux's great brewery. Its fame was wide, for food, drink and entertainment of a high quality. She had often paused to read the bills posted outside: Mdlle. Manietta, Mr Levy Hime, Mr Sims Reeves the celebrated tenor, Mr Arthur Lloyd the *lion comique*, (who will render his famous ballad *'Immensikoff'*), Mr J.H. Stead, 'The Perfect Cure', Mr Delano, the prestidigitator – whatever could that mean? It was enough to give one wild dreams.

'I couldn't, Uncle. What could I tell them – or Mamma, for that matter? It would never do. Oh, dear.'

Gil looked sly, laying his forefinger alongside his nose.

'But if they didn't know, my dear? If you told them a little story?'

Eleanore thought hard. Out in the evening, in the dark – alone. What little story could account satisfactorily for that? An idea dawned. 'I could say I was going to a confirmation class at St Pancras Vicarage. They don't know when the classes are, or what time. Only I shouldn't have to be out long.'

'Seven o'clock to eight. Just an hour! There'll be something doing even as early as that, now they do two houses a night. No need to eat there, it's not compulsory, you know.'

They were agreed, Eleanore excited but nervous, Gil jubilant. And, as though fortune favoured the wicked, nobody asked any awkward questions. Amy was pleased at her daughter's apparent upsurge of piety, Eudora and Minerva full of warnings about the perils of the evening for solitary young ladies. But Patty could not be spared to accompany her, and Eliza-Ann, when asked, developed a sudden painful bone in her leg which would prevent her from walking as far as the New Road.

'Mayn't I come with you, Nell?' Harry pleaded. 'I could wait for you, or come in and listen, because I shall be confirmed myself some day, shan't I?' Eleanore hardened her heart and refused. She would willingly have taken him with her to her real destination, but there just might be something in the entertainment which would be harmful to one so young. Her heart fluttering and her step light, she set out alone.

And, after all, Gil had been too optimistic. The performance had not started, would not start for another hour. On the wide stage above the rows of tables being set for supper men in aprons scuttled about dragging scenery flats into position, shifting a grand piano and a harp, shouting and whistling as they worked. But Eleanore hardly noticed them. Enraptured, she stared about her, at the galleries with their brass rails, the intimate caves that were the private boxes, the soaring pillars leading the eyes up to the forty-two foot high ceiling, carved and gilded, with – wonder of wonders – twenty-eight great stars of crystal, hanging like spiders. But unlike spiders, they glowed and sparkled with the miraculous glow of gaslight, creating a brilliance such as Eleanore's eyes had never seen before within doors. Their radiance was thrown back and doubled by a huge sheet of plate glass rising behind the stage. It was as though the Indian sun had somehow been captured and brought to this gorgeous place to solace Londoners weary of fogs and rain.

Gil was also staring around him, but not at the splendours of the theatre. Waiters were darting about, arranging cutlery, making the tables handsome for those who would sit at them later. Gil eyed them longingly.

'Y'know, I could do with a drink. You stay there, that's a good gal.' Eleanore hardly noticed that he had vanished in the direction of the bar. She was lost in her surroundings, possessed by a feeling that she had not had since the first year in England, when she had wept in her sleep with longing to go back to the warm bright land of her birth, the kindly brown faces and soft voices of the servants, the flowers and the colours. Somehow, this place was like that – her dream of home. Yet how could it be? No Indian building had ever been like this. Instead of the scents of the Careys' 'English garden', of which her mother had been so proud, there was a strong redolence made up of size, back-stage carpentry, gas, beer, tobacco smoke, patchouli, onions and last night's audiences. The management had not thought of airing the premises. But Eleanore sniffed it, inhaled it, loved it, revelled in it like a pit pony put out to grass.

A young woman came on to the stage from the wings followed by a stage-hand bearing a small table. He put it down, flung a black cloth over it, and the girl arranged on its surface a number of objects, none of which Eleanore could identify. Then both went off and returned carrying a wooden box some six feet long, which they up-ended. Again and again they made the trip, with a painted screen, a large wicker basket, and something they placed behind one of the four classical statues which stood guard over the stage. Eleanore noticed that these seemingly massive figures and their plinths could be moved as easily as things of cardboard.

She was not aware of how long she had been standing there, watching. A hoarse voice beside her asked, 'Anything you want, missie?' She came back to herself with a start.

'Oh – no, thank you.'

'Waitin' for someone?' The management was more than broad-minded towards assignations made during the course of the evening, for they encouraged trade, but lone ladies soliciting were another matter.

'Yes, my uncle.' Before the waiter had time to raise cynical eyebrows Gil had appeared from the bar, wiping his lips. The waiter drifted away, but Eleanore stood, her eyes on the stage, a dazed look on her face.

'Sorry for bein' so long, m'dear, got talking, you know how it is. Here – compliments of the management.' Another waiter was behind him, bearing a wineglass on a tray. 'Nice glass of brown sherry, make it up to you for being left high and dry. Won't be dry after that, eh?'

'Oh, but I'm not – I mean I mustn't. The aunts will know.'

'Don't they hand out booze at the parsonage, then? Come on, drink it up, gal, it'll put roses in your cheeks – not but what there's some in 'em already.' He surveyed her curiously. 'Feelin' all right? Not goin' to swoon or anything?'

'Good gracious no. Uncle — what are those people doing on the stage?'

'Eh? Oh, settin' up for a magic act – Nostro, or Nostramus or some such name. Can't be up to much as he's first on the bill.'

'Magic – what sort of magic? Like the rope trick that the jugglers do in India?'

'Couldn't say, I'm sure. Come on, then, if you've got to go, I'll see you to the door. Forgive the old man for bringing you here under false pretences, my love, and spoiling your treat. Thought there'd be something going on. You can't have enjoyed yourself much, all alone in this barn of a place.'

Eleanore clasped his arm with both her warm hands: 'Oh, but I have, I have!'

Nothing was said when she got home, out of breath and flushed. But she knew, when saying good-night to Eudora and Minerva, that they smelt the sherry. She was caught out in a lie and would be punished. Perhaps it would be the cellar again. When they merely presented cold cheeks to her she was disconcerted. Something would come of her escapade, but what?

Two weeks had passed before she found out; two weeks of April weather, tempestuous showers and sudden benisons of warm sunshine that turned the raindrops to diamonds on London's trees, their fresh green triumphing over the winter's black. Eleanore's spirits were at their highest. She felt as though some marvellous change were about to come over her life. Perhaps the aunts were mellowing, for they had spoken to her only mildly since the music hall episode, had even taken drives together in a hired brougham instead of remaining as oppressive presences in the house, day in and day out. A missionary campaign was being waged at Bethesda, whose lady members were busying themselves with the stitching of elementary garments to be worn by heathens, who would have otherwise continued to gambol in shocking nudity. Neither Amy nor Eleanore was asked to help in this worthy undertaking, for which both were grateful.

It was a beautiful May morning, with a thrush singing at the top of the stunted tree outside the parlour window. 'We should go out and enjoy ourselves,' Amy told her children. 'What would you like best? the ducks in the Regent's Park, or the soldiers in Whitehall?'

'The soldiers,' said Harry eagerly. 'I'm going to be a soldier like my papa.'

'Then you'd better eat up your pudding every day instead of leaving it, or you'll be too little and thin. Now hurry up and get your coat.'

They were almost ready when a sharp rap on the door announced Eliza-Ann. 'The mistresses would like to see you in the droring-room, please, M'm.'

Amy said, 'Bother' under her breath, and aloud, 'We were just going out. Is it urgent?'

'D'reckly, Miss Eudora said.'

'Tell her to say we've gone already,' hissed Eleanore.

'Of course not. Very well, Eliza-Ann, we'll come down.'

The sisters were sitting one on each side of their fireplace, upright and expressionless. 'Come in,' Eudora said, 'and sit down.'

The three of them ranged themselves on a sofa with an uncomfortably low-railed back. 'We were just about to take the air, as the morning is so fine,' Amy said. 'Will whatever you have to say take long?'

'Not long. It is simply this – we have decided that Harry must go away to school.'

In the silence that followed three faces turned white as marble. Then Amy began to tremble, and Eleanore, between her and Harry, put an arm round each of them.

'I don't think we heard you correctly, Aunt,' she said. 'Have we not agreed long since that Harry is too delicate to be sent away?'

Eudora threw her a quenching glance. 'Possibly he is too delicate because he is mollycoddled, cosseted, over-indulged by you and his mother. Do you want the boy to grow up into a spineless ninny?'

'He is learning nothing,' put in Minerva. 'You never had much brain, Amy, and I fear you are incapable of teaching any child. Harry will have to make his own way in the world, which he certainly will not be able to do if he remains in your charge.'

'How dare you speak to my mother like that!' Eleanore raged. 'You never even take any interest in Harry's lessons, and Mamma teaches him very well indeed, and I've brought him books from Miss Sutton's, and ...'

'Hold your tongue, miss! Your recent behaviour has set no sort of example to a young child, and we think it better than he should not live under the same roof as one so rebellious and ill-conducted. Is that not so, sister?'

Eudora nodded. 'It is. You may think we are blind, miss, and see nothing of your conduct. Young women who tell lies and enter this house smelling of liquor and tobacco smoke are little better than – a word I cannot bring myself to speak. A servant who behaved so would be dismissed.'

'But as you can't dismiss me you are punishing me by sending Harry away.' She clutched her weeping brother tighter and gave Amy's shaking shoulders a reassuring squeeze. 'Very well, then, I'll admit everything. I *have* been disobedient, I *have* been naughty, I *have* told lies – well, one lie. But I was only with Uncle Gil, and you mustn't blame him. It was just one small brown sherry, and ... So you can punish me as much as you like and treat me as Harry's whipping-boy again. I don't care what you do, only don't let these two suffer for what I did. They're good, they've done nothing.' She faced them proudly, already feeling the cane across her shoulders and seeing the cellar-rats running over her feet.

'What a deal of ranting nonsense,' Eudora said.

'I never heard such stuff,' Minerva concurred. 'You talk like a wicked play-actress, which I daresay you will finish up being, if nothing worse. Pray don't imagine yourself a story-book heroine, for you are nothing of the kind, but a self-willed child, dependent on our charity. You may be humbly thankful to us both for sending your brother to a school where he will learn to be a man – perhaps.'

Eleanore was silent. Amy pulled herself together enough to ask haltingly, 'Where is this school you have fixed upon?'

'Oh, none of the famous schools, in case you had imagined Eton or Harrow for your boy,' replied Eudora. 'We have chosen a modest private establishment in Highgate, kept by a Mr Channer.'

'A most respectable man,' added Minerva.

'Recommended to us by a gentleman we much esteem, Mr Manfred Pye. Mr Pye is a Justice of the Peace, and is confidently expected to become an Alderman of the City of London.'

'*So* well-known,' said Minerva, 'for his piety and charitable works. He is a highly respected deacon of our chapel, and an occasional preacher.'

'But what is the school like? Will Harry be comfortable? Is it clean? Will they be kind to him?'

Eudora laughed shrilly. 'Dear me, Amy, you must think very badly of us if you imagine we would send our nephew to some kind of penitentiary. I hope we can be trusted a little farther than that.'

'Of course ... But – shall I be able to see him often?'

'As to that I can't say.' Eudora had already ascertained that Mr Channer did not encourage holidays or visits home by his pupils. Harry clung to his mother, his face hidden against her breast.

'Since you are already in your walking-clothes,' Eudora continued, 'it would be a convenient time for us to drive to Baker's in the Tottenham Court Road and purchase a school outfit for Harry, since his own clothing is so unsuitable.' Her eyes raked disparagingly the outgrown jacket and trousers which Amy had not been able to afford to replace, instead letting down turn-ups which were now showing signs of raggedness, and the shirt with a frill at the neck which Amy favoured. Harry's thin childish ankles and wrists protruded pathetically, the white skin of his fragile neck showed up the yellowed linen of the frill. He looked like any waif from the poorhouse, thought Eleanore bitterly.

'You will not be accompanying us, Eleanore,' Eudora informed her. 'The brougham only holds four with comfort.'

'I would prefer not to accompany you,' Eleanore retorted with truth.

From a front window she watched the expedition depart, Amy and

Harry clinging together like birds on a frozen bough. Two red spots of rage stood out on her cheeks, and from her lips flowed silently a stream of invocations to the gods and spirits of her native land: Kali the Terrible, with her necklace of skulls, Rudra the Archer, whose shafts despatch his victims to the next world, Ravana, chief of the evil Rakshakas, and an assortment of powerful demons. If these beings had immediately obeyed her instructions the brougham would have reached the premises of Messrs Baker at 137 Tottenham Court Road with two of its passengers mere heaps of charred ashes among the straw on the floor. But they gave no sign: perhaps their influences could not pierce the cold clouds over London.

The day Harry went to school was the blackest one in the Careys' life since their arrival in Gower Street, almost five years before. Then, Harry had thought it the ugliest place he had ever seen, and had cried to go back to India, in spite of all the chaos and fear of their flight from the Mutiny. Now it was his home, and he cried bitterly at leaving it. In his new uncomfortable Rugby suit of tweed, and the shirt with the stiff collar, he felt quite dreadfully strange even to himself, and clung to everything familiar. He made a last trip down the basement stairs to take a farewell of little Patty. She was the only other child in the house, and they had been friends. They wept in each other's arms, under the disapproving cold eye and red nose of Eliza-Ann.

'Oh, don't, Master 'Arry, don't go on so. It won't be that bad – not as bad as 'ere.'

'It will, it will. Schools are awful, Patty! You haven't read *Tom Brown's Schooldays* and I have. The big boys beat the littler ones and – and torment them, and I don't know what. Sometimes boys die ...'

'If 'twas so the missuses wouldn't 'a sent you, now, would they?' (But secretly she thought they would.) 'You'll find it won't be 'alf like what you think. An' you got your Mamma and Miss Eleanore to come back to, mind. I ain't got nobody if they was to send me away.'

The kitchen cat, washing her paws on the rug, raised her head at the unusual note in the human voices. Harry flung himself down beside her and hugged her hard, to her discomfort.

35

'Tibby, don't forget me, Tibby. You were always nice to me and I saved you bits of sardine, and now you won't get them.' Harry's tears fell on her striped head, but she bore the dampness patiently, not struggling, for this human had indeed taken more notice of her than had any of the others, except the big one with the long red fur. She gave his hand a perfunctory lick.

The labouring horse toiled up Highgate Hill, pulling behind him what Eleanore thought of as the tumbril. It contained herself, the silent Harry and Amy, and Eudora, in charge of the firing party. Past the Old Crown, the first resting-place for horses, past the mansion called after Cromwell, up into the narrow High Street of neat little houses, shops and inns, past the Gate House. To this village Amy and her children had come in the happier past for refreshments at the Spaniards tea-house. The wide expanse of the Great North Road stretched before them, sparsely bordered with dwellings. A mile or so along it the driver pulled up outside a large double-fronted house faced with grey stucco, its narrow front garden railed round, a brass plate on the brown-painted front door. Harry, who had imagined some huge building with frowning battlements, was faintly relieved, and Amy felt that it could not be so bad if it were indeed a house, not an institution. Eleanore regarded it grimly, prepared to judge it on its merits, if any.

A starched maid opened the door. Yes, Mr Channer was in and expecting them. From a room on the right of the hall came a buzz of voices in unison, the boys at their lesson. The maid showed them into a small, stuffy parlour lined with books, which looked as though they had not been taken down from their shelves for the past forty years.

Mr Channer was as colourless as was possible for a human being, as if Nature had given him the ability to merge unseen with the pages of the dusty books. His bald head was not pink, but brown-mottled, his fleshy-jawed face was like lard, his eyes, behind pebble lenses, were as glassy as goats' eyes. Even his suiting was no longer black, but faintly greenish with age and wear, the collar speckled with dandruff, and his cravat the hue and texture of parchment. When he greeted Eudora his thin voice held a strong tinge of north London. 'No gentleman,' thought Eleanore. He did not shake her hand so much as enclose it briefly with his own cold flabby one; she saw Harry draw back from his touch.

'So this is Master Carey,' he said. 'Not Carey Major or Carey Minor, but Carey Solus, eh?' He tittered at his own joke, made whenever a new pupil without brothers was presented to him. Laboriously he took down the details of Harry's background, stooped over his desk.

'I hope,' said Eudora, 'you will be able to effect a Marked Improvement in my nephew, Mr Channer. He has been brought up largely without a father's influence. You will find that he lacks Moral Strength, for he has been greatly over-indulged and petted – ' Amy gave a faint mew of protest. 'Petted, I say,' repeated Eudora, with a quelling glance. 'I rely on you and your assistants to put some manliness into him. He requires the constant company of males, having been reared in a female household with no strong, noble example before him.'

Harry piped up in a trembling voice. 'My papa was a soldier and I'm going to follow *his* example.'

'Are you indeed.' Channer slid his spectacles down his nose and regarded Harry over them. 'I think we'll take your education in hand without more delay, young man.' He banged a handbell on his desk. The maid who had opened the door appeared, genie-like.

'Fetch Lyon, Clara.'

'Yessir.'

Lyon could not have been far away, for she was back in a moment with a tall youth, more man than boy, slender and shabbily dressed. Eleanore's thoughts darted to *The Life and Adventures of Nicholas Nickleby*. Was this a Smike, the Poor Drudge, or a Nicholas, the Penniless Usher? She saw a thin face, bright expressive eyes of clear blue, curling brown hair worn long over the ears, long delicate hands that were certainly not covered with blisters or chapped with menial toil. Nicholas, without doubt.

'You sent for me, Headmaster?'

'Ah, Lyon. I want you to take Master Carey and show him where he's to sleep, and the classrooms and playground and all that. Now,

Miss Carey, as to terms ...' He waved a dismissive hand towards Harry, who got up and went towards Lyon, with a wild look back at his mother and sister. Eleanore, on impulse, sprang to her feet.

'I would like to see where my brother's to live, Mr Channer. Perhaps I may accompany him.' Without waiting for permission, and ignoring Eudora's protest, she followed the two into the corridor, shutting the door firmly behind her. Lyon smiled at her, a smile of singular sweetness, and she smiled back, a sudden illumination of beauty which caused him to stumble on the bottom step of the staircase, well though he knew it. Pretty girls were rare flowers in the neighbourhood of Yew House, and Lyon had set eyes on very few of them in his whole life. He looked with pity on the child with burnished hair like hers, now clinging to her hand as though she were an angel conducting his soul through stormy skies.

'This is the dormitory,' he told them. In a private house it would have been a large double bedroom, no more. Somehow it accommodated twenty narrow pallet beds, mere mattresses on planks, covered with the roughest of blankets. The only decoration was a text framed in poker-work, THOU GOD SEEST ME, and a huge staring brown eye to point the moral. A door opened into what had been a dressing-room, in the house's better days: Eleanore could glimpse a single wash-stand, with ewer, basin and a cake of yellow soap, towels hung on a clothes-horse beside it.

Harry's face was horror-struck. 'I can't sleep *there*! Will there be boys in all those beds?'

Lyon nodded. 'Twenty, junior and middle. Us older ones are in the attics, and the masters that live in sleep over the coach-house.'

'Where,' asked Eleanore grimly, 'are the baths?'

'Baths, ma'am?'

'You mean to say there are none?'

'No, ma'am. It an't very cleanly, but they're not provided.'

Harry, used to his tin bath being lugged up the stairs by Patty so that he could bathe comfortably and pleasantly before the sitting-room fire, broke into a howl. Eleanore and Lyon exchanged helpless looks. He had been through such scenes many times before, but this occasion involved a beautiful and angry young lady, and was worse than usual. 'You'd better see the classrooms,' he said, leading them downstairs.

The classrooms were in fact the front and back half of a one-time drawing-room. Small desks, battered, scratched and inky, stood in ranks close together. The other furnishings were the master's desk, a blackboard, and a few tattered maps on the wall. Only the front classroom was occupied by a dozen or so boys chanting a Latin declension in monotonous chorus. To Eleanore they all looked shabby, dirty and under-fed. Among them Harry would be like a graceful young robin in a gaggle of city sparrows, and soon he would lose that appearance and look as they did. The master was a short, swarthy man who would have seemed quite at home in a gipsy encampment. Eleanore disliked and feared him on sight. She whispered to Lyon to close the door of the back room before Harry's sniffs attracted attention.

The playground had once been a garden. Now the grass of the lawns was trodden down, worn away by feet, the flower-beds overgrown, the only colour and brightness the green leaves of a straggling rambler rose on the wall and the pale yellow of leggy late daffodils. Lyon said 'Perhaps Master Carey would like to see the horses.' He led them through a gate into a small stable-yard, where two heads, brown and bay, turned towards them over the doors of their stalls, and a whinny greeted Lyon. He caressed the brown muzzle while the bay's soft mouth gently lipped his shoulder.

'Tennyson and Dickens, they're called. Good pair of names. I look after 'em – they're the best part of this place. When the carriage isn't wanted I take them out for exercise – there's capital galloping on Finchley Common. Better than dinning dates and figures into boys' heads.'

'Are you a teacher, then?' asked Eleanore. 'I thought you were a pupil.'

'Sometimes one, sometimes the other, ma'am. I try to pick up all the learning I can so that one day I can move on somewhere better.'

Harry was watching the horses with the first signs of interest and pleasure he had shown. 'I'd like to ride Dickens and Tennyson, too. Do you think they'd let me?'

'I doubt it. Why, can you ride?' At a glance, Harry looked too small and slight to sit a horse.

"Course I can. I rode since I was a baby, in India. I had my own *syce*, (that's a groom) all to myself, and my own pony – he was called Nandi. And Nell used to ride with us sometimes, in breeches like a boy. Oh Nell, I wish we were back!'

Into Lyon's mind flashed a picture compounded of his imagination and memories of the illustrations to *The Arabian Nights' Entertainments*, which had been among his grandfather's books. The old man had been only a clerk, with little money to spend on the child he had brought up after the death of the young parents, but he was well-read, and could at least hand on his own delight in books to Barnaby. The picture had shown a young bejewelled prince on a white horse. Only the long limbs in the baggy trousers of sparkling gauze were a girl's limbs, hidden now by the forbidding crinoline, and the face was the lovely one he now beheld, framed in its chestnut hair and crowned by a black pork-pie hat. Lyon was young and romantic and starved of love and beauty. A blush spread from his throat to the roots of his hair, and Eleanore too began to blush as their eyes met and lingered. Harry, on tip-toe, stroked the velvet noses of the horses.

'What's your name?' Eleanore asked abruptly. 'I mean your Christian name?'

'Barnaby, ma'am. I believe it came from a favourite book of my mother's.'

'Barnaby! But how extraordinary. You see ...' But the tale of little King Edward's whipping-boy was too involved to tell. 'Mine is Eleanore, but you can call me Nell,' she declared, mentally cocking a snook at Eudora, who would have paled with horror at the idea of a young lady inviting a quite common youth, a mere usher, to use her Christian name at first acquaintance or even a later one. 'Barnaby, listen, there's not much time. I want you to promise me upon your honour to look after Harry for me. He's too young to be sent away from home and it was done from spite, but never mind that, and he's very delicate because he was brought up in India and England is far too cold and foggy for him. I daren't imagine what might happen to him in this awful place. Will you do that for me?'

Barnaby Lyon would have promised to do single-handed combat with a fire-eating dragon for her. Solemnly he vowed that he would take care of Harry in every possible way, at all times. He knew, though he did not tell her, that it would be difficult, sometimes nearly impossible.

'Thank you, Barnaby. I knew I could trust you. And please will you contrive to get word to me? I live with our mother and our aunts at 142 Gower Street, Bloomsbury. Can you remember that?'

Remember it? Already it was engraved on his heart in letters of burning gold.

'If anything goes wrong, you know, or if Harry needs something?'

'I know. And I will get word to you, ma'am.'

'Nell.'

'Nell.' Why had he not realised before that Nell was the sweetest name a girl could be called by? 'I think I should take you back now. These – interviews – are pretty short as a rule.'

'Very well. Harry ...' Nell dropped to her knees on the cobbles, hugged her brother in her arms and whispered to him reassurances and comforts and promises, covering his face with kisses. They were both weeping, and sympathetic tears started to Barnaby's eyes. Getting to her feet, she said to Harry, 'Trust Barnaby. Go to him when – if – you need help. Promise me?'

'I promise, Nell.'

'And always be brave – remember Papa. I shan't say any more to you in the house. Shall we go?'

They went indoors, the tall girl and the tall boy, with the child clinging to a hand of both.

III

Barnaby rides out

The task that Barnaby Lyon had undertaken for his lady's sake was not a light one.

Mr Channer's school was, in fact, no worse than many other of its kind. Parents who could not afford to send their sons to one of the great public schools made no objection to the private sort, converted residences like Yew House, with no special facilities for the comfortable accommodation of many boys, and staff who were largely unqualified. Eustace Channer had gone into the education business entirely for profit, as a man might breed chickens or rabbits without having any particular fondness for those creatures. He crammed into Yew House as many pupils as could be got, rejecting with regret only those who would have had to be bedded down in the stables or cellars, for the shocking exposures of the Yorkshire schools in *Nicholas Nickleby* were not forgotten, and the eye of the law was upon headmasters who might be thought to take after Mr Wackford Squeers.

Some of his scholars, the fortunate ones, were local and non-resident, brought every morning by servants and returned home every evening. Their treatment was a shade better than that of the boarders, since they could complain directly to their parents; the boarders' letters were censored. The day-boys sat at a separate table for meals, and the superior food (which was saying very little) went on to their plates.

Of the small staff, only two had been to universities, and had left them without degrees. The rest had taught at similar schools or been private tutors. They had enough learning to pass on rudimentary knowledge, but no more, and as no examinations were held their deficiencies were never found out.

But alas for Harry, Aunt Eudora's words had been unkind but true: he was quite uneducated. His mother's gentle teachings had been largely scriptural and historical, Eleanore's no more than lively story-telling. As neither of them ever punished, Harry was quite unacquainted with discipline. He knew hardly any boys, and no man at close quarters other than his Uncle Gil, who indulged him with sweets and tips. In the world of Yew House he was like a lamb in a cageful of hungry tigers.

It came as a dismal surprise to him that he was expected to rise from his painfully hard bed at six in the morning, summoned by a clanging bell, and that if he did not immediately get up he would be unceremoniously pulled out and have his head banged on the floor to liven him up. Washing consisted of a brisk scrape of the face with a communal flannel and piece of soap, at a communal basin which was emptied only when all twenty boys had washed. Sanitary arrangements shocked the modest child, reared in a prudish household, so much that in the first days at school he became ill from refusing to make use of them.

Why, he wondered, had he ever complained of the food his aunts provided? Breakfast at Yew House was thin, watery porridge, called by the boys skilligolee, after prison-fare, and even thinner beer, brewed in the school cellars – from nettles and dandelions as well as malt and hops, some said. For dinner (he was jeered at for calling it luncheon) there might be a slice of fatty boiled bacon with potatoes over-boiled to a mush, cabbage cooked until yellow and limp in quantities of water, meat stew or broth made from joints which had themselves been served upstairs. Supper, the last meal of the day, was two slices of bread and scrape (butter applied and then removed) and a grudging layer of jam or treacle, served with the luxury of tea, even though it was what servants called water bewitched. For Sunday dinner came a treat – Resurrection Pie, made from scraps left over from what had been served during the week, upstairs and down, whether they blended or not, fried up and served hugger-mugger in a dish.

On this fare Harry grew thin and pale, and suffered frequent and embarrassing digestive upsets. There was no school doctor, no matron; a physician would be called only in the case of serious illness. Mrs Channer, immensely stout and lethargic, regarded herself as something of an interesting invalid far too fragile to be concerned with the troubles of boys, and the servants were an unfriendly lot to whose hearts the only key was bribery.

But if the details of daily life were disagreeable, they were as nothing to the tortures of the classroom. It was soon clear to teachers and boys that the new pupil was completely ignorant, a fair target for scorn and derision. Questions were fired at him from the Beak's rostrum.

'Carey: in the reign of which king was North America discovered? Name the chief battles of the Peninsular War ... the rivers of England ... the monarchs of France ... What do you know of decimal fractions? Between what years was the Younger Pitt prime minister? Pray conjugate *ignoro* – come, that ought to be an easy one for *you*.' (General classroom titter.)

To all of which Harry could only shake his head or mutter that he didn't know, making matters worse by forgetting to add 'Sir'. Those dreadful volumes, Mangall's *Questions* and Pinnock's *Catechisms*, teemed with facts every boy should know and one boy did not. Useless to be acquainted personally with India, its manners, customs and speech – these things were of no account, it seemed, the only information imparted to the boys being that its inhabitants were weak, indolent and effeminate, as befitted its climate. Quite useless here were his poor little scraps of knowledge – verses, hymns, stories and fables, acquired as he sat by his mother, or lay in his bed while she read or sang to him, her hand holding his.

For his ignorance Harry was caned daily, and never failed to cry with the pain, however hard he tried; much to the satisfaction of his fellow-pupils. It was a regular game for any boy who sat beside him to pinch his arm or leg or run a pin into him, so that he would give an involuntary squeal and earn himself another caning for making an unseemly noise. It was not that the boys were in themselves evil, merely that they were members of a herd, conditioned to turn on the weakest among them. Muff, Duffer, Jackass, they called him, and

The Swell Young Nabob, and Mamma's Precious Popsy-Wopsy, teasing him at the same time with fiends' ingenuity. Lighted matches would be applied to his still-long hair, 'to barber it a bit', and allowed to burn down on his neck, brushes forced into his bruised and blistered hands, chopped-up earthworms slyly introduced among his food to sicken him.

Barnaby Lyon watched, and grieved and fumed, and could do very little. For more than two weeks he was not fully aware of the extent of the persecution. Then, in a play-time, he came suddenly upon a small knot of boys in a secluded corner of the garden, enjoying an interlude of quiet torture, with Harry on the ground in the middle. A warning cry of 'Nix!' went up, but too late – he was among them.

'What's this? What were you doing?'

'Nothing, Lyon.'

'It looked like something, to me. What are those matches being used for, Nugent?'

'Er – just striking, Lyon.'

'Give them to me. What were you doing to Carey?'

Nobody answered. Harry scrambled to his feet, mopping his tear-stained cheeks with the back of a sleeve.

'Very well,' said Barnaby, 'I'll tell you. You were tormenting him, as you've tormented new boys before. Now, Carey is younger and smaller than you, and has not had the advantages of your education. You're no better than a gang of bullies and cowards to set on him, and if I catch you, or any other boys, at it again, I will beat you personally. Understood?'

'Yes, Lyon.' Defeated and shamefaced, they melted away. They understood perfectly. A leader of the pack had spoken, and the pack must obey. It seemed curious to them that such a despicably weak animal as Carey should be exempted from their rough justice, but the leader knew best. Carey would not be tortured again – at least, not when Lyon could possibly catch them at it.

'Thank you, Barnaby,' Harry whispered, dry-eyed now.

'Lyon, not Barnaby.'

'But Nell called you that.'

'I wouldn't mention your sister here, if I were you, Harry. But she

45

asked me to look after you, and I will. Now, why did you not come to me and tell me how those oafs were treating you?'

'It would have been sneaking. Papa said that when I went to school in England I shouldn't ever sneak on anyone, because an English gentleman didn't.'

It was not always possible for Barnaby to be present at classes, but he was able to gather enough knowledge of what Harry underwent there, especially at the hands of Mr Hughes, the swarthy bad-tempered Latin master. He requested an interview with the head-master, who appeared surprised to see him. Mr Channer was used to summoning this useful jack-of-all-trades rather than being approached by him.

'Yes, Lyon?'

'Sir – I was wondering if you could possibly be so kind as to say a word about young Carey. To the other staff, that is.'

'Carey? Why, has he been giving trouble?'

'Not exactly, sir. That is, in a way. He is punished very frequently for what he cannot help.'

Channer frowned. 'Punishment an't given without cause in my school.'

'No, sir. But Carey is caned every day for not being able to answer the questions put to him.'

'Then why don't he apply himself to his studies?' Channer snapped.

'He has not the … ' Lyon floundered. 'He has been taught nothing that's of use to him here. At home he had no tutor or governess. He knows nothing of Latin, or arithmetic or the globes.'

'Let him learn 'em, then.'

'It's not easy, sir. There is no preparation time, and his mind is quite untrained.'

Channer leaned forward. 'Laziness, plain simple laziness. From what I've seen of him the boy's a muff, pampered by silly women. He came here to learn, and learn he shall, even if learning has to be caned into him. Now don't waste any more of my time.'

'But sir. The canings do no good. The child's hurt and unhappy and too afraid and low in his spirits to learn of his own accord. I feel –

46

and pardon me, for it is really none of my business – that something should be done to help him.'

Channer sighed ostentatiously. 'What, then? And it *is* none of your business.'

'I should like, if you please, sir, to have a little time with him after classes are over, and give him a few lessons – tutor him, as it were, though I'm aware I am not a qualified teacher. But I have been through the school, and I think I could introduce some knowledge into his mind without frightening him.'

Channer favoured him with a hard stare. 'Pretty boy, an't he.'

Lyon's ready blush flooded his face. He knew all too much of one disagreeable but inevitable facet of boarding-school life, and was not going to waste words in refuting the implication. 'I think I could help him, sir. And it would make things easier for the other masters.'

The headmaster had lost interest. 'Very well, if it don't waste your time when you should be occupied with other matters. Do as you like.' He turned to his favourite task, the making out of bills to be sent to the boys' parents, loaded with extras for Music, Dancing, Washing and Mending, Boot repairs and Medicine.

'Thank you, sir. It's very good of you.'

Harry was touchingly grateful for the offer of extra coaching from the only friend he had at Yew House, and responded to it better than Barnaby could have hoped. He had become convinced that he was naturally stupid, and encouragement provided the spur which punishment could not give. After a week or two the rudiments of Latin grammar began to sink into his mind, the map of the world held fewer terrors, and the fearsome army of dates became less impossibly difficult: as Barnaby pointed out, it was always the same ones that were asked for. The time came when Harry was not caned for days together, and the cowed look he had worn lightened a little.

Then dark clouds encompassed him again. His concentration began to slip, and answers he should have known would not come to his lips. Barnaby found him one day in the empty classroom, slumped over his desk, sobbing.

'What is it, Carey? Mr Hughes been after you?'

A shake of the head.

47

'Aren't you well? Come on, tell me.'

But no amount of coaxing would extract an admission from Harry, who from that time became withdrawn from his friend. The canings began again, for inattention now as well as ignorance.

Barnaby was greatly troubled. He was only eighteen, without authority in the school, liable to punishment himself if he interfered too much with the daily life of another pupil. He was at his wits' end how to help, and he had promised to help.

Suddenly, as he lay awake in the stuffy attic room he shared with three senior boys, an idea came to him. He would ride up to London and consult Eleanore. All he needed was the opportunity.

It came on a Sunday afternoon, soon after he had made his decision. The day was wet, a heavy summer drizzle from grey skies. The whole school had been to church, Resurrection Pie had duly appeared in all its grisly complexity on the boys' tables, and Mrs Channer had announced that she did not propose to take her usual Sunday afternoon drive in such inclement weather. Barnaby's time was his own until the evening. Leaving a message that he was going to exercise the horses, he gave his chin an extra shave, brushed his hair until it curled like feathers, put on his cravat and saddled up Dickens. Leaving Tennyson disappointed in his stall, they rode out: not towards Finchley for the usual gallop, but down the Great North Road, through quiet Highgate towards the New Road and his destination.

His heart was beating fast, from the realisation of the rash thing he was doing, and even more from the anticipation of seeing Harry's sister again. Would she be as beautiful as he remembered her? Would she be permitted to ask him in, perhaps entertain him to tea, and if so, how long would they spend together? He hoped his accursed habit of blushing would not be too much of a pest – yet she had blushed too, how charmingly ... Before he knew it he was riding down Gower Street, and here and there a curtain would be withdrawn slightly as censorious eyes peered at the horseman who seemed to be travelling for pleasure, on the Sabbath Day, judging by his ardent face and eager glances up at the tall houses.

It was unfortunate that Eudora and Minerva had also decided that the weather would not permit them to take their usual walk, an exercise perfectly permissible before evening chapel. When Barnaby pulled Dickens up outside the house they were seated in their front parlour, near enough to the window to watch any passing traffic and comment on it.

'There's a young man riding past now. Quite ordinary. Nobody we know. Sister!' Minerva sat bolt upright with a squeak. 'He is stopping at our door. Who can it be?'

Both pressed their faces to the window to watch the rider tie up his horse to a post and walk lightly to the front door.

Little Patty answered the bell, red-faced from sleeping in front of the kitchen fire. She stared uncomprehendingly at the stranger.

'Is ...' Barnaby gulped. 'Is Miss Carey at home?'

'Dunno, sir. But the Miss Cordwells is, both on 'em. Who shall I say?'

Dismay invaded him. Both! She must mean the aunts, that Gorgon who had brought Harry to school and the other one he had mentioned.

'Er. I meant young Miss Carey – Miss Eleanore.' Fool, to have gone about it so clumsily. Patty gawped at him.

'Couldn't say, sir. Never seen her go out.'

'Then ... '

A shrill voice floated downstairs. 'Who is it, Patty?'

'A young man for Miss Eleanore, mum.'

'Bring him up at once, Patty. *At once.*'

Cursing himself, Barnaby followed the maid up to the parlour. There, the blush well in evidence, he stood confronting not one Gorgon but two, the other one fat and flaccid but no less piercing of eye.

'Well, young man? I hear you enquired for our niece.'

Barnaby began to stammer. He had come from Yew House to give Miss Eleanore news of her brother's progress. He thought she would like to have news. He was sorry to intrude, and if they would kindly let him have a word with Eleanore he would not take up any more of their time.

He was not asked to sit down, and Eudora allowed a silence to elapse that would reduce him to an even worse state of nerves before asking, 'What possible interest can anything you have to say have for our niece? She requires no news of our nephew, from you – whoever you may be – or anyone else.'

But the door had flown open again and Eleanore herself was standing in the doorway. She was every bit as beautiful as Barnaby remembered, her fine shape outlined by a tight-fitting day-dress of soft violet, her hair glowing through a woollen snood.

'Barnaby, it's you!' she cried. 'Yes, I *do* require news of Harry, Aunt. Why was I not told Barnaby was here? How is Harry? Did he send me a message? When can I see him?'

Before Barnaby could speak Eudora had interrupted. 'This is all most unseemly, most unseemly. Eleanore, we do not know this young man and we cannot imagine how you come to do so.'

'Quite improper,' put in Minerva.

'I saw him at the school – you saw him yourself –'

'Be quiet. My niece has nothing further to say to you, Mr – Barnaby.' Eudora rang the hand-bell violently. Patty, who had gone only a few steps down in order to listen, appeared, wide-eyed.

'Show this person out, Patty. Eleanore, return to your mamma. We will speak to you later.'

Before Eleanore could detain him Barnaby went past her with a wild look and a head-shake. He was helpless against these forces. Eleanore, also powerless for the moment, watched him down the stairs. Then she turned to her aunts.

'How could you? How *could* you?' And like a flash of lightning she was gone, down the stairs, through the front door, out to the pavement where Barnaby was untethering Dickens. She ran to him and clasped his arm.

'Oh, Barnaby, I'm so sorry – the wretches, the beasts, after you'd taken the trouble to come here, and then to treat you so and not let me hear – oh, how is he?'

'Not happy, ma'am. Very unhappy, indeed. I've done what I can, but – he has been much punished for what was not his fault. There seems no more I can do. I came to speak to you, to seek your help.'

'If only I could give it! I'll do my best with them, but you see what they are. Tell Harry you've seen me – give him my dear love – say I promise to do something, anything.'

'I will.' Barnaby was looking down into her eyes, her hand still warm on his arm. Between them, through the cloud of her anxiety and his defeat, still shone the light that had been kindled in the stable-yard at Yew House, weeks before. Youth to youth, chivalry to beauty, and in both the tenderness for a loved child that bound them together: these things fought the darkness of the house behind them. The rain put diamonds in Eleanore's hair and crisped Barnaby's into closer curls as they gazed at each other for a long moment. Then he gently disengaged himself.

'I must go, ma'am. I'll tell Harry.'

'My love and Mamma's to him. And thank you, thank you, Barnaby.'

She could not watch him ride away, for they had both come out and dragged her indoors between them.

Amy was brought to listen to the indictment of her infamous daughter. Bold, shameless, unwomanly, stubborn, disobedient, without modesty or any sense of fitness; no wonder her brother had disgraced himself, as he must have done for that person to be presumptuous enough to come and report it to her. Eleanore kept her hands clenched by her sides, determined to fight reasonably while she could. When she could get a word in edgeways she said, 'Harry has not disgraced himself. Barnaby, Mr Lyon, came to tell me that he is unhappy and ill-treated. You should never have sent him to that school, Aunt, you must see that. He is not fit for a school of any kind. Please, please, will you not take him away and let him study with a private tutor? Mamma, you think so too, I know – say something!'

But Amy only trembled, twisting her fingers together, though she longed to speak for her son and support her daughter.

The two sisters had no need to confer, they were so perfectly in accord.

'Have you finished?' coldly asked Eudora. 'Then you may listen to me. Harry will not be removed from school; he must stay and fight his own battles. If anything were seriously amiss with him Mr Channer would have informed us, I am sure. You will not communicate with him, nor you, Amy. And if the person who called upon us today should repeat that impertinence a constable will be sent for and Mr Channer informed.

Eleanore drew a deep breath. Then, with the vestige of a smile, and speaking in soft tones, she said in Hindi: 'Daughter of an unclean pig, descendant of ten thousand monkey-devils, fornicatress with beasts and defiler of thine own flesh, companion of scavenging dogs, eater of gutter-filth, may thy nose drop off as thy mother's did after she had slaked her lust with numerous diseased beggars. May the great Kali drain thy blood and add thy skull to her necklace, may Surya withhold the light of the sun from thee, may snakes gorge thy veins with their poisoned tongues, may the royal elephant of Buddha trample thee under foot to the thinness of a *chupatti* and thy soul be torn for ever by demon tigers. And,' she added, turning to Minerva, 'that fate be thine, also.'

Amy, who had understood every word, gave a little shriek of mingled horror and mirth, jumped up and ran out. They heard her hysterical laughter growing fainter as she reached her own room.

Eudora had not understood the words, but the tone was unmistakable. She had been cursed, and terribly, and so had her sister, her ally. Under Eleanore's baleful stare she seemed to shrink in size, and her face was ashen. For the first time in her life she was very frightened. Minerva's lips were moving soundlessly, the lines of a childish hymn she had been taught long ago.

Eudora addressed Eleanore, who was watching with satisfaction the result of her tirade. 'Out,' she said. 'Get out of my sight, you wicked heathen.'

'Oh, I am not a heathen, Aunt,' returned Eleanore. 'If you want a text from Scripture, you can have one. "Whoso shall offend one of these little ones which believe in Me, it were better for him that a millstone were hanged about his neck, and that he were drowned in the midst of the sea."' Turning on her heel, she walked calmly out, closing the door quietly behind her.

A few days after this scene, Eudora and Minerva were taking tea with their respected friend, Mr Manfred Pye of Highgate. He it was who

52

had recommended Yew House School to them. His new and expensive house was just down the hill from the Village, in Swains Lane, built to the acme of fashionable taste in the High Gothic style, with steeply sloped roofs and profusion of gables, windows with pointed arches, small turrets which resembled dovecotes but were not, and an imposing porch. The general effect was ecclesiastical, appropriately enough, as the house faced the picturesque grounds of Highgate Cemetery, that elegant celebration of affluent Death, and the tall spire of St Michael's Church loomed above, pointing all good villagers to the skies.

Mr Pye was a personable gentleman. Tall, well-made, he had kept a trim figure and a face little lined by his forty-four years. His hair was thinning now, receding from his high brow, but that only gave him an air of intellectuality, just as his prominent arched nose suggested an imperious nature, though his manner was polite, even suave, to his equals. Beneath the nose a pair of remarkably full lips contradicted any ascetic look he might otherwise have had. Admiring ladies had been known to say that sculpted in marble he would make a perfect Caesar; though it might have surprised them to learn that the Roman emperor he most resembled was the infamous Tiberius.

His large pale eyes the ladies found particularly fascinating. His gaze once caught, it was almost impossible to look away, and the eyes of those who spoke to him were often fixed upon his luxuriant whiskers, or the elaborate gold watch-chain which was festooned across his waistcoat.

He drank tea as daintily as he sipped wine, as he often did at the City banquets which, as a prosperous stockbroker, he attended. At Guildhall he had supped on the luscious green fat of the turtle, beheaded to make soup for the Lord Mayor and his Aldermen; and enjoyment of the feast had not prevented him from picturing himself filling the Lord Mayoral seat. To become Lord Mayor, it was necessary first to become Alderman, as his neighbour Sydney Waterlow had done. Perhaps that was not far off ...

His gaze flickered across the opulent tea-table, with its Royal Worcester china and silver spirit-kettle, to where his wife Claudia sat in her upright chair, her back supported by cushions, for she was seven months pregnant. Claudia was very slender in her normal state, delicate-featured, long-necked, not pretty, too sharp-looking for that by half, thought her husband. Her mouth quirked easily in laughter or mockery, one eyebrow had an expressive and critical life of its own. Her small head was elegant in its lace cap with the flowing lappets and small knots of rosebuds above the ears. Thank Heaven she was wearing her best one today, and straight, and the buttons of her bodice were all in the right holes. Even in company her dress was sometimes deplorably slovenly; she thought more of her silly little writings and notes than she did of the business of being an ornament to him.

He hated her for her pregnancy. Last time it had only produced a whining girl, not the son he wanted. He had tolerated her grotesque figure then, just as he had tolerated her silly whimsicalities for the fortune she had brought him. But now he could hardly look at her. In such an ugly condition she should not be showing herself to people, particularly two unmarried ladies. Catching her eye, he smiled. Instantly she returned the smile, with one that made her face beautiful.

He set down his teacup. The sisters Cordwell did the same.

'Now,' he said, 'to the matter in hand, the matter of your dear niece. What is it that you require of me, ladies?'

'Your advice, sir,' Minverva said. 'Once again, your advice.'

IV

The Master of Ashurst Lodge

He listened to the tale of Eleanore's misdemeanours, with no comment beyond the blink of eyelids or an occasional slight shake of the head. Claudia listened eagerly, eyes flickering from one narrator to the other, then to her husband, estimating the situation, weighing the danger.

'You see, Mr Pye,' concluded Eudora, 'it is no longer possible for us to keep the girl under our roof, since she has flouted our authority so often and we clearly have no control over her.'

'We are not a home for delinquents,' said Claudia softly. Pye flashed a look at her.

'My wife means,' he said, 'that we must be sure your niece would respond to my authority. She is not dangerously violent, is she?'

Eudora shifted uneasily. 'Violent, no. There is no insanity in the family. But I might describe her as ...' she glanced at Minerva.

'Self-willed. Contentious. Undutiful.'

'Surely,' said Claudia, 'these are fairly natural things in a growing woman of any character.'

Eudora bridled. 'I hope, ma'am, she has had examples of proper behaviour in my sister and myself.'

'Oh yes, indeed. Patterns of virtue.' It was said with a barely perceptible curl of the lip which neither sister missed. Minerva flushed and Eudora reflected how very much she disliked Mrs Pye and pitied her splendid, noble husband for being shackled to such a shrew. Manfred Pye smiled upon them both.

'Your virtue, dear ladies, is incontrovertible and unchallenged, as I am sure Mrs Pye meant to imply. May we take it that your niece's is the same – that her wildness does not extend to ... bad companions?'

Both sisters tacitly decided to forget the episode of the Sunday afternoon caller. 'Most thankfully there is no stain on her character,' Eudora said. 'She has been brought up as a lady, and protected from all such temptations, by her mother as well as ourselves.'

'Then why is her mother not with you today?' Claudia asked.

There was a silence before Minerva answered, 'We thought it too distressing for her – she is of a nervous disposition.'

'No doubt the reason why we have not had the pleasure of meeting her,' Claudia said sweetly. It was quite clear to her needle-sharp eyes that these harridans were ashamed of their poor relations, and she wanted so much to make Manfred see it as well and know that he was being deceived. He was so clever, so brilliant, and yet to be taken in by such hypocrites … And the girl – what kind of threat would she present?

'I hope,' she said, 'your niece is agreeable in appearance. I couldn't endure to have one of those hideous plain governesses in the house. Poor things, of course they can't help their looks, but one doesn't wish to have one's spirits continually dashed by the sight of a face like a fiddle.' She was gazing pointedly at Eudora's own face. Minerva saw that her sister could scarcely speak for anger, and answered, 'Oh, she is presentable enough, though her hair is an unfortunate shade of red.'

'Often the outward and visible sign of angry passions,' said Eudora viciously. Manfred Pye was looking dubious. Angry passions might be an obstacle to the fulfilment of his wishes. But on the whole he preferred to trust in his own urbane charm to soothe the savage breast. Or breasts …

'On the whole,' he said, 'I think you have convinced me, Miss Cordwell. We will be happy to offer your niece a place in our household as nursery governess to our daughter Caroline. And later, if she proves satisfactory, to …' But it would be indelicate to refer to his wife's condition, and he preferred not to dwell on it. Then he surprised the sisters and Claudia. 'The boy, her brother. Is he also of an intractable nature?'

'Harry? Not at all. Rather the reverse.' Eudora sniffed. 'A sickly child, quite girlish in his ways.'

'Then,' said Claudia swiftly, 'what is he doing at school?' Pye flashed her a glance which was for once approving.

'Precisely what I was going to say myself, Mrs Pye. Why should not the brother join us too as a companion for Caroline and a pupil for his sister?'

'Quite impossible,' Minerva snapped. 'Under her influence he would come to no good at all – he has been under it far too long already.'

'*Far* too long,' Eudora echoed. 'And you did recommend the school yourself, Mr Pye.'

'Yes, of course.' How he wished he had not. A nubile girl and a pre-adolescent boy: if the one did not serve, the other might. But the old women were mulish, he could see. No use to press them further now. Perhaps later he might work on them.

'Now, as to practical arrangements,' he said. 'I will be happy to pay Miss Carey a small emolument –'

'Of which my sister and I feel we should receive a proportion,' put in Eudora rapidly, 'in compensation for the amount we have spent on her education. She will need no money of her own, living in this handsome establishment, with everything found for her.'

'Don't you think,' Claudia asked sweetly, 'that she might like just a *little* money of her own, to spend on trifles – ribbons, bonnet trimmings, small presents, for instance?'

'She has quite enough. Vanity in girls is not to be encouraged.'

'We shall see. The wages of our domestics are in my hands, but I'm sure Mr Pye would agree.'

'As you say, my dear.' It was not his intention to quarrel over details, and he was heartily bored by the company of the two Miss Cordwells, for whom the only thing to be said was that they had a niece, who might be exceedingly useful to him in a project he had in mind.

'I do hate to leave you, Mamma,' Eleanore was saying as they corded up her small trunk of clothes. 'What will you do without me? Those two will eat you alive, if I'm not here to protect you.'

'I shall do very well, my love. I hope I am not entirely without character. Indeed, I fancy I may be rather better treated, if you are not about.' Amy's gentleness did not extend to the point of stupidity. She realised that both her children had been used to get at her – what they had suffered, she had suffered. Now she would have no hostages, and perhaps Eudora and Minerva would ignore her.

Eleanore hugged her impulsively. 'That's my brave, dear, pretty Mamma. When I'm earning money you shall have all I can spare, and perhaps if I do well they'll raise my salary and I can buy you – oh, all sorts of things. Look at you! That collar is a disgrace and that skirt has been turned I don't know how many times. I declare,' and she banged the lid of the trunk noisily shut, 'I'd give anything, anything, to find a nice, rich, kind man to marry you and take you away from this place – yes, I would. You're so pretty, and it's such a waste.'

'Eleanore! Pray don't say such shocking things. An old woman like me, with grey hair – well, nearly grey. Besides, after your dear father … '

'My dear father would want nothing more than to see you married again and taken care of. Come, you know he would. And if he's looking down from Heaven at us he'd be – glad – glad to see … ' Suddenly she was weeping, on her knees by the trunk, her head on her arms, and Amy wept with her.

Everything was ready for her departure, the cab summoned, Eudora waiting impatiently downstairs to accompany her. But Eleanore hesitated.

'Mamma – there is something – I don't like to ask you, but I would so love to take it … '

'What, my dear?'

'That.' She pointed to the picture of the Lady Jacquette Brome. 'I've always felt that she and I belonged together, though of course that's silly, but she would be a sort of company for me – do you understand?'

'Of course I do.' Composedly Amy took down the little picture from the wall, not without a pang, for she had dearly prized her only family portrait. But perhaps, in better days to come, she would see it again. 'There. Wrap her in your old cloak – no, in this one of mine – be careful, the wood is very fragile.' Goodbye, Lady Brome, she silently said. Bring good fortune to my daughter, and keep away evil from her. The dark painted eyes seemed to shine and sparkle before the cloak covered them; but that, of course, was only a trick of the light.

Eleanore was less impressed by Ashurst Lodge than her aunts had been. It seemed to her a very ugly, pompous sort of house, and in her downcast mood after parting with her mother she was prepared to dislike everything about it. But the comfort and warmth of the drawing-room into which she was shown was immediately cheering to her spirits.

Claudia, embroidering by the fire, looked up sharply as 'Miss Carey' was stiffly announced. But the first glance was enough to tell her that this was not one to be feared. She knew too well the type of beauty Manfred admired in women. This shabby girl, with her childish mouth, wary eyes and theatrical colouring, would certainly not attract him. Or she hoped not, touching the wooden work-table beside her.

'Come in, my dear,' she said. 'Sit down and tell me about yourself.'

Eleanore too had been nervous about the interview, for different reasons. The employers of nursery governesses were a legend for harshness, as their offspring were for mischievous cruelty; Miss Sutton had told her plenty of tales of both. But she liked Mrs Manfred Pye on sight, sensing kindness and intelligence behind the features sharpened by pregnancy. She was not one who bloomed as her baby grew; Amy had done that while carrying Harry, but this woman was being drained of vitality. Eleanore was sorry for her.

Briefly she told Claudia the scanty details of her education and family background, unconsciously revealing far more than she said. Claudia had met the aunts and heard about Harry; she recognised a passionate spirit and a fighting nature. Eleanore wanted very much to keep her sympathy, but truthfulness drove her to risk her chances by saying, 'I'm afraid I am not a good teacher. I tried to teach my brother, but I fear it has done him no good at his school. Do you think I should be more successful with your daughter?'

'You had better meet her before we decide that.'

59

The child brought in by a nursery-maid was seven years old, as small and slightly-built as Harry, pale-faced and red-nosed, and unfortunately plain of feature. She had, Eleanore was to discover, an almost perpetual cold, caused by infected tonsils. Eleanore received the impression that her mother did not like her, and that the child knew it. Yet again her sympathy was called upon, though she knew nothing of either mother or daughter.

'Curtsey to your new governess, Caroline,' said Claudia. 'Her name is Miss Carey.' The child dipped a wavering curtsey, righting herself in time to blow her nose yet again. She did not meet Eleanore's eyes.

'Tell Miss Carey what lessons you learned with Mademoiselle Patrice.'

Caroline shuffled her feet, sniffed, glanced furtively at her mother, and muttered something inaudible, which she was sharply ordered to repeat.

'Fredch. Jography. Twice tibes.'

'Very well, that will do. Go along with Ada.'

When the child and maid had gone Claudia shrugged and smiled wryly, the wilfully expressive eyebrow shooting up towards her cap.

'You see? Plenty of room for improvement.'

'Yes.' Eleanore was deeply embarrassed. It was all turning out differently from the imagined interview. She had no idea what to say next, and was painfully conscious of her feet, hands, tight boots and bonnet slightly askew where she had caught it on the door-frame.

'You see, too, what a curious family we are. Not a case of *mater pulchra, filia pulchrior.* Both very plain and odd.'

Eleanore looked blank, bringing a laugh from Claudia.

'Never mind – scholarship is not popular in this house. The Three Rs will do very well.' Her tone changed suddenly. 'So you left India when the Mutiny broke out. Tell me, what was it like? But before you tell me, do take off that bonnet which I see is making you most uncomfortable.'

When Manfred Pye entered his drawing-room on his return from the City he found his wife, her face alight with animation, raptly listening to a tale that had begun with alarm in the night and was

60

ending with the flight of a terrified young mother, her children and their *ayah* before the advance of shrieking natives, torchlight and shouts coming nearer and nearer. 'And then one of our servants, the only one who'd stayed faithful, got us out and into a little boat he had moored at the bottom of the garden. Mamma and I were dreadfully frightened, but *ayah* had given Harry a dose of poppy-juice, so he slept through it. They would have cut us in pieces, you know, as they did any women and children they caught. At the *Bibi-ghar* they chopped them all up with swords and threw them down a well ... '

A cool voice broke in. 'What a pretty tale. Pray do continue.'

Eleanore spun round to see Manfred Pye gracefully poised in the doorway. His wife's attention had left the story. Her face was glowing with pleasure, transformed, almost beautiful.

'Mr Pye! How early you are.'

'I hope I am not interrupting a solemn conference.' Her hand was stretched out to him in welcome, but he neither took it nor appeared to notice it, but dropped the merest ghost of a kiss on her hair — perhaps even on the border of her cap.

'Miss Carey was telling me the fascinating story of her escape from the Mutiny, my dear. You have not met, have you? This is my husband, Miss Carey. We have been getting on together extremely well; I am sure we shall suit.'

Pye was summing Eleanore up, and she him. Imposing, yes, she thought. Handsome, no, but thinks he is. A cold fish to that poor creature who clearly worships him. And yet ...

A startling young woman, thought Pye; what they call a stunner, I suppose, though very raw. Still, all the better for that. While her gaze was on his face, he took the opportunity of trying out a singular accomplishment he had discovered in youth and had by now perfected. Staring into her eyes, he made his own glow with a strange pale light. It was a trick performed by widening those large, slightly prominent orbs to their full extent while standing where the light from window or lamp shone through them. But none of those on whom he had tried it knew it to be a trick: he had had some very satisfactory results of a mesmeric nature. By now he had come to think of it as a phenomenon produced by his own powerful will.

61

The effect of it on Miss Carey was acutely disappointing. She had seen some very odd things in India, one very similar to this performed by a so-called holy man, the second cousin of her mother's cook. He had been able to fascinate snakes with it, and even a tiger cub. Eleanore was interested to meet it in a Highgate drawing-room but not in the least impressed. Coolly she stared back.

She was never to know how nearly she was dismissed on the spot.

But Manfred Pye was not one to accept defeat easily. Perhaps the refraction of light had not been quite perfect, or his own powers not at their best late in the afternoon. He flashed her a charming smile. 'So, you are to join our household, Miss Carey? Excellent. I am sure our daughter's education will benefit.'

'Thank you, sir. I hope so.'

When he had gone Claudia said, 'Your aunts called you Eleanore, I think?'

'Eleanore, ma'am.'

'What a long and dreary name – it quite bores me. From that awful Tennyson poem, I suppose. I shall call you Nell – if you don't particularly object to that.'

'Oh no! I like it far better.'

'Good. Now I shall ring for Ada to show you to your room.'

Life at Ashurst Lodge was a distinct improvement on the routine of Gower Street. Nell missed her mother, and the cheerful presence of Patty, for the servants in the Pye household were not given to frivolous gossip, and to them a governess was only a little elevated above themselves. Meals were taken in the nursery, except when Nell was invited to dine with the Pyes downstairs. She enjoyed these evenings, only finding them embarrassing when the stresses between husband and wife became too apparent.

Slavish adoration at one end of the table, cold detachment at the other. Claudia was very well educated (her father, a Classics scholar, had given her her Roman name) and, pathetically, could not resist showing off her learning in little Latin or Greek quips which in academic society would have earned her a reputation as a ready wit. But Manfred Pye was not an academic, and resented someone being cleverer than himself at his own table. The joke that fell flat, the sage observation on current affairs curtly contradicted or ignored altogether, all left yawning holes in the conversation. Nell learned to say as little as she could, afraid of provoking one of these painful clashes.

She noticed, too, that Pye hardly glanced at his wife, and when he did it was to criticise her appearance. 'That is a very unbecoming cap, if I may say so. I hope it will not appear too often. And do you think the cut of that bodice entirely suitable ... at the present time?'

'But it is so very hot, my dear – and I feel the heat so much, just now.'

A disdainful silence would follow, causing Nell to keep her gaze intently on her plate rather than seem to notice the flush on Claudia's high, sharp cheek-bones. She sensed that this displeased Pye. His barbed, sarcastic remarks were meant to impress her favourably and ally her with himself. In fact, they had exactly the opposite result. For this Claudia was touchingly grateful, showing her gratitude in small rewards – a pretty lace collar and cuffs, a fan 'found at the back of a drawer', a pleasant tea with conversation in the drawing-room on a wet day. Nell wished that Amy could have joined them; they three would have got on famously.

Caroline was proving a better pupil than Nell had expected. She was backward, far from bright, childish in speech and limited in conversation. But who would not be, almost completely ignored in the household? The reason for Claudia's coolness towards her daughter was hard to guess, unless it had begun in jealousy of the attentions she might get from her father. If so, the jealousy had been entirely unfounded. Manfred Pye was unenthusiastic about children in general, but he had wanted a son. Every successful man should have a son; to prove a credit to him and carry on the family fortunes. He had tried for one often enough before and after Caroline's arrival, but his unsatisfactory wife had been disappointingly infertile. Caroline was of the stuff of old maids and of not the faintest interest to him.

Nell set about the task of improving Caroline. First, by encouragement. For each right answer given in a lesson the child got a compliment: 'How bright you are today, Caroline! Why, I could hardly have answered that myself when I was your age.' Very, very slowly her confidence was built up, until she began to smile as she had never done before, and to greet Nell spontaneously with an embrace, when they met each morning in the schoolroom.

It was, alas, a rather damp embrace, for the child's nose never ceased running. Nell soon discovered that she was given no exercise except playing in the large garden, or walking to the shops with Betsy the nursery-maid, whose mind was on the meetings she might contrive with her sweetheart, a young gardener at one of the big houses in the village. Nell, with Claudia's casual permission, took things in hand.

'Caroline, we will go for a walk every day, you and I. And we shall start this afternoon, by taking a stroll on Hampstead Heath. Would you like that?'

'Oh yes, Miss Carey.'

The stroll became something more like a gallop, the freed child gambolling on ahead of Nell's brisk stride. Off came the stiff hard hat, at Nell's suggestion, letting the lank hair tortured into ringlets fly in the summer breeze. Off, too, came the heavy poplin coat, to be carried by Nell, warm though she was herself. At first Caroline looked back continually, to see whether she was to be reproved or recalled: then, finding she was not, she began to run – down through the orchard, up the steep slope which led eventually to Lord Mansfield's house, Caenwood. As she ran she breathed deeply and quickly. Nell smiled to herself. The ugly chrysalis would produce a butterfly yet, if she had her way.

They explored the Cemetery, Caroline darting away from the level paths to examine a grandiose, mysterious tomb, a tired old horse drooping its stone head, the sleeping lion of Wombwell the circus-master, mourning angels and wistful cherubs. Their melancholy beauty charmed the child as it did Nell. Here Death seemed to shed its terrors, and the stings of Life grow blunt.

'I should like to be dead in here,' Caroline said. 'Would I have a little baby angel, like that one?'

'I don't know. Perhaps. But I should not wish to be dead yet, if I were you, when there's so much life to be lived.'

'What sort of life?'

'You'll find out. Better than you think at the moment, perhaps.'

Caroline threw up a questing bird-like glance. She had not thought much at all, about life or anything else, until her new governess came to Ashurst Lodge.

As they left the Cemetery through the main gate Caroline said, 'Can we go and see Harry one day?'

Nell's heart jumped. Why not, since they were free to go anywhere in their leisure time? She began to plan: it would be a long way for the child to walk, but they could rest in one of the inn gardens on the way. She would write to Barnaby first, then he would contrive to bring Harry to the stables ...

A carriage swept round the bend of Swain's Lane so swiftly that Nell had to drag Caroline aside to avoid being run down. Pressed against the wall, they had a clear view of the two people the carriage contained: one was Manfred Pye, the other a woman, young, richly dressed in shades of deep purple, mauve and violet, darkly handsome with a face in which indolence kept insolence company. The passengers were engaged in talk, neither noticing the girl and the child in the road, though the driver shouted an oath at them.

'That was your papa, surely?' Nell said. 'He should not let the driver go so fast in a narrow lane like this.'

'Oh, it is not his driver,' returned Caroline indifferently. 'That's Mrs Wynne-Gaskoin's carriage. She always drives fast.'

'Does she, indeed. Who is she, Caroline?'

'Oh, just a lady. She used to come to our house when there were dinner-parties, but now Mama doesn't receive. She's very rich. I heard Betsy telling Mary-Ann. Papa likes her.' Caroline could not have explained why she knew this.

Strolling up the steep lane, empty of vehicles, Nell pondered. Mrs Wynne-Gaskoin (what a name!) was young, languorously lovely, widowed, to judge by her half-mourning dress, very rich; and Papa liked her.

The pieces of a puzzle began to come together in her mind, and the pattern they formed was an ominous one.

65

V

The Secrets of New Georgia

She would have been saved a great deal of speculation if she had been able to attend as an unseen presence at an encounter in a graceful, stately house in a Georgian terrace at the foot of Highgate Rise, less than an hour after the near-fatality at the Cemetery gate.

The time was four o'clock. It was the hour dedicated to afternoon tea, but, though the finest porcelain had been set out with delicate bread and butter; cakes and sandwiches, and the best Lapsang infused gently in the most elegant of teapots, Manfred Pye and Olivia Wynne-Gaskoin were not partaking of these dainties. The sofa was wide, accommodating them both comfortably so long as they jointly took up the room of only one person, as they were doing, with enthusiasm restrained by the thought that servants have sharp ears.

At length the gentleman, with a prolonged sigh of satisfaction, rolled off towards the supporting back of the sofa, and the lady's ecstatic moans died away into deep-drawn breaths. Soon there would be all the fuss of dressing: corsets to be re-laced, buttons fastened, the grim lobster-pot of the crinoline frame to be stepped into once again, the complexities of drawers, petticoat-laces, trousers and boots to be dealt with and overcome, all without the assistance of maid or valet. Until that moment came they would enjoy a brief respite, a few content, close moments of pleasant conversation.

'If she were to die in childbirth ... ' mused the gentleman.

'No such luck,' responded the lady. 'Few mothers are lost nowadays, since these new ideas of cleanliness came in.'

Manfred Pye gave a shudder of distaste. 'Pray don't talk about such things.'

'Oh, but I find them fascinating. One speck of infectious dirt, and

66

we win – a thorough scrub with chlorinated lime, and we lose. All a gamble. I love a gamble – and a gambler.' Contentedly she nibbled his neck. He responded automatically with some skilful palpation which almost re-started the activities just ended.

'My delicious Olivia,' he murmured into a plump white shoulder. 'All woman. Yet so stately, so dignified ... My love, when you giggle like that you cause me the most intimate discomfort. I am quite aware that our present posture is not a dignified one. What I am saying is that you are so entirely fitted to be an ornament to a man of ambition – his queen, his consort, his helpmeet. Unlike that ... No, I can hardly bear to talk of her.'

'You've tried ... everything?'

'Everything discreet. Sudden shocks. An infusion of the fungi I told you of – she is uncommonly fond of mushrooms *au gratin*, and the cheese disguises the taste. But I fear they were not the right kind ... I reduced some of the contents of her smelling-salts bottle to a liquified state, and added it to a spiced breakfast-dish, but she was instantly sick. She is continually sick, even at this late stage.'

'It is not uncommon. Well, then, what next?'

'The thing I mentioned to you.'

Olivia raised on one dimpled elbow, interested. 'You told me hardly anything about it. *Is* it magic, really and truly?'

'Ssh. Someone might overhear.'

'I should think they would have heard quite enough already, in that case. Come, don't be a tease – do tell. You know how inquisitive I am.'

'Not even you, my love; it must be a dead secret. I think, I believe, I have the right helper now, the one without whom this could not be done. Intelligent, innocent – indeed, a virgin.'

Olivia raised dark eyebrows. 'You know that?'

'How could I possibly know? I assume it.'

'You don't intend to find out for yourself?' Her voice was barbed with jealousy.

'There is no need for coarseness. You must leave all this to me.'

'With pleasure. It all sounds very dubious, and dangerous too.'

'Ah, now, perhaps. But when I take up residence in the Mansion

67

House, with you by my side, my Lady Mayoress in the finest of furs and diamonds, will you remember the danger then? Oh no, my lovely one. *Then* you will be glad of all I have done for you, dubious or dangerous. The prize will be ours, the risks are all mine.' He did not add that he was looking forward to those risks, relishing the thought of practising the black arts he had studied so carefully, proving himself as the magician he was sure he had the power to be. Olivia would not understand.

Olivia shifted and gave a tiny yawn. Manfred did talk so, in a twopence-coloured manner she found amusing sometimes and boring at others. She would like nothing more than to be Lady Mayoress, or even the wife of an alderman. The life of a widow, even a rich one, was not enviable to a full-blooded experienced woman in her ripe thirties. It was a nuisance to have to be always discreet, always pretending, never able to go upstairs together openly to the soft feather-mattressed half-tester bed she had once happily shared with her stockbroker husband. But she wished that Manfred would not go about the business of freeing himself for her in such a fantastic way. Delicately she forebore to ask herself what other way would have met with her approval.

'I think,' she said, 'I hear someone on the stairs.'

Nell was reading to Caroline. The books provided in the nursery she considered on the whole dull, pompous and sentimental. It could not do a child any good to be told continuously of other children dying of wasting diseases brought on by their own wickedness – such as sewing a doll's frock on the Sabbath. Instead she had chosen a *Child's Domestic History of England*, which dealt pleasantly with interesting things and used picturesque antique language. Today they were in the age of Elizabeth, wandering in the pleasure-garden of a gentle-man of quality.

'"At the back of the house,"' Nell read, '"it was neither field, nor garden, or orchard, or rather it was all of these: for they came into a place cunningly set with trees of the most taste-pleasing fruits. But scarcely had they taken that into consideration ere they were suddenly stepped into a delicate green; on each side of the green a

68

thicket, and beside each thicket again new beds of flowers. In the midst of all the place was a fair pond, whose shaking crystal was a perfect mirror to all the other beauties —"'

The nursery door opened. Manfred Pye stood there, watching with mild amusement the red hair, now neatly drawn back into a knot, bent over the book. What a picture of maidenly meekness; it was time to test her armour.

'I fear I interrupt your studies, Miss Carey. But if you can spare the time, I would like to show you some features of this house which you have not seen and may find instructive.'

Caroline's face fell. She would like to have known what lay beyond the flowery thickets and the crystal pond.

Nell rose obediently. 'If you wish, sir. We will finish the chapter tomorrow, Caroline. You may tidy away the books now.'

Without any further word Pye led her down the two flights of stairs to the hallway, then paused, and to her surprise produced a key, and inserted it into the carved border of one of the panels that lined the hall in imitation of the baronial style. The panel, border and all, swung gently inwards. Within a short flight of stairs led down to a dim passage. He turned to her with a smile.

'Ashurst Lodge is full of surprises. I dare say you wonder where we are going now?'

She was, and, more anxiously, whether she should be accompanying a gentleman without the protection of some other female. Surely he could have invited Caroline to come as well? But he had taken no notice of her.

Nervously she said, 'I imagine Mrs Pye would approve of my ... of ... Perhaps she would wish to accompany us ... '

'Mrs Pye has no interest in this part of the house. She has a dread of subterranean regions and has always refused to visit it,' he answered brusquely, as though it were a matter of annoyance to him; as indeed it was. 'Follow me – it is not very dark.'

The passage was quite dark enough, with the door shut behind them, Nell thought, but fortunately it was a short one. At the end of it lay another door. She heard him unlock it and followed him into the room beyond. Telling her to stay at the door, he struck a safety-match and lit a gas-lamp, then another and another, until ten in all were glowing with a greenish light. Each was contained in a green globe, but Nell did not notice that, only the strange, eerie effect.

She moved cautiously forward and looked about her. What she had expected, it would have been hard to say. An exhibition of priceless pictures, perhaps, or a gallery of statues? But the walls were bare of anything but a striped wall-paper. An ordinary-looking wooden chair with arms stood by itself, and a smaller one some distance away.

Nell was beginning to suspect that she was being hoaxed, or that she had been lured to this strange empty room for some evil purpose. In the back of her mind was the thought that a man who plays tricks with his eyes might well be capable of other slippery deceptions. She began to be afraid.

'I see nothing remarkable, sir,' she said.

'No, of course not. But you will, you will, Miss Carey. Won't you take a seat?' He waved her towards the armchair.

Reluctantly she sat down poised to start up again if he made a move towards her. But the moment she was properly seated, her arms along the arms of the chair, two iron bands shot out from the wood and clamped themselves round her wrists, while another sprang from under the seat to enclose her thighs in its grip.

Nell gave a loud scream. Manfred Pye began to laugh as though he would never stop. Between gusts he gasped out, 'Very – very neat, an't it? Have you ever – found a chair so welcoming?'

She was very frightened, but fury surged up from the fear that should have struck her dumb.

'This is some very bad joke. Please release me at once.'

The laughter quietened. Mildly he said, 'Of course.' What he did she could not see, but the iron clamps receded as suddenly as they had emerged. Nell got to her feet and made for the door. But it was firmly shut, and there was no handle to turn. She stood with her back against it, glaring at her employer, who had never appeared more amiable or happy.

'You are right, Miss Carey. It *was* a joke, if a bad one. Are you very, very frightened?'

She would not let him think her a coward. 'No, merely alarmed.'

'You think me very eccentric, no doubt. Well, well, perhaps I am. But I entreat you to bear with me a little farther in my small experiment. Come towards me. So, just a few steps more. Look at the wall on your left.'

She turned towards it. A whole section of it slid down, and out from it came a human skeleton, which seemed to glide rapidly towards her, then stopped a few inches away. Again she screamed, confronting the yellowed bones, black pits of eye-sockets, gap-toothed grin. Manfred Pye was chuckling and smiling broadly.

'Well done, oh well done – most young women would have fainted away.' He tapped his foot and the skeleton disappeared into the wall.

Girl and man faced each other. Nell swiftly summed up the situation; it was a talent she had acquired in a country where it was always likely that one might turn a corner and confront a poisonous snake. For some reason Manfred Pye was putting her through a test – unless he was merely tormenting her for fun. In either case it would not do to let him win by breaking her nerve.

'What next?' she asked coolly, though her knees were trembling.

'You might find this seat more comfortable than the other.' He indicated the smaller chair. Nell walked to it and sat down. For a moment nothing happened. Then suddenly, sickeningly, the chair dropped several feet below the ground, jolting every bone in her body and taking her breath away. She was in a narrow pit, but not alone. The faint green light from above showed that she was ringed round with the snakes she had been thinking of only a few moments before. There they were, the enemies of her childhood – cobras, vipers, kraits, rattlesnakes, pythons, all menacing her, with necks reared, huge mouths gaping, poison fangs sharp and ready. It was the most terrifying sight she had ever seen, would ever see.

Fortunately for her resolve, she was so paralysed by fear that she could not even scream, as helpless as though the venom had already entered her blood. It took a supreme effort of will to focus her eyes on the hooded cobra, the most fearful of all, long enough to realise that its head was not swaying in preparation for the kill. It was motionless. So were they all, for they were models.

The chair began to rise, more slowly than it had descended. Pye

71

was waiting for her, alight with curiosity. 'You didn't scream,' he said disappointedly.

'Why should I?' She felt that her voice was coming out as a croak. 'Very clever toys. Did you make them?'

Pye surveyed her face, from which all the colour had drained, leaving it a greenish-white, even to her lips. Her hands were clasped tightly together to stop them shaking. She dared not trust herself to get up from the chair, and he knew it. Yet she had not screamed or fainted. A woman he had chosen to frighten for his amusement had died from the effects of his little experiment in terror. Her heart had simply ceased to beat in the snake-pit, and he had had the devil of a job explaining the presence of a corpse in the hall, where he had dragged it, leaving his secret domain locked behind him.

If only Claudia could have been persuaded to venture through the panel! He had tried to coax her, with promises of a strange and pretty collection, including some rare books and prints. It was not like her to resist him when he coaxed, and he would never know why she did. Perhaps it was from maternal instinct, urging her to protect the child she carried. What a pity. Claudia was of a nervous disposition at the best of times, and he might well have sent her over the edge of reason. But then she would merely have gone mad, and he would still have been fettered to her, unable to marry again.

'No, I did not make them,' he told Nell. 'I bought them, from a dealer in curiosities. He told me they had come from a cottage called New Georgia, near the Spaniards Inn, in Hampstead. The owner was Robert Caston, a notable eccentric who made a living by showing off his little mechanical contrivances for the diversion of visitors.'

'I hope they were suitably diverted.'

'Yes, indeed. Some people enjoy being frightened, you know. But others were less charmed, and he had to close the place almost a hundred years ago. There are other delights, beside those you have seen – if I release a panel on that wall a huge stuffed bear, much larger than a tall man, will advance to embrace the visitor – not fatally, of course ... No?'

Nell found the strength to stand up. 'No, thank you. I should like to leave now, if you please.'

'Certainly.' As they returned to the hall he told her proudly of how he had the New New Georgia specially built, trapdoors fitted, every modern mechanical aid supplied to add to the shocking effects of old Robert Caston's ingenious diversions.

When Nell regained her room she lay down on the bed, waiting for her nerves and muscles to quieten. Manfred Pye was mad, quite mad, and she was in his power. Two choices lay open to her: to go to Claudia, tell her all, and resign from her position, or to keep quiet and see what happened next. Possibly nothing more would happen. Pye had enjoyed himself giving her a good fright; and that might be the extent of his intentions towards her. She very much hoped so.

A few days later a letter came from Barnaby in answer to one she had written. He had arranged for Harry to be given a riding lesson on the following Saturday, and would contrive to bring him to a meeting-point in Highgate Wood, not too far for Caroline to walk.

Saturday was fine and warm, a perfect day for strolling gently to a meeting which Nell longed for with all her heart. Caroline too was excited. At last she was going to see the brother her dear Miss Carey loved and talked of so much. Her fancy created a younger version of Nell, but dashingly male, one who might even graciously condescend to admire her a little, now that her nose was no longer so red. She wore her new yellow muslin dress, which she thought the most beautiful one she had ever possessed. She was almost eight, conscious for the first time of being female.

There they were, visible through the light screens of summer leaves, in the clearing Barnaby had described, by a great hollow oak. A bay horse and a hired brown pony, and two figures – Barnaby, looking eagerly about him, but – the other?

Nell stood still, clutching Caroline's hand. This could not be Harry, this boy at least an inch taller than he had been, and so thin that the once smart tweed suit hung loosely on him. Even his hair seemed faded, or perhaps it was never washed. His pale face certainly looked unclean, with spots, like small boils, disfiguring his brow. He was staring ahead of him, as though lost in a gloomy reverie.

'Harry!' She ran forward over the yards of ground between them, and clasped him in her arms. He smelt musty, like the miasma of old clothes which whiffed out at one from shops in certain low London streets. His arms came round her, but only limply, then fell away.

She looked a startled question at Barnaby, who shook his head warningly before greeting her.

'Miss Carey, how well you followed my instructions. I thought I might not have made them clear enough.'

'Oh, perfectly. Caroline, this is my friend Mr Lyon. Barnaby, Harry, this is Miss Caroline Pye.'

Caroline made her best little curtsey and extended her hand to both. She thought tall Mr Lyon charming, with such fetching curls and nice eyes, but she was bitterly disappointed in Harry. Perhaps Mr Lyon had brought the wrong boy?

'I think Miss Caroline and Harry might like to get to know each other,' Barnaby said. 'Take Miss Caroline for a walk, Harry, and show her where the wild roses grow.'

'All right. Come on.' Harry said ungraciously.

Alone with Barnaby, Nell asked urgently, 'What in Heaven's name is the matter with him? Is he ill? I thought he'd be so glad to see me, after all these weeks, yet ... oh, what is it?'

'How I wish I knew! I told you he was unhappy, bullied. I tried to stop that – indeed, I thought I had. He seemed to be getting on better in class, and I was giving him a bit of help myself. Then – and this is why I came to see you in Gower Street – the whole trouble seemed to begin again. Last week he was beaten by Mr Channer himself for 'silent insolence', and there was nothing I could do to stop it. I've wished he could catch a fever, to be away from it all in the sickroom. Anything.'

Nell sat down suddenly on a tree-stump, her head in her hands.

'What a beast I am, what an unfeeling beast! Barnaby, when you came to see me that time I promised, *promised*, to do something for him, and I've done nothing, just thought about myself and my own affairs and my new position at the Pyes'. How could I not have not tried to see him, do something?'

'It would have done no good. I'm afraid it will do no good even

74

now, your coming here. If Harry refuses to talk to me, whom he
trusts, then ... '

'"Whom he trusts?" Doesn't he trust me, then?'

'I ... what can I say, Miss Carey? He muttered something about
your deserting him, one day when I tried to talk to him.'

Nell tore off her gloves, screwed them up into a ball, then threw
them from her. 'Oh, I could kill myself. Barnaby, what shall I do?'

'Suppose I take charge of Miss Caroline, then leave you alone with
Harry. That will at least give you a chance to talk, with nobody
listening.'

Soon he returned with the two children, who seemed not to be
speaking to each other, though Caroline clutched a handful of wild
roses. Offered a pony-ride, she was shy and nervous and excited all at
once, but went off readily enough with Barnaby towards the wide
path that made the wood easy for horses. Nell thought what a good
father Barnaby would make some day for his fortunate children.

She had longed to be alone with Harry, but now the time had come
she felt numb and powerless. She took the grimy hands in hers,
seeing with pity the bitten nails; he had always had such pretty
hands, as a little boy. But he was not a little boy any more, just a
youth who was almost a stranger to her, who looked at her with dead
eyes and set his mouth in a sullen line.

'Harry ... darling. What is it? *Did* you tell Barnaby you thought
I'd deserted you?'

One shoulder shrugged. 'You never came.'

'Dear, I couldn't. I have to work now – you know, I wrote to you.'

'You didn't.'

'But I did write, Harry. Just a few days after I moved to Mr Pye's,
telling you all about it, and about Caroline, and saying I'd come and
see you as soon as I could get away, but it might be difficult.'

He shook his head irritably. A shocking thought struck her.

'Have you had any letters at all – not just that one?'

'No.'

So it was true, her suspicion. Those unspeakable beasts at Gower
Street had given orders for Harry's correspondence to be intercepted,
and the hateful Channer had agreed. Such rage boiled up in Nell that

75

she struck her fist against the bark of a tree as though it were the face of one of those three. Harry watched uninterestedly.

'I saw Mamma,' he said.

'Mamma? Where? You mean she came to see you?'

'In the road. Outside the school. Just standing there, crying. *She* didn't desert me, you see. But they wouldn't let her in.'

He spoke flatly, without emotion, as though past feeling, past hope. Nell was near to despair; it seemed that Harry was caught in the jaws of a trap which she was powerless to open. She tried a last gambit.

'Can't you tell me about it, dear? I mean about what is so awful at Yew House – not just the letters from Mamma being shut out, but the rest of it. There is something, isn't there? Something bad?'

Yes, something very bad, too bad to tell his sister, even if she did seem to him like a figure in a dream, not the old dear Nell. How could he find words, or say them, to describe what awaited him every night, after the dormitory door had shut behind the master in charge?

His early tormentors had taken notice of Barnaby's threats, and left Harry alone in the playground and the classroom. But Barnaby, in his uncertain status, neither quite boy nor quite master, had not authority to enter the younger pupils' dormitory, a natural place for the continuance of the persecution. Harry's foreign background and reputation as a sissy and a mother's pet would have been forgiven and forgotten if he had fought back at first. But the others were too strong for him, and despised him all the more for his weakness.

So they had continued to torture him physically, in ways that humiliated him to the depths of his being. Nothing was too crude or lewd for them to do to him, a child who knew nothing of life, nature or sex. Two of the bigger boys, Tapworth and White, took it upon themselves to educate him in these respects, by practical demonstrations and verbal assaults. In their mouths his mother, his sister, his aunts were turned into gross monsters, things worse than beasts. Tales of the brutalities practised on women and children in the Mutiny, so near to his own memories, were told to him until he screamed, even in his sleep. Very capably, by word and deed, these

76

two young fiends destroyed Harry's innocence and his self-respect.

When they finally let him be at night, he lay awake wishing himself dead. There was a school legend about a boy who had hanged himself in the wash-house, years before. Harry wondered how he did it, and whether it would be very difficult. He had even been into the wash-house to work out the possibilities. If he stood on the copper, and threw a loop of clothes-line up to one of the hooks on the ceiling, it might be just possible, small though he was. He would try it one day, when there was nobody much about.

So when Nell asked him about the 'something bad', he shook his head and tightened his lips.

Barnaby was coming back to them, leading the pony on which the delighted Caroline was still sitting, her skirts tucked up so that she could ride astride. When she had been lifted down Nell led Barnaby aside.

'It's all much worse than I thought. Oh, he won't talk to me, but I know. Something *must* be done, Barnaby, before he goes mad – or worse. I didn't know, oh, I didn't know ... '

Barnaby's arms were round her, and he was patting her shoulders as though she were a frightened horse.

'Don't let Harry see you cry,' he said. 'Smile. Talk about something ordinary. Keep your head clear. Harry depends on you, and only you – I can do nothing more without getting turned away from the school, and that would do no good.'

'*I* shall do something,' said Nell, between her teeth. 'I shall get him away from that place, if I have to commit murder to do it. Just let me have the chance, that's all!'

It came sooner than she had expected: that same night.

VI

The Black Spell

A light was shining into Nell's eyes.

For a half-dreaming second she thought it was the morning sun filtering through the curtains. Then, fully awake, she knew it for candle-light. The holder of the candle was Manfred Pye, standing beside her bed, peering down at her. He wore a dressing-robe and a tasselled smoking-cap, rakishly tilted, and carried a large book under his arm.

'Don't scream,' he said softly. With one sharp pull he threw the bed-clothes down to her feet, uncovering her completely. She gasped with shock, though her body was hidden from neck to ankle by a voluminous cotton nightgown, close-frilled at throat and wrists. Her arms went protectively across her breasts as she stared wildly up at him.

Pye smiled and nodded. 'That's what I wanted to see. Not your charming undraped form, my dear, but your virginal shrinking from inspection. You *are* a virgin, are you not?'

'Sir! Get out of my room at once!'

'Answer my question. Are you a virgin?'

A chaos of answers rose to her lips, but she could only nod. He pulled the bedclothes up again and patted them down like a nurse putting an infant to bed.

'Good, as I thought. And don't fear that I came to your room with the intention of altering that happy state. Such an act would no doubt be highly pleasurable, but it would entirely defeat my object.'

Nell was now quite sure that he was completely mad. She must keep calm, treat him as a reasonable being.

'What object, sir? Pray keep your voice down, the nursemaid sleeps in the next room.'

'Certainly. I have no more wish to be compromised than you have. May I sit?' Without waiting for permission, he took the small bedside chair. Nell sat up, so that her arms were free should he make any sudden move. Her hair, plaited into two thick ropes, hung over her shoulders, making her seem years younger than her age; an appearance Pye approved greatly.

'My object,' he said. 'Well, to tell you the whole story of that would take time. Very briefly, I require the assistance of a young person who must be completely chaste – I'd like to wager you've never even been kissed, my dear? Pray don't flash your eyes at me like that, handsome though they are – completely chaste, in order to carry out an experiment, an experiment in the occult. You don't know what that is? Another name for something commonly known as witchcraft.'

'I see,' Nell said calmly.

'Do you? This is nothing to do with flying through the air on broomsticks, and yet – yes, there was a form of ointment used in that, too. I have to perform a ceremony, you see, which cannot be performed alone. I shall be the priest, you the acolyte.'

Nell wished very much she had kept up her confirmation classes at St Pancras Church. 'Perhaps you would tell me what it is, sir.'

'Indeed. Quite simply, we shall need to remove a corpse from its coffin in one of the Catacombs in the Cemetery, obtain various bones, and subject them to a process which will ... extract a fluid which I shall mix with ... certain herbs and powders. I shall then use this for my own purposes, which need not concern you. Oh – and an incantation must be said by the acolyte during the preparation. It is called the Black Spell.'

A long pause followed as Nell incredulously took in the information.

'Well?'

She drew a deep breath. 'I absolutely refuse. I will *not* take part in anything so ... so irreverent. Yes, and so disgusting. I can hardly believe I heard you properly, sir. Surely such horrible practices don't take place nowadays – not in England. In India I expect the natives did such things, though I never heard of them. But here, now, in

London … And you think I'd be a party …' She remembered that she was talking to a madman, and lowered her voice. 'You must excuse me.'

Pye left the chair and sat on the side of her bed, causing her to move away from him.

'I know what it is,' he said. 'You doubt my powers. You think I am only fitted to play with the mechanical tricks you saw downstairs. But it's not so, I assure you. I am – ' he straightened his shoulders and said with pride, 'I am a warlock. An incantator, a *veneficius*, a magician.'

'Yes, I'm sure you are. And a very … powerful one, too. But that makes no difference, I'm afraid.'

'You refuse to do what I ask?'

'Yes.'

He sighed. 'Oh, what a pity. I thought you would be more reasonable. Let me put something to you. I see in you a young lady very much troubled on behalf of a relative. A brother. More than ever troubled, during the day just past. Oh, you may look surprised, Miss Carey, but I know this not by divination but by word of mouth. You see, my small daughter talked to me yesterday evening, when I paid a visit to her at her bedtime. She told me, with a little prompting, how she and you had met your brother at an appointed spot, and how unwell and out of sorts he seemed, and how you shed tears on the way home and said some very wild things. Children do notice, Miss Carey, and can be persuaded to repeat things. Your brother is ill?'

'I think so.'

'And ill-treated?'

Nell forgot caution. 'Almost to the point of going out of his mind.'

'And you are quite desperate to get him away from the school which I so unwisely recommended to your aunts? Yes, I see that. Well, I offer you two alternatives. If you still refuse to help me in my experiment, at no danger to yourself, I will dismiss you from your post and return you to your aunts, who will certainly not help you to remove the boy. If you are sensible and do as I ask, I will myself take him away from the school and bring him here, to be under your care and educated by a private tutor. Your aunts will agree if I put the thing on a basis of money: I think I know those ladies. Come – an easy night's work for such a reward?'

Nell was thinking hard, making a desperate decision. Even if Pye were stark staring mad he was capable of carrying out either threat or promise. The whole fantastic operation might be a figment of his imagination; she had only to go through with whatever nonsensical actions he demanded, and Harry would be saved. She herself risked very little. Whatever it was, it would be worthwhile.

'Very well,' she said. 'I have little choice, have I? If you will really and truly free my brother ... Then yes.'

'Well done! Decided very properly. I knew you were a girl of good sense. Be ready tomorrow night, at this time, fully dressed. I shall not come to your room, but you will meet me by the door at the end of the kitchen passage. Wear stout boots and a cloak that will not be conspicuous. Goodnight.'

He was gone, as swiftly and silently as the supernatural being he declared himself to be. The night was quiet. A soft wind stirred the garden trees; in the next room Betsy was snoring. Had it been a ridiculous dream, or had Manfred Pye really come to her room and made his fantastic proposition? Nell decided that she would lie awake all night to work out the implications of what she thought had happened. And, sliding under the warm bedclothes, fell asleep.

Even next day it seemed unreal. As the hours passed Nell began to believe that the visit had really happened, and that the man was sincere in what he had said, what he thought himself to be. But that his Black Spell would work she could not for an instant believe. On whom, or what, was it supposed to work? His career in the City? Some enemy – but whom? The thought of his careless manner towards his wife crossed her mind, but she dismissed it. He could intend no evil towards the woman who was just about to produce what might be his hoped-for heir.

She switched her thoughts to Harry. Harry, free from whatever horror oppressed him at Yew House; Harry, here with her to be soothed and loved and cured of the trouble that weighed on him, Harry taught as a delicate boy should be by a mild tutor. Harry ...

Claudia, pouring out tea, glanced over the table at Nell.

'*Post equitem sedet atra Cura?*' she enquired.

Nell started. 'I beg your pardon?'

'Black Care riding behind the horseman. That is how you look, my dear. Preoccupied, your thoughts somewhere else. Is that so?'

'No, not at all. I was thinking of ... my brother, and other things. I'm sorry if I was inattentive. Mrs Pye, are you feeling well?' Claudia had suddenly twisted into an awkward position, one hand in the small of her back, her face sharpened with pain. The spasm, or whatever it was, seemed to pass, as she said, 'Quite, thank you. For a moment I thought ... But it was nothing.'

How vulnerable she looked, thought Nell, such a small lady to be carrying such an enormous child. The child of Manfred Pye. He must not, must not, be planning some evil against her.

'If I should die – ' Claudia began, startlingly echoing Nell's thoughts, 'oh don't look shocked, it happens. I am not young, and Caroline's birth was difficult – if I should die, give me your promise to stay here and take care of them both. Caroline and my dear husband. I see now, since you came, what a bad mother I've been to my child. It has not been her fault; I think I've loved her father too much to have room for her. Nell – ' she stretched out a thin hand, and Nell took it – 'he will miss me.' The devil he will, thought Nell, echoing a favourite phrase of Papa's. 'I know I'm not ... all he would wish, but he does care for me a little. Promise me you'll be his angel, when I'm gone, Nell.'

'I promise.' Nell did not specify what kind of angel she would be. 'But you mustn't talk like that, Mrs Pye. Everything is going to go very well.'

That night, as St Michael's clock was striking twelve, she was hoping earnestly that the same would apply to the expedition she was about to make with her employer. She was wrapped in a dark mantle which completely covered her dress, and a black scarf hid her hair. A sick loathing for what she was about to do filled her with something near

82

to nausea. She looked long and hard at the portrait of Lady Jacquette, and talked to it, her only confidante.

'Was I right to agree to this awful thing? Would you have done it? Yes, I suppose you would, three hundred years ago. And it will mean so much to Harry if I can only make myself do it. Please give me a sign that I'm right.'

How useless, talking to a painted panel and a woman long dead. Nell turned away, listened for a moment to Betsy's snores, and hoped earnestly that Caroline would not waken with a nightmare, as she sometimes did, and want comforting. Then she went softly to the door, glancing back into the room, in which the only illumination came from the gas-lamp in the lane, throwing flickering shadows on the wall.

What an odd shadow it made on the wall where the portrait hung. Jacquette's face, the wide ruff and and the heart-shaped head-dress seemed larger, life-size, and below was the dark shape of a Tudor dress, wide skirts falling from a wheel farthingale set below the pointed waist, sleeves puffed at the shoulder. The figure was quite motionless, except that something colourful sparkled above the face. The jewelled coif, of course. Nell could make out red and blue points of light, and the milky sheen of pearls. But those colours had been hardly visible in the painting, obscured by the smoke and grime of centuries. Nell stared and stared, blinked – and the illusion was gone: just the dark square of the picture remained, and a shifting pattern of leaves.

No time now to wonder and reflect on what she thought she had seen. Shutting the door softly, she went downstairs without a single creak of floorboards or a missed step. What a mercy the house was new and stoutly built.

He was waiting where he had said, by the door that led from the kitchen quarters to a yard where coals and wood were stored. Silently he opened the door, already unlocked, and ushered her out and across the yard to a gate from which a pathway led round to the tradesmen's entrance and the front of the house. Beyond it he paused.

'Well done. The butler and the page sleep beyond the kitchens. They can have heard nothing. Here.' He unscrewed the top of a flask and poured some of the contents into it. 'This will help to calm your nerves. Drink it down.'

It was brandy, which Nell had seldom tasted. She half-choked on the fiery spirit, coughed, recovered herself, and felt a welcome warm glow inside. Pye drank from the flask himself, picked up the carpet-bag he had brought, and whispered to her to walk beside him and not to talk.

The summer night was moonless but light enough to show them the road. Pye turned right, towards the top of Swain's Lane and stopped at a small gate at the farthest end of the Cemetery, by the North Lodge. Producing a key, he unlocked it. With a raucous squeak the gate opened, and they entered. They were now on the broad clear path that led to the Cemetery's showpiece, the Circle of Lebanon, a ring of vaults below ground level, surrounding a great cedar tree, all that remained of the garden of Sir William Ashurst, whose house had been demolished to build the church.

Nell had wandered round the Circle by daylight, gazed in awe at the massive iron doors of the vaults, reflected morbidly on their contents, and passed on to the pleasanter surroundings of the walks and flower-plots outside. Tonight the earthy smell of the vaults was strong and she had an almost irresistible impulse to run away.

But Pye sensed it, looked round at her warningly, and, pausing at the entrance to the vaults, took out from under his voluminous cloak a dark-lantern, and adjusted it so that its beam shone out on the low gate under the archway, and on his own figure, like a huge bat with folded wings. Again he produced a key-ring, and unlocked the gate.

'How did you get the keys?' Nell ventured to ask.

'There are ways.'

They were inside the Circle of Lebanon, the massive old tree looming overhead, the stone doors, facing each other, on either side of them. The dank smell of earth was stronger now. The third key on the ring, a large, heavy one, Pye inserted in the lock of a vault on the right-hand side. It was rusty, and only strong pressure finally persuaded it to turn. He pushed the iron door, which at first refused to yield.

'Help. Put your shoulder to it,' he commanded. Their joint weight finally moved the door inwards, far enough to allow them to enter.

The lantern-light showed Nell a small, cave-like apartment with shelves along its walls. On the shelves were coffins: she counted seven. So they were not, after all, going to dig one up out of the earth; that was a relief, if anything could be in such a situation. Pye put the lantern down and rubbed his hands.

'Excellent. Exactly right. No one placed here for many years.' He peered at the name-plate of one coffin. '1845. That should serve nicely. Open my bag.'

Nell, on her knees on the damp floor, fumbled with the clasp of the carpet-bag. The cold was intense, striking up from the stone, and the scent of death was becoming more oppressive every minute. Trying to think of nothing, she produced from the bag the few tools it contained – a wrench, a screw-driver, a small claw-hammer and a tin bottle, filled with lubricant oil. The only other object was a folded sack.

'Come here, hold up the lantern,' he ordered. Under its light he went to work. Nell tried not to watch, but her eyes kept returning to the coffin-lid, as he loosened it all round after removing the screws, which were rusty and reluctant to leave the holes they had occupied for eighteen years. At last, with a triumphant cry, he wrenched the lid off.

Nell pulled the scarf off her head and tied it round her nose and mouth. Pye was working inside the coffin, at a yellowish cloth covering something she could not yet see. Pulling it open.

She made an incoherent sound and pushed past him, through the door and into the comparatively fresh air of the path between the catacombs. She heard him calling her, but nothing would have got her inside again. She leaned against the doorway, trying to control her rebellious stomach, until at last, after what seemed hours, sounds inside told her that he had finished whatever he was doing. Tools clinking, scrapings and shufflings indicated that the coffin was being closed and pushed back into place, and a faint unmusical whistling proclaimed that Pye was satisfied with his work.

He came out, shutting and locking the door. The carpet-bag seemed full now, and heavy, as he picked it up again.

'Queasy, miss?' he asked her in a jocular voice, quite unlike his own. 'Never mind, I contrived nicely without you. Now we will go home, and you will keep quiet on the way. No puking, mind!'

As they began to retrace their steps the church clock under the tall steeple struck two.

VII

What the Gardener saw

'We shall conduct our operation in the garden,' Pye told Nell, as they re-entered the gate of Ashurst Lodge.

'Not the kitchen?' She doubted that he would catch the sardonic inflection in her voice, and he did not.

'I think not. The servants rise so early.' He led the way round to the farthest end of the gardens. Nell could make out the shapes of one or two sheds, a small conservatory, and a table-like object which proved to be an incinerator built of bricks. Pye felt the fragments of charred leaf and flower inside it. 'Quite dry. Capital.' He set down the lantern, its beam turned away from the direction of the house, and unfastened the carpet-bag. Inside, at the top, was the cloth she had seen before, now rolled up around something. Nell watched with horrified fascination as he lifted it out and unfolded it. A quantity of bones fell with a clatter to the ground. Nell had thought of bones as white, but these were dark, yellowish. She stepped back, her hand over her mouth. She could not distinguish most of them, but there was no mistaking the skull!

They were to be cooked, it seemed, in a large iron pot, the sort which in a large kitchen would be suspended over a fire. At Pye's command she helped him lift the heavy thing to the top of the incinerator, which he had filled with twigs from a basket in the potting-shed. He must have had a whole range of aids to his experiment stored in there; Nell wondered what the gardener thought. A large watering-can was tilted over the cooking-pot. When it held enough water, Pye dropped the bones into it, one by one, muttering under his breath, and lit the fire.

When the odour of the boiling became unbearable Nell took

refuge in the potting-shed and shut the door, disregarding Pye's call to her to come back. She huddled her cloak tightly round herself. It must be long after two o'clock. She should have been tired, longing for her bed, but tension, fear and disgust fought any desire for sleep.

Rancid smoke filled the air round them and drifted away in clouds. Surely someone would smell it — someone in Sydney Waterlow's spacious estate which adjoined Pye's garden, sleeping with a window open to the summer night air? Nell wondered what the penalty for grave-robbing was now, and whether her youth would be taken into consideration when their case came up in court.

The fire, glinting through the bricks of the incinerator, was dying down. Pye lifted the pot down by its handle — thank goodness he had not asked her to help him with that. As she watched apprehensively he poured some of the liquid contents into the ground, set the pot down, and with a pair of long fire-tongs extracted the bones, and laid them side by side on the ground. The predawn light was growing; Nell looked away from the ghastly sight. Then, to her alarm, she saw that he was approaching the potting-shed, opening the door.

'Now,' he said gleefully, 'comes our great moment.' He fetched in the lantern. 'Here are the ingredients.' He displayed a handful of foliage, shredded fine. 'I collected them with much care. Hemlock — aconite — the leaves of poplar — chimney-soot — and — a medicinal powder.' The powder was arsenic, obtained by a servant for the ostensible purpose of poisoning rats. 'Into this bowl I pour a little, only a little, of the sacred ichor.' He did, and the shed was rank with the stench of it. He paused. 'Now, child, kneel.'

'Kneel?'

'You heard. Be quick before the ichor cools. Now repeat after me the spell, word by word.' Slowly, solemnly, he intoned, echoed by Nell.

'*Lazos — Athame — Calyolas — Samahac — et Famyolas — Harrahaya*! Now, the sacred names — and bow the head at each one. *Leviathan — Balberith — Sonneillon — Carreau — Rosier — Beelzebub*!'

All this time he was stirring the leaf-mixture into the stinking bowl. When it was all mixed in, he bent over it and muttered words Nell could not hear. Then, holding the bowl before him as reverently as though it were the blood of a sacrifice, he stalked out of the shed in the direction of the house. Nell called after him.

'Come back! What about the mess? Are you not going to tidy up? Oh, come back, do!'

Slowly he turned and looked, but she thought he hardly took in the smoke still hanging in the air, the great pot on the ground, the bones.

'Ah,' he said, 'yes. They might well notice. Er — what shall I do?'

'*Do?* Bury — those, for a start. Rinse out the pot. Put some more branches, or something, into the incinerator, and clear up the shed. I'm going back to the house.' Looking back over her shoulder she saw that he was obeying her, moving slowly, like one in a trance.

As she walked she came to a firm conclusion. The events of the night had shown her that Manfred Pye was even madder than she had guessed: mad enough to have been prepared to leave such open traces of his act on view that detection would have been inevitable. He was no warlock, merely an amateur bungler playing with dark forces. There had been no feeling of supernatural evil in the shed, only one of physical nastiness. Not for a moment did she fear that his Black Spell would work on its intended victim. She had been the instrument of a would-be villain who was also a colossal fool. And she would make him pay for it.

She waited for him by the door of the kitchen passage. When he came in sight she went out to meet him.

'Listen to me, Mr Pye,' she said quietly. 'You have just subjected me to a horrible experience. I've gone without sleep, lent myself to some sort of evil magic that could get me turned away from any Christian church if it were known, put myself in jeopardy of punishment by the law — I don't know what, perhaps a long spell in prison. And you face that too, remember.'

'Yes, yes, What are saying to me? Make haste.'

'I'm saying that I want my reward. You promised you would have my brother taken away from school and brought here to be educated by a private tutor. Well, I demand that you do that — now. At once.'

'But ... ' He looked vaguely up at the brightening sky. 'The time ... so early ... '

89

'The servants will be up soon. Go up to your room, write a letter to Mr Channer asking that my brother be brought here, this morning, on urgent family business. Then waken the page-boy and give him the note to take. Afterwards you will write to my aunts and tell them what you've done. Do you understand?'

'Yes. Yes.'

'Then go and do it. If you don't, I shall go to the police, and your Black Spell will have no chance to work, because your precious ointment will be thrown away.'

Pye stared at her, open-mouthed. 'I will do it,' he said, and went slowly past her into the house, bearing the bowl.

How easy it was, how wonderfully easy, to make people obey one, even mad people – perhaps especially mad people. Her mind a turmoil of feelings, with relief uppermost, Nell went swiftly and silently up to her room. The water in the ewer was cold, left for overnight refreshment, but she poured it into the basin, stripped, and bathed herself all over with a sponge. Then, shivering, she put on her nightgown and fell into bed. In a few moments she was asleep.

She was awakened by being violently shaken. The under-housemaid, Jane, was standing by her bed.

'Oh miss, get up please, do! They're askin' for you downstairs and you never come down to your breakfast.'

Nell dragged herself out of heavy sleep and Heaven only knew what dreams. 'What – what time is it?'

'Near eleven. You an't ill, are you, miss?'

'No, no. I'll get up now.'

'I brought your hot water, miss.'

Washed, dressed, still stupid with sleep, Nell went downstairs. Mrs Vokins, the housekeeper, was hovering in the hall with a scowl on her fat face. 'A nice time to come down. There was talk you'd died in your sleep. There's two people waiting for you in the small parlour and Miss Caroline's been taken for a walk.'

The sight of the two people in the little parlour off the hall brought a cry of joy from Nell. 'Harry! Barnaby! Oh, how quick you've been – I never expected you yet. How wonderful to see you.'

She flew to Harry and hugged him. 'My goodness, you're hot. Have you been hurrying? You didn't walk all the way, did you?'

Barnaby said gravely, 'No, Miss Carey. I rode down on Tennyson, with Harry up in front – I had to hold him on. He isn't well at all; indeed, Mr Channer thought that was why you'd sent for him.'

'Not well? What's the matter?'

'There's a sort of fever running through the school – aches and pains, spots, bad headaches. Several boys are ill with it – if it spreads the school may have to be shut down.'

Nell took Harry's listless hand. It was burning hot, as was his brow, and his eyes were inflamed and watery. 'How do you feel, my dear?'

'My head,' he said, like the child in the Bible. 'My head, my head.'

'I don't know what it is. I would have let you know, but he was only taken ill yesterday,' Barnaby said anxiously.

Nell gave him her most radiant smile. 'It was not your fault. Indeed, believe it or not, all this is most providential. I shall take care of everything, and there's not the slightest need to worry. Harry, cheer up, darling – you aren't going back to that school, now or ever, and I shall take care of you here, myself.'

For the first time a faint smile came to Harry's flushed, swollen face. 'That's lovely,' he said hoarsely.

Barnaby was still anxious. 'It seems highly infectious, Miss Carey. Do you think you should nurse him?'

'I said I would take care of everything.' She pulled the bell, and requested the maid who answered it to bring a large glass of beer and a cup of cold milk. 'Now I shall leave you for a few minutes – enjoy your drinks.' Looking back at the door, she saw that Harry's head leaned against Barnaby's shoulder, as though against a father's.

Mrs Vokins was surprised to be sought out by the governess, and even more surprised to be given what amounted to orders. She was, said Nell firmly, to prepare one of the small rooms in the wing at the back of the house as a bedroom, with another one beside it for the nurse.

'Nurse? What nurse?' Mrs Vokins bridled.

'A trained nurse – from the same agency that supplied Mrs Pye's monthly nurse, perhaps. I'll ask her, and arrange it. My brother has an illness that needs great care, and isolation from other people in the house.'

'Ho! and might I ask what it is?'

'An infection quite common to people who have lived in India,' Nell said airily.

'I don't know what the master'll say, I'm sure, bringing infectious sick people here,' grumbled Mrs Vokins. 'I'll have to ask him before I lifts a finger to get rooms ready and go to such trouble.'

'He is perfectly willing to have my brother here – indeed, it was his suggestion – and when I tell him the circumstances he will agree to any arrangements,' Nell said with confidence.

The monthly nurse, now in residence to attend on Claudia's confinement, disclosed that she came from the Aesculapian Medical and Surgical Home in Bentinck Street, Cavendish Square, and that the Home had twenty-five outdoor nurses available, one of whom was sure to be free. Her pleasant, capable manner and clean appearance were reassuring: the days of Sairey Gamp were long past, the day of Miss Nightingale and her trained nurses had happily come.

'Of course, Miss Carey,' said Nurse Pepler earnestly, 'I must make it clear that the other nurse and I must have no contact, no contact at all. It is strictly forbidden, since the link between' she lowered her voice 'deaths in childbirth and sick-nursing was understood. Would you believe it, that a doctor might go straight from tending on a gangrenous wound to a mother's bedside? Now matters are very different, and not before time. What is the nature of your brother's illness, by the way?'

'Typhus fever,' said Nell.

In the kitchen a battle was raging. The cook, Mrs Petch, a little ferret of a woman with sharp black eyes, had never been the best of friends with Mr Wooley, the head gardener. A running feud went on between them about the picking of vegetables and flowers by the kitchen staff before Mr Wooley judged them to be ready – which, in the case of flowers, was hardly ever. This morning they fought on a new ground.

' ... nasty stuff all over my rubbish-burner,' he was saying, not for the first time. 'Nasty, black, sticky stuff what wouldn't come off, and more of it in the potting-shed, not to mention a stink fit to flatten you.'

'I don't know nothing about it, Mr Wooley, like I said before and I'll say again, no more do any of the girls.' The kitchen-maid, scrubbing pans at the sink, shook her head vigorously.

Mr Wooley snorted, 'Likely story. Truth seems to me some dish got spoiled and whoever done it poured it away where it wouldn't never be seen, in *my* rightful part o' these premises. Cunning as monkeys, girls are – oh, don't tell me.' He laid his finger alongside his nose.

Mrs Petch set her arms akimbo, all five feet of her trembling with temper. 'Such a slander I never did hear. You look at this, Mr Smart Wooley.' She marched to a drawer, brought out a notebook, and waved it at him. 'My Menu Book, this is. Made up every day between Mrs Vokins and me, that is if Madam don't want anything special. You take a look at yesterday, now, all writ down nice and clear. Dining-Room Breakfast – mutton cutlets, grilled, sheep's kidney, two rashers of bacon and a sausage. That was for the master, Madam only took toast and a coddled egg. Dining-Room Luncheon, there wasn't none, Master being out and Madam taking broth and a Semolina Cream in her bedroom. Dinner, a clear soup followed by stewed sole and fillets of beef with veg., and a Royal Pudding. Nothing in *that* to spoil and make a nasty sticky mess, I hope?'

Mr Wooley was not going to concede defeat easily. 'No sheep's 'ead?' he asked with a significant leer. 'Not even for the kitchen's dinner?'

'Certainly not.'

He beamed triumph at her. 'Then how come I look where someone's been diggin' and turn up a lot o' bones?'

'Bones? what sort o' bones?'

'This sort.' He produced from the pocket of his apron a fragment which had undoubtedly come from a head of some kind, since it had two teeth attached to it. Mrs Petch stepped back.

'That's been buried a long time, if you ask me. And it don't look

93

like sheep, more like a -- what do you think, Ada?'

'A dog,' young Ada suggested.

'That's it, a dog. People often buries dogs in gardens, and they gets turned up years after.'

'Big dog it must 'a been, then, from some of them bones. And what about all that black stuff on my rubbish-burner, what it'll take me weeks to get off? I tell you straight, Mrs Petch, there's rum doin's been at work in my garden, and I don't 'alf like it.'

'Well, they wasn't nothing to do with me nor my staff, so just you clear off and stop making nasty incinerations.'

Mr Wooley went, still convinced that there had been just what Cook had unintentionally described: nasty incinerations.

In a curtainless, carpetless room, off a landing from which a staircase ran down to the ground floor, Harry lay ill. A large pail of carbolic acid solution stood in the room, ready for his next change of linen to be plunged into it and carried away, and for the hand-washing of the nurse. That estimable woman, Mrs Ann Wyburn, sat patiently by his bed, clad in a loose cover-all and tight-fitting cap, as the rules of the Home prescribed, reading or knitting. A fire burned steadily in the grate for the consumption of the scraps of rag used by the patient for handkerchieves. Beyond the door hung a sheet moistened with double-strength carbolic solution, to catch any germs on their way to other parts of the house.

Nell, suitably carbolicised, looked in occasionally, but made no attempt to nurse Harry herself; there was no point in two patients suffering from the disease. He tossed, muttered, raved in delirium. Some of the ravings were audible, and told Nell things about his ordeals at Yew Lodge which he would never have told her had he not been ill. She would never breathe them to a soul, but, angry and pitiful, heard and understood, innocent as she had been before of such wrongs.

The patient was progressing well, Mrs Wyburn told her. The fever was burning itself out, the rash disappearing, the muscular pains almost gone.

'I've seen it in India,' Nell said. 'What causes it?'

Mrs Wyburn turned the heel of a sock. 'Lice, in the main,' she said. 'Fleas, sometimes animal ticks – general dirty conditions. I fear I've had to shave off your brother's hair, but I feel sure it will grow again, and as curly as ever.' She looked up brightly. 'By next week he may be allowed egg-custard, and a little beef tea.'

While Harry's slow recovery progressed, more dramatic scenes were taking place in the master-bedroom of the house. Suddenly, in the middle of the night, Claudia went into labour. It was the opportunity Pye had been waiting for. The monthly nurse had kept him away from his wife as effectively as the fiercest watch-dog, partly on principle, 'husbands are not acceptable in the mother's bedroom', and partly from an instinct that this particular husband was not of the sort to cheer and encourage his wife.

But he was there now, at the grey hour of dawn, perched on the side of their bed, the bear's-grease pot containing the ointment in his hand. Already Claudia was too preoccupied with her contractions to take much notice of what he did. Stealthily, under pretext of holding her hand, he smeared the ointment from the pot on her arm, from elbow to wrist, then on her hot brow.

So: it was applied. It would begin to work. He muttered the Black Spell, praying that the young bitch of a governess had not somehow confused the sacred names or the words of the rite. He dreamed as he sat, of Olivia, not Claudia, lying in that handsome bed, laced and frilled and scented, awaiting him with open arms, a languorous Peri. Claudia would take the infant down to death with her, he felt sure, but what of that, when Olivia was young and healthy enough to bear him many more.

'Manfred ... ' breathed the woman in the bed, her head moving restlessly.

'Yes, my darling?' (In his imagination she was still Olivia.)

'Go away.'

The bubble of his dream broken, he went, pausing first to deposit more ointment on her shoulder. Nurse Pepler entered, a bundle of small flannel garments over her arm. She sniffed.

'There's a funny smell in here. Mr Pye, have you been smoking?'

'No, Nurse.'

'Then I don't know what it can be, but I think it would be better if you left Mrs Pye now. She'll be perfectly all right with me, so don't worry yourself – I see no dangerous symptoms.'

Don't worry, indeed! He was only worried that Claudia might be perfectly all right. But with a spell of such strength, it could hardly be possible. *Invocatio atritae*: it was all-powerful, the spell of Blackness. He returned to his comfortable bachelor bed in the dressing-room, and dreamed of happy things.

Claudia's labour was prolonged and difficult. She was weak, having eaten very little in the preceding weeks, and having taken almost no exercise. The doctor tut-tutted at her thin, monstrously-swollen body. He prescribed drinks of nourishing broth, weak brandy and water, hot bricks to the feet, and settled down by the fire rather than leaving the patient to the attentions of the nurse; the family was wealthy, and he was too well-known in the district to let his reputation be damaged by losing a patient.

'She's carrying a big child, Nurse,' he observed, when Claudia had been gasping and moaning for some four hours. 'I don't like it, in a frame like hers. Better prepare the morphine.'

But Claudia's moans and struggles became more urgent as the minutes and hours passed. The sun was high in the sky, the household about its business, when the doctor mopped his brow, washed his hands yet again, and said, 'I am going to use chloroform, Nurse.'

'*Chloroform*, Doctor?'

'It was good enough for Her Majesty, it must be good enough for her subjects. Lay a cloth on that table. Now, the cotton wadding ... '

In a few moments a powerful scent filled the air, making the nurse cough. She had attended only a few cases when this dangerous but miraculous new pain-killing anaesthetic had been used. Breathlessly she watched as the soaked pad went over the patient's nose and mouth.

Some twenty minutes later the child slipped comfortably into the doctor's waiting hands, and, being slapped, cried lustily. But the mother slept on peacefully. The nurse, who had turned pale, looked anxiously at her.

'Don't wake her,' the doctor said. 'It's perfectly natural.'

'About all that is,' she muttered, about her duties of bathing and dressing, though her practised hands were trembling. Several minutes passed before the mother stirred, yawned, and opened her eyes.

'Oh, I must have fallen asleep,' she said drowsily. 'Never mind, it's refreshed me wonderfully. Though I do feel a little sick.'

'You have no need to exert yourself any more, Mrs Pye. The baby is safely born.'

'Born? How wonderful! But I didn't know ... What is it?'

'A boy, a large healthy boy.' To her cry and look of joy he returned a shifty glance.

'Where is he? Can I hold him?'

'All in good time, all in good time.' He hurried into the next room, where the nurse was settling the baby into its cot. He stood beside her, and both gazed down, speechless, at the large, wriggling, sturdy child. He was the colour of milky coffee: tight curls of black hair clung damply to his head.

The doctor returned to the mother's bedside. 'Mrs Pye, I must prepare you for strange news. Now don't agitate yourself, ma'am ...'

Two storeys below, in the kitchen regions, a rumour spread from servant to servant. Not of the birth, for no one yet knew of that. The words they whispered to each other, more and more loudly, were, 'The police! The police are here, asking for Master!'

VIII

Shades of the Prison-house

Mr Wooley the gardener had a son, Albert, who followed his father's trade. He was regularly employed at one of the grand houses in South Grove, near the church, where he contrived as often as possible to be working in the front of the house when Betsy the nursemaid passed with her charge, Caroline. Many a tender exchange passed between them over the gate, for Betsy was a pretty girl.

She was eager to tell him of his father's suspicions and of the scene he had created in the kitchen. Albert already knew something of this, from his father's growled account at supper, cut short by his wife's interruption: 'Oh, give over, do, Wooley, when we're eating of our vittles – you and your nasty black stuff and your old bones. I dessay you was right and one of them gels had thrown out some meat-stock or some such. Never mind it now.'

Betsy was more forthcoming, having heard a lively version from the kitchen-maid, and passed on all the horrid details to Albert. It so happened that the next day Albert heard at the Flask Inn of some extra gardening work that was being done at the Cemetery – the laying of a new flower-garden near the Egyptian Avenue. They were paying good money, said his friend who regularly worked there. Why shouldn't Albert make a few bob helping out, as they were looking for extra hands?

The head gardener at South Grove was a kindly man who privately thought his employers skinflints. He gave Albert the day off, and the boy duly joined those who were digging and planting late autumn flowers almost in the shadow of the great arch, built to look as if it framed the entrance to Egyptian royal tombs, and guarded by twin obelisks.

Late in the morning a funeral cortège wound its way up the path towards him, the first that day. The black garb of the mourners and the purple of the coffin-pall contrasted curiously with the brilliant sunlight and the late summer reds and golds of the flowers in bloom. A clergyman walked in front, the undertakers' mutes in their stove-pipe hats, black-streamered, behind. Albert and the other gardeners swept off their caps respectfully and paused to watch until the last black form had disappeared into the gloom of the Egyptian Avenue. A well-heeled toff, or toffess, they thought, someone who could afford to pay £100 and more for a place in one of the vaults.

It was some minutes before an un-funereal commotion interrupted their resumed work. One of the undertaker's men had reappeared, looking flustered.

'Who's in charge here?' he demanded. 'Any of you fellows?'

No, one of them answered, they were under-gardeners and jobbers, with no authority.

'Well, you'd better find someone who can tell us what's been going on here. Mr Smart's in a right taking, and so are the family – in a proper lather, they are.'

'Why, what's up, mate?'

'Marauding – grave-robbing, that's what's up.'

In no time the news had spread to everyone in the immediate neighbourhood. On the vault being unlocked to receive another member of the family, a much older coffin was found on the floor, opened by force, with only the shroud and parts of the body it had contained left. A young cousin had fainted at the sight. The whole solemn ceremony was in confusion.

When the worst of the chaos had died down, Albert and some of the other gardeners sauntered up the Egyptian Avenue to the Circle of Lebanon to see for themselves. The vault had been left unlocked, ready for the arrival of officials. The young men peered in, with the permission of the mute left on guard. They gasped and whistled at the gruesome litter inside, speculated on the reason for the vandalism – gold and jewellery buried in the coffin, a family secret, a document? They were still clustered, whispering, when the police arrived.

'Now then, you lot, clear off,' the constable in charge told them.

'Nothing more for you to look at. Get back to your work.'

Albert's mind did not function quickly, but it had been quietly ruminating on the scene before his eyes. 'Bones ain't all there, are they?' he enquired of the constable.

'No, they ain't, and what's that to you?'

'Only my guvnor come across some, buried in the garden what he works. O'course, they'd be animals' bones ... '

The word spread like wildfire. Within half an hour a policeman from the little station that backed on to Pond Square presented himself at the door of Ashurst Lodge. Of course, there might be nothing at all in it, but the police were bound to investigate any clue to the shocking affair. As the master of the house was out, they would return when he came home from the City, and meanwhile some questions would be asked of the staff. There appeared to have been a grave infringement (no joke intended and none suspected) of the Act of 1861 dealing with Misdemeanour in any street, square, churchyard, or burial ground.

Nell heard the news as she and Caroline were having nursery luncheon. The food seemed to turn to ashes in her mouth and her heart began to thud. So the deed was discovered already, by a stroke of bad luck. She imagined herself and Pye both taken into custody, put in prison – for how long?

It was not a pleasant prospect, but an even less pleasant one was the possible fate of Harry. With her removed and disgraced nobody was likely to assume responsibility for him. He would be returned to the school, or even to the aunts. And with the prison-slur on her reputation she would never get another job as governess.

When the maid came to take the trays Nell asked her casually, 'Did the policeman say much when he was here?'

'There was two of 'em, miss, an old 'un and a young 'un, and the young 'un stopped for a glass of beer and talked quite a bit. Said as there hadn't been a grave-robbing case for years, and the magistrates was sure to make an example of whoever done it.'

Nell folded her napkin neatly into a series of perfect squares and pushed it slowly through its ring. 'Did he mention what the punishment was likely to be?'

'Ooh yes, miss, he said it might be six months or a year – so as to give 'em time to think over what they done.'

So her fears were justified, and there was only one thing for it. She must get away, and take Harry with her.

There was no time to be lost, for they must not be in the house when its master came home. Fortunately it was raining, so Caroline's afternoon walk would not be possible. The child must not be told until it was too late for her to draw attention to the flight by her distress. Nell set her to copy pictures from an old fashion-book, a pastime which kept her happy, and went up to her own room.

There she packed up hastily her own few clothes and possessions. The picture of Lady Jacquette had to go in her portmanteau – it would never do to be seen going out of the house with it.

Four o'clock. Tea-time, for Nurse Wyburn. Now that Harry was so much better she took her meal downstairs in the servants' hall, where she could enjoy a little company. Today she would certainly linger over it, to hear as much as she could of the enthralling gossip; even worthy nurses are not free from human curiosity. The baby's colour was now common knowledge. It provided the most entertaining news the staff had ever heard. How could that poor little thing have been born to the mistress? Nobody could suspect *her* of hanky-panky, whatever the master might have got up to. It was a subject never exhausted, and it would become a legend. Nell hovered at a point from which she could hear the sick-room door open and close, and Nurse's quick footsteps pattering downstairs. Then she ran, portmanteau in hand, to Harry.

'I can't explain now, darling, but we have to leave this house. Now.'

'But Nell ... '

'Can you walk?'

'Oh yes! I walk every day, all round the room. Nurse says I'm quite strong.'

'Good. And you haven't a fever today?' She felt his forehead. 'No. Quite cool. Come along, get dressed as quickly as you can.'

Harry had grown so used to obeying commands at school that he obeyed her without question. She helped him scramble into his clothes, laced his boots for him and helped with his necktie. There was nothing to pack except a bottle of medicine which stood on the wash-stand.

'Now. Very quick and quiet, remember. Keep hold of my arm.'

As his thin arm linked with hers she realised that he had grown even during his illness. The child who had clung on to her hand could now walk beside her, his head almost level with her shoulder.

They were lucky with the stairs and the back door into the garden, lucky in seeing nobody as they left the grounds of Ashurst Lodge. The rain had kept Mr Wooley away from the gardens and the servants indoors. They turned into Swain's Lane, Nell looking across it, with a shudder, at the Cemetery wall.

After a few yards Harry asked, 'How far do we have to go, Nell?'

'Not very far. Only down the hill to the end of the lane. Can you manage it?'

'Yes. Only my legs feel rocky ... '

By the time they had reached the main gate of the Cemetery his steps were slowing, the effort it cost him to walk more obvious. Nell put one arm round him, the other taking the weight of the portmanteau. Her hooped skirt felt ridiculously cumbrous, sweat was breaking out on her forehead; every moment she dreaded to see a carriage coming up the lane with Manfred Pye in it.

It was a nightmare journey which brought them at last to the end of Swain's Lane. Mercifully it had all been downhill, or they would never have completed it. Nell was half-carrying, half-dragging Harry by the time they emerged into West Hill.

'Just a little farther, dearest – only a little farther.'

The most beautiful sight she had ever seen was the Duke of St Alban's tavern, posting-house and terminus for omnibuses. And there, even more beautiful, stood a yellow omnibus, the 'Highgate', fresh horses between its shafts and the coachie chatting to an ostler.

Seated at last in the half-empty omnibus Nell collapsed against its comfortable upholstery. Her whole body ached with the strain of supporting Harry, and her arm felt pulled out of its socket. Harry was leaning against her, his face a whitish-green, eyes shut. She prayed hard that she would not live to curse herself for a fool when she had elected to run from Ashurst Lodge. If he died, it would be worse than anything that could possibly have happened.

She gently shook him, saying, 'Harry.'

He opened his eyes and gave her the faintest of smiles. 'Nice to sit down.'

'Very nice.' She tendered fourpence to the conductor for their fares.

'Mealy, the nipper looks,' the man said. 'Proper die-away. Ain't got nothing catching, I 'ope?'

'Oh no! He's very tired. We – we have not eaten today.'

The conductor scrutinised her strained face, damp with sweat and yet, he thought, as pretty as a picture. 'Ere,' he said gruffly, 'buy a bun or summink.' She found one of the pennies pressed back into her hand. Before she could thank him he was at the other end of the vehicle, helping an old woman to alight. What a kind man. She hoped the incident would not cause him to remember her if enquiries were made.

The omnibus stopped for them in the Tottenham Court Road, at the end of Great Russell Street. Once on foot, Nell felt less conspicuous. In London nobody stared at a young woman supporting a half-fainting child. Thank Heaven Uncle Gil lived not very far up the street, opposite the end of Bedford Square.

The bookseller's shop was open, the proprietor up a step-ladder arranging volumes on a high shelf. For all his short sight he recognised her at once and came hurrying down.

'Miss Carey! And Master Harry. Why, what ails the boy?'

'He's been ill. Mr Vigo, is my uncle at home?'

'I think so – I'm almost sure … ' He opened the door at the bottom of the stairs that led to the upper floors. Faint strains of music floated down: someone playing, on a scratchy flute, *The Girl I left Behind Me.*'

'Oh, thank goodness.' Nell heaved a sigh. 'Please, may Harry sit on your chair while I go up and speak to him? Things are … we're in difficulties.'

Mr Vigo pushed his glasses down his nose to see her better, nodding emphatically. He had always had a weakness for old

Cordwell's pretty niece, and taken sides against two arrogant old women who had visited him occasionally – who had once brought him back from their home, singing-drunk, and vented their wrath on his landlord, for letting him behave so scandalously and live above the income left him by their father's Will.

'Of course, of course. Would you like a mint-humbug, laddie? Very refreshing. I always keep them for emergencies.' As Harry struggled to make conversation, Nell hastened upstairs and knocked at Gil's door. The music stopped, and the door was opened to her.

'My God ... fathers! Little Nell! Where have *you* sprung from? Come in, come in. Why, you're all of a lather. Sit down, my love.' Nell was pleased to note, as she kissed him, that he smelt less strongly of spirits than usual, and that the bottles of Old Tom and brandy were still more than half-full. She threw off her hat and dropped thankfully on to the shabby sofa.

'Uncle Gil, I want to tell you what's happened. It's a very strange story and I don't suppose you'll be able to make sense of some of it, so I'll tell you quickly now.'

What, indeed, could a listener make of such a tale? But Gil was a lover of melodramas and penny-dreadfuls; the ghastly details of the exhumed corpse and the Black Spell delighted him. It was the most interesting thing he had heard for years, but there was no denying that it put his beloved niece in some danger.

'So we came to you,' she ended. 'I hope it's not too awkward. But there was no one else, you see. Perhaps I was silly to run away, with poor Harry so weak. Only I couldn't face going to prison and leaving him.'

'Of course not. Absolutely right. You'll want to stay?'

'If we can.' She looked round the untidy bachelor room, and thought of the still more untidy bedroom behind the folding doors of what had once been a Georgian drawing-room. 'But – oh dear – I don't know where.'

Gil took a quick nip of brandy to sharpen his brains.

'Tell you what, my love, I've got a notion. Let's get old Vigo up here.'

Mr Vigo, suffering from a shortage of customers, was only too

104

pleased to lock up the shop and join them, bringing Harry, who was for once in his life allowed brandy as well. It brought colour to his face, and Nell ceased to feel quite so anxious about him.

Vigo had been a scholar in his time; his brain was sharp, and he did not share his lodger's weakness for the bottle. Nell spared him the full story, but gave him enough of its outline for him to realise her plight. The solution of it occurred to him without effort. Five years before, his wife had died. Their only son was in South America, and Vigo was a lonely man. He had let the first-floor rooms to Gil Cordwell partly for income, partly to have some company in the house, though if he had known of Gil's habits he might have hesitated. His own bedroom, and his wife's parlour, on the second floor, were now deserted, untouched, except by the woman who came in to clean once a week. He slept upstairs, but otherwise spent his time in the shop, among the books that were now his life. Why should not those desolate rooms house the young fugitives? He put the suggestion, timidly enough. Nell leapt at it.

'But that would be wonderful! If you could really spare the rooms. They are your home, after all ... '

'No, Miss Carey. Not since I lost my wife. They bring back too many memories. I would be so happy to let you have them – and as for sleeping, there's an old turn-up bedstead in the attic that used to be our son's. I could easily bring it down to the shop – indeed, I would be happy to sleep there.'

An awful thought occurred to Nell. 'But – I couldn't pay you. All I have is what Mrs Pye kindly let me keep of my salary. It was supposed to go to my aunts, but she said that wasn't fair.'

'Good thing. Greedy hags,' put in Gil.

'So you see I haven't any money for rent.'

'The rooms are standing empty. I've had no money for them in the past – why should I need it now?'

'But coals – light ... ' Nell was sure it cost a lot to live in rooms, judging by the way her aunts had complained of what it cost them to keep the Carey family.

'I'll do that,' Gil said. 'Glad to. Use up me spare cash.'

Nell hugged him. 'You're an angel. Wait till I get some work, and

I'll pay you both back, see if I don't.'

Nobody enquired what kind of work she hoped to get. People did not hire a governess off the streets, nor were sewing-women recruited that way, or ladies to serve behind shop-counters. But optimistic youth thought nothing of such quibbles.

'Please,' Harry said, 'I'm so tired. Could I go to bed, Nell?'

The rooms on the floor above Gil's delighted Nell. They were low-ceilinged, modestly but attractively furnished with things that had been in fashion when the Vigos married, long before the Great Exhibition had brought in thick knobbly legs for furniture and portraits of the Prince Consort in woolwork upholstery. Miniatures and black silhouettes hung on the walls. Nell mentally arranged them so that Lady Jacquette would hang above the parlour fireplace.

Harry, the recent invalid, was to have Mr Vigo's bedroom, while another turn-up bedstead was borrowed for Nell. As she tucked him up that night he said sleepily, 'Tell me a story.'

'Of course, dear. What kind would you like?'

'One of the old stories.' She sat down beside him, holding his hand, softly repeating one of the Indian legends he had known since babyhood. Very soon the hand relaxed in hers and he breathed slowly and steadily.

Nell studied the face on the pillow. It was a child's once more, the sharpness gone, and the look of suffering. The hair, cut during his fever, was growing again into tight curls, clean and bright as new copper. She knew that the illness had been a blessing, since it had blotted out the memory of what he had undergone. In his delirium he had raved it all away.

Two days went by in peaceful enjoyment. Gil was so cheered by his young company that he drank little; Mr Vigo felt his deserted rooms had come to life, as Nell cleaned and mended for him and Harry browsed among the books, particularly the old atlases, which held a fascination for him. 'You'll be a traveller, my boy,' Vigo prophesied.

'And what will I be?' Nell asked.

The old man studied her. To any other girl he would have answered, 'A good wife and mother, I hope, in time'. But there was something about this girl which made that particular prophecy a little shadowy in his imagination. Something ... dashing. That was the word which came to him, but he dismissed it as inappropriate and altogether improper.

Mr Vigo particularly enjoyed having supper in company, now that a charming young person was there to provide it. One evening it had been a nice rabbit pie, the next a tasty stew – Gil had bought the ingredients from the butcher round the corner, since it seemed unwise for Nell to show herself in daylight so soon. But habit was hard to break, and on the third evening he was still in the shop sorting out a new consignment of books when the meal was almost reaching perfection. Nell went downstairs to summon him.

Almost at the door into the shop she halted abruptly. A familiar voice was hectoring Mr Vigo. Eudora's voice.

'I demand to see my brother! Don't prevaricate, man. Of course he is here, and so I daresay is my wretch of a niece. Let me past at once.'

'I really don't know, madam, that Mr Cordwell is in,' Mr Vigo was saying placatingly. 'Doubtless he will not be long, but I couldn't positively say ... '

Nell flew back upstairs and burst into her uncle's parlour, where Gil and Harry were waiting.

'Aunt Eudora's here,' she gasped, 'and asking for you, Uncle. You must go down to her at once – she mustn't come up here – and Harry, get upstairs quickly. We'll both hide up there with the door locked. And Uncle, tell a good story, please try!'

'By Gad,' said Gil, 'by Gad! Here, is she, the old vixen. I might have known. Don't you fret, m'dear, I'll lie faster than a horse can trot.' With a speed to suit the words he was on his way downstairs.

They were both there, as he had expected, Minerva sitting, frog-like, on the shop's flimsy chair, Eudora standing over little Mr Vigo like a tigress over its prey.

'*There* you are, Gilbert. Now we shall have the truth.'

Not if I know it, Gil assured himself. He was soberer than he had been for years, only one small brown sherry to sharpen his appetite for supper, and he was not going to babble away the freedom of his niece and nephew to these two Gorgons. His heart beat fast, but his face was blandly innocent.

"Evenin', Eudora, Minerva. To what do we owe this pleasure?'

'You know perfectly well, Gilbert, don't pretend with me.'

'Know you wouldn't be calling on me unless there was something up. Well fire away!' He was pleased to see that Vigo had composed himself and shrunk into the background, leaving his friend to face the attack.

Eudora was just a little daunted by his open countenance and cheerful tone. She had never seen him like this; it was not at all what she had expected.

'Eleanore,' she said.

'What about her? Miss the child, since you whisked her off to some slavery or other. Not ill, is she?'

Minerva spoke. 'Not ill. I can hardly believe you know nothing of what has happened, Gilbert.'

Gil perched himself on the corner of a solid table covered with books; it gave him the advantage of being comfortable while under fire.

'How the devil can I know anything? You even kept the child's whereabouts from me. I got the address, though – from Amy, so I've sent her a scrawl now and then, just to raise her spirits in case she was lonesome.'

The sisters glanced at each other. By now, they silently agreed, they could almost believe that Gilbert was in ignorance.

Eudora said, 'The employer to whom we entrusted Eleanore has proved unworthy of that trust. He has proved to be a criminal of the worst kind.'

'God bless m'soul!'

'He has committed ... ' Eudora shut her eyes. 'Grave-robbery. Violation of the dead. Satanic practices of the most obscene kind.' She shuddered delicately. 'And our niece – your niece – was his accomplice.'

She paused for effect. Gil contrived to look blank.

'Don't understand what you're talkin' about. Black magic – or Burke and Hare stuff? Thought all that had gone out since the quacks got bodies properly, by law. Anyway, what would Nell want with grave-robbin'?'

Eudora shook her head impatiently. 'How thoroughly stupid you are, Gilbert. I am telling you plainly that this man – Mr Pye, committed this crime with Eleanore's help – it seems that she consented on condition that her brother was removed from the school to which we had sent him. He admitted that to the police.

'School! The penitentiary, that would be.'

'The *school*, the excellent establishment which would have made a man of the little milksop! Well, he was removed, and has vanished with his sister. The police want to question them both and a search is out.'

Gil stroked his moustache. 'What's happened to this dodger, Pie or Puddin' or whatever his name is?'

'The police have him in the cells. He is to be examined for lunacy.'

'Ah, dotty, is he? Don't wonder poor Nell's run off.'

Minerva had been staring at her brother. 'Gilbert, *why are you sober?*' she asked keenly.

'Me? Sober? Well, m'dear, evening's young yet. Give me time and I'll be as lushed as you like, if it'll make you happy.'

Minerva addressed her sister. 'Eudora, I think we should look upstairs. I am not satisfied.'

Gil flashed a look at Vigo, trying to convey that he was not to panic. 'Look away,' he said amiably. 'Just don't eat my supper, will you.'

He watched the two women go upstairs, Eudora stalking, Minerva lumbering. Then he darted to Vigo's side and whispered, 'They're in the bedroom, locked in. Table's not laid. Nothing to show anyone's in the house but us – I hope to God!'

The sisters stared round the dining-parlour. They had not been familiar with it before, so its unusual neatness did not strike them. A cloth was on the table, but no cutlery, and the savoury contents of the pan on the hob might well have been for Gil alone. Nell kept her few possessions in her room upstairs, the one where she and Harry were now crouching, still as frightened mice, listening to the hated voices downstairs.

'I do believe the creatures are not here, sister.'

'It seems not. Well, we must not ... ' Nell missed the rest of the exchange as her aunts returned to the shop.

Eudora fixed Gil with a steely eye, driven back but not defeated.

'Very well, we accept that you are not hiding those two. But we feel perfectly sure they *will* come here, and that you will harbour them if you can.'

'Perish the thought,' Gil dared to say. Vigo's head was buried deep in an encyclopaedia.

'I know you. And I know – that girl,' Eudora said. 'We have agreed, Minerva and I: a watch will be set on this place, day and night, though it will cost us good money. Nobody shall enter without our knowing of it, depend on that. And when they come, we shall have them. That girl must be exposed for what she is.'

'Pity they've stopped standing culprits on the Stool of Repentance,' Gil mused. 'Should have thought your Chapel would have brought that sort of thing back.'

Eudora flushed. Some form of public shame for Nell had been in her mind. 'Don't mock what you don't comprehend,' she said.

The two stiff figures marched out. Vigo was pale and trembling, Gil considerably less confident than he had appeared.

'All bosh, of course,' he said later, reporting the conversation. 'Who's going to keep watch? Not the peelers, they've other fish to fry. That stringy old servant of theirs, what's-her-name? No, depend on it, a lot of huff. You're as safe here as you would be in Buckingham Palace, gel.'

'Yes, uncle,' Nell said.

And, much later, 'Harry, my darling, we must go. It's not safe to stay, for us or for them. Listen ... '

At earliest light, before the shabby man in the ulster had taken up his post in the street, sister and brother were gone.

IX

The Streets of London

The police most certainly wanted to question Nell.

When Pye returned home on the day of her flight, late in the afternoon, the patient Inspector Wardell was waiting for him in his study. Pye had wondered from time to time during the day how his wife's confinement was proceeding. It was odd that no messenger had been sent to inform him, particularly if, as he hoped, the birth had been fatal to her. But a hearty and prolonged lunch with colleagues at a City chop-house created in him such a state of euphoria that all anxiety faded from his mind. The Black Spell must have worked – nothing else was possible. They were afraid to tell him, that was it.

He was faintly surprised not to see drawn blinds at the windows of Ashurst Lodge. But perhaps all was not yet over. The butler met him in the hall and took his hat and coat with a grave face; but then Baker always looked grave,

'Ah well, Baker?' he enquired. 'Mrs Pye … ?'

'I couldn't say, sir. The nurse is still upstairs.'

'I see.' So it was not all over. He went, as usual, straight to his study, where a nondescript-looking man was reading *The Times*. Politely, the visitor rose, announced himself to be Inspector Wardell of the local constabulary, and begged permission to ask Mr Pye a few questions.

Pye heard with an unmoved face of the horrid discovery in the Cemetery and the connection with it which had been traced to his own house. What confounded bad luck, a burial so soon after his operations in that catacomb. But the police were too stupid to make a thorough investigation; it would all be dismissed as a piece of kitchen nonsense. Wardell did not miss the slight jump he gave when told

111

that a constable had taken the liberty of digging near the incinerator, and had turned up a quantity of unmistakably human bones.

'Great Heavens! Well, Inspector, it seems some nasty jiggery-pokery has been going on. You have my leave to question all my household – except my wife, of course, who is at this moment confined. Indeed, I must – '

As though on cue, a brisk knock announced the entry of Nurse Pepler.

'If I could speak to you, sir.'

'Of course, of course. Is there news?'

'Yes, sir.'

Pye looked at the policeman, who began to get to his feet, but Mrs Pepler said, 'I think you'd better come with me, sir.'

She walked quickly in front of him up the stairs to Claudia's bedroom and paused at the door.

'I beg you not to disturb Mrs Pye more than you can help, sir.'

His heart sank. So the infernal woman was not yet dead. Aloud he said, 'I'll do my best.'

With a shock, he saw that Claudia was sitting up in bed, reading a book and looking perfectly healthy and more or less her usual size. The birth had clearly taken place. She gave him a nod and a smile.

'Ah, Mr Pye. Come to see your offspring?'

He pecked her cheek. 'And you, my dear. You're – well?'

'Never better. It went on a long time and I got rather tired, but Nurse Pepler has been splendid. Go and look at baby.'

The nurse, grim-faced, was standing by the lace-draped crib. She lifted out the sleeping child and drew the shawl away from its face.

The shock Pye received was cataclysmic. Dry-mouthed, he stared at the small, shining brown face and the tight-curling hair. He reached out and opened the shawl further. Tiny brown hands, tiny brown feet. With a kind of groan he staggered to a chair and sat, clutching his head. Claudia was watching him with a slight, amused smile.

'A fine boy, isn't he?'

Pye stuttered 'But he ... he ... A mulatto, half-caste.'

'Octoroon, or something of the sort.'

'It must come as a shock to you, my dear.'

'Brandy,' Pye muttered. The nurse poured a draught from the bottle that stood among the medicines. He drank it at one gulp, and met Claudia's mocking eyes.

'Please don't suspect my virtue, Mr Pye,' she said. 'I assure you I have not erred and strayed from my ways like a lost sheep. Indeed, I'm not aware of any gentlemen of colour nearer than the East India Docks – are you? Not hard to account for, however. My grandfather Amos traded in black gold – slaves, you know – on the coasts of West Africa. He married several times, siring my aunts and uncles by his first wives. But Papa's mother, my grandmother, died before I was born, and I never heard much of her, nor did Papa seem to remember her well.'

Pye helped himself to more brandy.

'I think we know why the poor lady was rather hushed up in our family history. There is my hair, you see, for one thing.' She pulled off the lace nightcap. 'I have never had to curl my hair – it crinkles naturally.' She ran her fingers through it, then held out one delicate hand. A faint tinge of blue ran round the base of the nails.

'Like his, you see?' She gestured to the cot. 'They told me it was a heart weakness. Now I know it is not.'

'Caroline ...' Pye muttered thickly.

'Yes, Caroline. She is like you, the strain has not passed to her. Nature is truly remarkable.'

'I never knew, I never noticed. You ...'

'You never truly looked at me, Mr Pye, because you never loved me, only my money, the money that came through black gold. Isn't that an irony?'

'You're bewitched, madam.' Out of sight his fingers were making the old sign that was supposed to ward off the Devil.

'Am I?' Claudia laughed lightly. 'It must be that stuff you smeared on me when I first fell into labour. Nurse complained of the unpleasant smell, and when she brought candles we saw some very nasty-looking marks which she washed off thoroughly. I hear that some curious experiment or other has been made in our garden.'

'What?'

'Just kitchen gossip that filtered up here – Nurse didn't mean to chatter, did you, Pepler. It gave me all sorts of strange ideas, as I lay here; about customs I've read of – you always thought I read too many books, didn't you, Mr Pye.'

With a choking sound he got to his feet and ran out of the room.

In his study the inspector was still patiently waiting. He had been going round the bookshelves, and become quite interested in the number of works on demonology and the like. But there was no need for him to reason out conclusions, for Manfred Pye confessed in full to what he had done, and why. 'And it worked!' he cried hysterically. 'The Black Spell worked, but against me.'

Inspector Wardell missed the point, but went on busily writing notes, as Pye went on to make wild accusations inculpating Nell Carey.

'I see, sir,' Wardell said soothingly. 'Well, the girl has run away, but I expect we can easily fetch her back and confirm all this. Meanwhile, if you wouldn't mind accompanying me ... '

Meekly Pye went with him, a young constable on his other side.

Alone again with her patient, Nurse Pepler asked guardedly, 'About the child, madam. Would you like me to make enquiries?'

'Enquiries? What do you mean?'

'About ... its future. The Aesculapian has connections with quite a number of useful institutions. There is the Orphan Working School in Cheapside, the Orphans' Homes in Southwark where the children are trained for service, the ... '

Claudia sat bolt upright, her cheeks flaming. 'What are you talking about? This child is not an orphan, he's my son and I intend to bring him up as such. I shall *enjoy* bringing him up.'

'But in a district like this – what will people say?'

'What do I care? Let them put their silly heads together and clack about each other's secrets, or the secrets buried over there.' She nodded towards the Cemetery. 'I have nothing to be ashamed of, nor has he. Give him to me.' She looked tenderly down at the mewing scrap in its dazzling white wool draperies, the son who had innocently freed her of her obsessive love for her husband, her would-be murderer; the son whose public bringing-up would punish him more than any other action she could have taken against him. It would not

114

be easy, it would be often difficult and painful, but she would do it. And to do it, she must stay alive.

Manfred Pye would be no threat to her in the near future, for at the Magistrates' Court he was sentenced to six months' imprisonment in the House of Detention, Clerkenwell, for the crime of grave-robbing and attempted poisoning (though this last was a somewhat nebulous charge.) While in prison, supplied with comforts from his own home and well treated, he slipped gradually over the edge of reason and became incurably mad, confined in a private asylum. Olivia Wynne-Gaskoin, at the first waft of scandal, had promptly accepted the hand of a wealthy brewer whose wife had already obligingly died without supernatural aid; poor Manfred had been quite exciting in his way, but so extremely eccentric. She would, she reflected, probably not have married him in any case.

It took only a very short time for Nell to realise that she had made a great mistake in leaving the shelter of Mr Vigo's.

'Where are we going, Nell?' Harry asked her as they began their hurried journey through the streets.

'Away from here. Somewhere they won't be looking for us.' They were heading south-eastwards, because Nell knew London's theatre-land better than any district outside Bloomsbury. She would feel at home there, both of them would be anonymous in the little crowded streets that ran off the Strand, where she had often wandered by herself, eagerly glimpsing a different, brighter world than the dull sphere of everyday life.

But her heart sank lower and lower as they journeyed. The theatres were all shut, sullenly asleep, cleaning-women the only evidence of life about them. Covent Garden would be alive and bustling, but Nell dared not venture so near Bow Street police station. Tramps and vagrants still slept, huddled on doorsteps. They themselves, Nell and Harry, were vagrants: what else, with no friends, no home.

Why, why had she run from Uncle Gil without thinking? Her mother had often said, 'My dear, your impetuous nature will be your downfall if you cannot learn to curb it.' (And oh, what was poor Amy feeling, with both her children Wanted Persons on the run, and no

115

news from them – except by way of Eudora and Minerva?) Remorse added itself to Nell's troubles as she trudged along, Harry gamely keeping up with her, strengthened by his two days of rest and good food.

They could have stayed hidden at Mr Vigo's. It would have done them no harm to keep out of sight until the watcher outside had abandoned his vigil. 'Daughter of an imbecile she-goat and an ancient tiger with no teeth, thou art wholly useless and fitted only to be a laughing-stock in the market place,' Nell said out loud in Hindi. Harry looked up. 'Are you saying rude words, Nell?'

'Yes, I am. Addressed to myself. It makes me feel a little better.'

Harry sighed. '*I* should feel better if we'd had some breakfast.'

'Oh, darling! We could have brought something with us – why didn't I think ... ? Look, there's a cook-shop opening. When the boy's taken the shutters down we'll go in and buy something.'

'Oh, please let's. I could eat skilly, I'm so hungry.'

The shop-boy must have been the slowest operator in London. He paused between removing shutters to stare at the window display, or around him, he snagged his finger on a nail, swore, and nursed it for quite a minute. Catching sight of the two who were eagerly watching him from the pavement across the way, he took a good long stare at them, as though early customers were some kind of unknown phenomenon. But at last the shutters were all down, and the hungry pair were able to go in.

Nell felt in the deep pocket of her coat. There were coins in it, but she had a cold apprehension that most were copper. They must be spent very, very carefully. For two-pence she bought a small hot pie for each of them. The shopman stared at her almost as pointedly as his boy had done.

Outside, Harry said, 'Let's sit on those steps to eat them.'

'But it's a house. Perhaps they wouldn't like us sitting on their steps.'

Harry had already perched on the lowest step of the tall house in Drury Court. Nell, feeling more and more like a vagrant, joined him. The pies were made of some unidentifiable meat, but savoury-smelling and tasty enough. She took out all her money and counted

116

it. Four shillings, two sixpences, and about a shillingsworth of pennies and halfpennies. She was too absorbed in her gloomy arithmetic to hear the door behind them opening.

'Aren't you cold down there, my dears?' enquired a pleasant, plummy voice. 'Cold stone gives people nasty troubles where they sit down, you know.'

A very fat woman was standing in the doorway, dressed in an elaborately frilled wrapper cheerfully patterned in red and blue check, a morning cap sporting several bows on her neat hair, which was quite black though her face was not young. She was smiling, and Nell felt a little better for seeing her. She began to make an excuse for taking up room on the steps, but the woman shook her head, laughing.

'It's no matter at all. Come in and eat your pies in the warm. Haven't had no breakfast, have you.'

The little hallway was certainly warm, in contrast with the chill outside. Even warmer was the basement kitchen to which they were led down a few steps. A huge old-fashioned fireplace and a shiny kitchen range provided the heat. On the hob a kettle was singing, and a porridge-pan bubbled gaily near by.

'Well, now, I'm Mrs le Bel,' said their friend, 'and if you'll tell me your names we can all be cosy together.'

Nell hesitated before answering, 'Ellen and Henry. Arkwright.' The truth seemed unwise. Goodness knows where Arkwright came from, unless it was from something to do with the steam from the kettle.

'There now, how pretty. Porridge – with cream? And a nice cup of tea.'

Mrs Le Bel scuttled about cheerfully, laying the big deal table with breakfast things. Harry, watching, wondered when Mr le Bel and the little le Bels would be coming downstairs. It seemed a very quiet house.

Trying not to eat and drink too eagerly, Nell parried the questions that came at her, revealing only that they had had to get up very early to travel to – imagination failed her – to London Bridge. To meet someone. Off a steamboat. She avoided Harry's stare of suprise. Mrs le Bel's extremely well-marked eyebrows rose.

'Bit early for that, ain't you? Sailings don't start till eight.'

Nell murmured something inaudible, biting into good bread-and-butter.

'Not mother and son, are you? No, much too young.' Suddenly Mrs le Bel reached across and pulled off Nell's hat. A tumble of hair came down with its removal. Nell put her hands up to tidy it, but Mrs le Bel said, 'No, leave it. My, what a colour. Used to be thought ugly when I was a little 'un, but they tell me now it's fashionable. Scotch, are you, or Irish? No? Well. I just wondered, seeing you've both got it, and that nice fair skin. How old are you, Henry?'

'Nine, nearly ten.'

She nodded. 'And your sister would be ... ?'·

'She's eighteen.' Harry enjoyed talking to this pleasant lady.

'Well, that's nice. That's very nice. Finished your tea? I can easy make some more. Not that I'm the cook, you understand, but she likes to lie in a bit sometimes, and I don't see why not, do you? 'Specially as we have supper-parties goin' on quite late, several nights a week. Oh, I see you stare, but I likes to have a bit of life about me of an evening. This is a gay house, you see.'

She looked fixedly at Nell for a reaction to a phrase which would have told anyone worldly all they needed to know about the establishment. But Nell only said politely, 'I'm sure it is, ma'am.'

'Come away from the table if you've finished, it's cosier by the fire. That's right, young 'un, pick up Pussy if you want to, she won't scratch you.'

'We had a cat at home,' Harry said wistfully, 'called Tibby. I miss her a lot.' He was caressing the large grey cat, which appeared to enjoy his attentions, kneading and purring with shut eyes.

'You could play with her all the time, if you were my little boy,' Mrs le Bel said. 'Like to live here, would you?'

Ignoring Nell's warning glance, Harry said, 'Yes, ma'am, I think I would.'

'That's nice. And what about you, Miss Ellen? Now don't be in a hurry to say yes or no, I can see you're a cautious girl. It's my opinion, you see, that you weren't going to no London Bridge, nor no steamboat, and there ain't nobody anxiously a-waitin' for you. I think you were runnin' off from somewhere, and it ain't my place to guess where. And I think what's more you've got no rhino.'

She burst out laughing at Nell's puzzled stare. Harry said, '*I* know what that means – money. The boys at … '

Nell interrupted. 'Quite right, Mrs le Bel, we haven't much money. But we hope to get some very soon from our relatives – we're not poor, indeed, whatever we may look.'

'Oh, quite so, my dear, and sorry if I touched your pride. But you could do with a bit of the ready, couldn't you, and a nice place to sleep – oh, and I could fit you out with some better clothes than them you've got on. Very poor cut, that coat, and you wants a bigger crinoline to show off your shape.'

'What should I have to do to return for all this?'

'Oh, very light work, very light – pleasant, you might call it. I've several young ladies living with me, all very well suited.'

As if in confirmation, the door opened and a head came around it, porcupined with curl-papers. ''Mornin', Ma - ow! Sorry, didn't know you'd company.'

'Go along back to bed, Phoebe.' Mrs le Bel told the head sharply. 'I'll bring you a cup of tea when I'm ready.' The head nodded and disappeared. Nell had noticed traces of carmine on the girl's lips, and blue shadows above the eyes, not washed off the previous night.

'Your young ladies are theatricals, I suppose?' she said. 'With all the theatres round here they must need plenty of lodgings.'

'Something like that, dear.' Mrs le Bel studied her guest covertly. Obviously very innocent, though sharp with it. She hoped she would not have to resort to the whiff of chloroform which was used when a subject proved too stubborn and awkward. Two people were needed to tie the subject down and administer the stuff, one of them necessarily being her lieutenant, Toby, whose talents would also be required when the subject was unconscious. After that, the girls never gave much trouble.

But this one looked more the kind to succumb to plenty of strong drink. A late supper, Toby in his best togs, a few compliments and a drop of something in the wine, and off comes another maid's ring – as

119

the saying goes. Yes, keep her happy till the evening, when the thing could be done.

And then the boy – what a bonus! Now there was a real innocent, young and tender, and pretty enough to tempt a good many gentlemen one knew. Not much trouble with him. Give him a shilling every time and he'll soon stop piping his eye, which they generally do at first ... Mrs le Bel beamed plumply on both of them, seeing her profits increase and multiply.

Nell saw the beam. Somehow it was not quite the smile that had greeted them. A cold suspicion touched her, and rapidly became a certainty. Mrs le Bel was not a theatrical landlady, but a brothel-keeper, a madam. The curl-papered head had belonged to a young prostitute, not an actress. The warnings Nell had been given when she had first been allowed to go out into London streets alone came back to her. Don't answer any strange men if they speak to you. Don't speak to any strange man or woman, even to ask the way. Never in any circumstances enter a public house. Never take a hansom cab alone. Avoid drunken people.

And so on. Nothing about entering what seemed to be private houses, but they should have thought of that. A powerful feeling of evil came to Nell from across that cheerful breakfast table, and she found herself very much afraid, a creature in a trap with its young to protect.

She studied Mrs le Bel's figure, fat but tall and doubtless strong, and the stout arms. A struggle with her would be a losing one; Nell had not the slightest doubt by now that there had been such struggles in the past.

'Please can't we stay, Nell?' Harry pleaded. 'It's so nice and warm.' Nell's mind was suddenly made up. Deception might work where resistance would not.

She leant back in her chair, loosened her coat so that more of her was visible, and gave Mrs le Bel the benefit of a wide smile. 'Of course, dear,' she answered Harry, 'I'm sure we shall be very happy, and make ourselves useful in all sorts of ways. You must thank Mrs le Bel for her kindness.'

Harry dutifully did so, though he knew his sister well enough to be conscious that she was playing some kind of part.

The trick worked. 'My, what nice teeth you've got,' Mrs le Bel marvelled. 'Aren't you lucky.' Greedy eyes travelled all over her; Toby was going to be lucky, too. 'Well now, as you're so cosy, I'll just make some more tea and take it up to my young ladies. Drat that lazy cook ... ' As she bustled about laying out cups and spoons on a large tin tray Nell was busy calculating the position of the front door and how it had been fastened. Just a knob to turn; the bolts were for night use. 'Can I help you?' she offered, praying that the offer would be refused.

'No, thanks, dear, I'm used to it.' The new capture was not going to see anything upstairs which she should not – not yet, anyway. The tea poured out, Mrs le Bel departed upstairs with it, lumbering yet speedy of gait.

Nell waited until a laugh and faint conversation told her that the woman had reached an upper floor. 'Come on, quick,' she snapped at Harry. Before he could protest he was being hauled out of the kitchen, up the six stairs to the lobby, and pushed out of the front door. Nell followed him and shut it behind her very quietly.

'Now run,' she ordered. 'Fast.'

Harry ran, Nell with him, down Drury Court into the Strand. Traffic and foot passengers were building up, buildings coming to life. Outside the church of St Mary le Strand a little bent old man was unlocking the gate. Nell pulled Harry by the hand across the road and through the gate, startling the old man considerably.

'Service isn't till eight o'clock!' he called after her reproachfully, as she made for the west door.

'Private prayer!' she shouted back. When the verger entered the church, looking suspiciously round for the unseemly visitors, they were almost hidden in a high pew, kneeling on hassocks and absorbed in what looked like reverent meditation. As he pottered about on his daily tasks they remained there, whispering very softly.

'But why, Nell? Why couldn't we stay?'

'Because she was a bad woman.'

'How?'

'You wouldn't understand.'

121

'I want to know!' Harry's lip was trembling.

'Well. She'd have turned us into ... into slaves. We'll find somewhere better.'

'Where?'

'I don't know.' She had thought of looking in Wych Street, cheap and cheerful and full of theatricals, but it was too near the place they had run from.

'I don't like all this. I want to go back to Uncle's.'

'And get sent to school again? Don't be a baby. Think of Papa. And as we *are* in church, we'd better say some prayers.'

When the congregation for Early Service came in, they stayed in their pew, joining in but not going up for Communion, since neither was confirmed. Then, unobtrusively mingling, they went out with the others.

The lodging they eventually found, after another weary trudge, was on the south side of Fleet Street in Bouverie Street, in the heart of the great newspaper world and close to the Inns of Court. It was cheap, being priced for poor law students, but it would still cost ten shillings a week for the two of them, without the usual benefits lodgers received – kitchen fire, gas, boot-cleaning, or attendance. All they had was a dingy room with a few sticks of battered furniture. The landlady, Mrs Parkins, was a small withered creature with a dreadful cough which Nell hoped was not infectious. She appeared too beaten down by the world to care greatly what they paid or what they did. Yet the money would have to be found, somehow, in all honesty.

A spirit of sheer daring drove Nell out that night to exploit her own talents, leaving Harry in their room in a sleep of exhaustion. She had a strong singing voice, though not a particularly musical one. Surely she could make it heard, even in a noisy company. And nobody had ever warned her not to go alone into a music hall.

The Middlesex, in Drury Lane, was perilously near the house of Mrs le Bel, but instinct told Nell that the lady would not be far from her house of an evening. It was best to go early, before the entertainment proper started.

The little theatre, once the Mogul Saloon, was already thronged with customers, top-hatted and cloth-capped men, women in bright, showy clothes, clerks and warehousemen and coves about town, with their own girls or girls who were nobody's and everybody's. The small stage was empty but for a piano and a harmonium, and the chairman was not as yet occupying his rostrum. The air, thick with smoke from cigars and pipes, made Nell cough almost as noisily as Mrs Parkins, but she summoned up enough breath to take up a position in one of the less crowded corners of the auditorium, and, in her loudest and clearest voice, began to sing a song everybody knew.

> 'Not long ago in Vestminister,
> There lived a Ratcatcher's daughter,
> Though she didn't qvite live in Vestminister,
> But on t'other side of the vater.
> Her father caught rats and she sold sprats,
> All rahnd and abaht that quarter,
> And the neighbours they all fell in love
> Vith the pretty little Ratcatcher's daughter.
>
> Both rich and poor, from far and near,
> In mat-ri-mony sought her,
> But ... '

A hard strong arm gripped her waist and a heavily-painted face was thrust into hers.

'What you think you're doin', eh?' shouted the girl in scarlet. 'You priggin' my patch?'

'I don't know what you mean.'

'You soon will, me 'andsome amachoor, when me bully kicks you through that door an' beats you up ahtside – if 'e don't kick you some more till you're the colour of a blackberry puddin'. Come on, scarper, beat the hoof, will you?' A violent push sent Nell reeling into a knot of people. None of them made any move to help her as she fell heavily among their feet, hitting her head against a chair. The girl in scarlet, triumphant, took up the place where she had stood, and embarked on her own song in a foghorn voice compared to which Nell's was a bird's trill.

'Now isn't it a pity
Such a cunning lass as I
Should ever die a virgin
Or for Roger have to sigh?
I will be a mot,
I shall be a mot,
I'm so fond of Roger
That I *shall* be a mot.'

Clambering to her feet, bruised and shaken, Nell could not help hearing the rest of the song, even through the din of laughter. She had never heard some of the words before, but their meaning emphasised with gestures, was only too clear. On fire with angry blushes she pushed through the increasing crowd and gained the door.

A man was following her, shabby, whiskered, and built on the lines of a gorilla. She glimpsed him out of the corner of her eye, and hurried into the street, but his strides soon brought him level with her. He gripped her arm in an iron clasp and propelled her round the corner of the building, into the street leading to the stage-door. There she found herself pushed against the wall and savagely, painfully assaulted.

If this was Ruin, it was more unpleasant than she could possibly have imagined, and quite possibly worse than death, as they said. She fought and struggled against the relentless pressure, but sheer brute strength was too much for her, and she began to wilt. Then, by a lucky chance, she was able to butt the man's chin sharply with her head. With a shout of pain he released his grip, and Nell screamed again and again, just as a small group of performers turned the corner on their way to the stage door.

'Here, what's all this?' said an elegant young man, his white top hat worn rakishly to one side. He was a sprite compared with the bully who was manhandling Nell, but his mere presence was enough.

124

Suddenly Nell was released, her attacker running into the darkening street.

She half-sobbed, half-gasped her thanks. The dapper youth stared, raised his topper saying, 'Don't mention it,' and passed gracefully on. Hardly noticing which way she took, Nell made her way back to Bouverie Street, and a bored, peevish Harry. She was footsore, empty, bruised, full of self-disgust, and she had not earned a penny. She had an unpleasant foreboding that she would never be able to earn a penny.

It was a disheartening thing wandering the London streets without money. In the old days she had been independent, enjoying temporary freedom but with a home to go back to, all expenses paid. Careless soon about the danger of being taken up by a policeman, she took to wandering farther afield, back towards the West End, over the bridges to the Borough, eastwards into Whitechapel. There, in the Jewish quarter, she read advertisements for sewing-hands in the workshops from which clothing came, clothing for the toffs who never saw the misery that went into the stitches. As she hovered in front of one such advertisement, a woman stopped beside her.

'I wouldn't if I was you, dearie.'

'Oh. Why, please?'

''Cause they're sweat-shops. You sweats eighteen hours a day in the Season, a bit less some other times. There's a dozen or so women to a room, fire and gas, not a breath of air. Kills you in time, even at your age. It's killin' me.' The woman was not, indeed, an advertisement for the trade. Painfully thin, hollow-eyed with sleeplessness, she wore musty ragged clothes which had come off a barrow in Petticoat Lane, and her hair was prematurely grey.

'Have you given it up, then?' Nell asked.

The answer was a raucous laugh. 'Given it up? And do what else? My youngest nipper's broke out with a fever and I daresn't go in to work, case I gives it to the others. That's right, get away from me.'

'How much do you earn – if I might ask?'

'Twelve shillin' a week with the needle, and that's Sundays as well. Four kids to feed on that. Think it over.'

125

She was suddenly gone, leaving Nell to stare at the ill-written paper.

In the New Cut, to which she had been drawn by the posters outside the Victoria Theatre, showing lurid scenes of melodrama, a coster offered her sixpence a day to skin rabbits and hares. Perhaps one could get used to the bloody work in time, but the flesh crept at it too much to risk the experiment.

Outside a West End wig-maker's a large, showy advertisement offered Good Prices for Human Hair, Length and good Condition Desirable. After a moment's pause, she went in.

The quiffed and monocled man in the shop asked her to remove her hat and take off the snood which confined her hair, then walked all around her, viewing the autumn-leaf fall of it with an expression which gave nothing away.

'Mm. Not a popular colour, only in artistic circles. Don't know that I've much call for it.' Secretly he thought it extremely beautiful, just the thing for some mouse-tressed Society woman wanting a sensational change. 'Tell you what – twelve-and-six, and that's being generous, miss.'

'For how much of it?'

'Well, naturally, the lot. You can't make wigs out of a few inches here and there, my dear. Something like this.' He indicated a spot just below her ears. 'Very handsome you'll look, you know. You could have the new curly crop, very fashionable. See? He pulled the mass of hair back and held a mirror up. An unfamiliar face looked back at her. She hated it. But one could do a lot with twelve shillings and sixpence. It would be over a week's rent, and some food as well. And hair grew again ...

As clearly as though it came from someone in the room, a voice spoke in her head. 'Do not do it. You will regret it always.' Nell looked round, startled. The voice had sounded foreign, French. Had the man a female assistant concealed somewhere? But there was no screen, no possible hiding-place. Yet she had heard the warning clearly.

She seized her snood and put it on, cramming her hat over it. 'Thank you, but not today.'

The wigmaker looked after her with unconcealed disappointment.

He could have got twenty pounds for a wig made of that.

Harry had usually been left behind on Nell's dreary searches for work. He was bored, fretful, and beginning to be rebellious. Nell was afraid that one day she would return to Bouverie Street and find him gone, back to Mr Vigo's. What might happen to him on the way was anyone's guess, so she took him to parks and or walks in respectable districts as often as she could.

One day, after eating their meagre lunch on a bench near the Chapel of the Savoy, they wandered along the Strand, pausing outside shops or theatres. It was a cheap amusement, almost their only one. Outside a little theatre of varieties a very large banner proclaimed 'A Grand Performance of MAGIC AND MYSTERY, for one day only. All Welcome. Poor Children Admitted Free. Performances at 2 and 6 o'clock.'

Harry pointed to it with a cry of excitement. 'Look, Nell, we can go without paying! Come on, hurry, before they start. Oh, come *on*!'

'I'm not exactly a poor child, Harry, even if you are. Perhaps they wouldn't let me in.'

'They will, they will!'

And they did. A few minutes later they were sitting on plush seats behind an excited crowd of earlier comers, waiting for the red spangled curtain to rise.

It rose, to a chorus of oohs and aahs. There, in a purple beam of light, stood a wondrous figure, some seven feet tall, it seemed, wearing a robe of crimson and black, worked with cabalistic signs in gold. He smiled benevolently on the assembly, and waved a shining wand. On to the stage bounded a small child, dressed as a fairy with gauzy wings.

'Ladies and Gentlemen,' it piped, 'may I introduce the Miraculous Merlin, King of Mystery, Magic and Mesmerism, the most wonderful man in the world!'

Nell clapped with the others. She did not know that her first disastrous brush with Magic was ended, and that she had moved into the glow of a new kind, which would transform her life beyond all dreams.

127

BOOK TWO
NELDA

X

The White Magician

Nell was held in enchantment from the first wave of the glittering wand. She had seen Indian conjurors, little brown men who did remarkable tricks, but the man on the stage – if he was a mortal man – came from a different world and wielded a far greater power. At his command miracles happened, things appeared and disappeared and were changed, transformed, surely by supernatural means. Merlin had been the Prince of Enchanters in the old times, the days of King Arthur. Had he risen from his long charmed sleep and come back? But that was too fantastic; of course he was real, just an entertainer.

Yet some strange influence flowed from him into the stuffy air of the place, enveloping her. Even through what she vaguely supposed must be theatrical make-up she was pierced by the brightness of his eyes, the witchery of his smile. Now and then the children round her laughed and made jeering remarks at which Nell was irritated, for to her it was all wonderful. Once before she had felt something like this, the beginning of a magic spell, in an empty music hall; and now the spell was working, binding her round in a skein of fascination.

The Miraculous Merlin, smiling with an austere benevolence perfected by years of practice, looked round the theatre. His ability to sum up an audience in a semi-dark auditorium was also professionally trained. He saw row upon row of small, dirty faces, round-eyed, eager, belonging to young persons unpredictable in the way they would react to his performance.

So far the children had given no trouble. The introductory music had been played with sinister verve by the one-woman orchestra, Mrs Seymore, who could extract from her harmonium sounds conveying Heaven, Hell, Fairyland or Unknown Regions, among which a sharp ear could detect fragments of hymns, operatic works and popular songs. Today her theme was Mystery, with a hint of dark powers; it usually kept them quieter than anything.

The indoor firework display had gone well, too. Lighting one from another, Merlin had waved wands from which flew living sparks, ignited fiery worms and caterpillars to crawl jerkily about the stage before expiring, set spinning a large catherine wheel which raised a chorus of admiration as it fizzed and sparkled itself to extinction against a dark screen. Some of the smaller children had been frightened, but that was no bad thing, and there had been the usual shout of 'Fire!' from a nervous mother, enabling him to give his usual calming speech at the end of the display.

His child assistants were not as young as they appeared. But they had to be small, for purposes of concealment in things, or under things, or behind things, and the smaller they were the better they looked as imps, nymphs, fairies or stage animals. The trouble was, he had run out of those invaluable children born of a long line of acrobats, circus performers, and pantomime artists. Often of Italian descent, they were wiry, sharp and skilled as English kids never seemed to be, creatures who knew instinctively how to seem to disappear, how to double up in small spaces and run round the back of the scenery like forked lightning.

At least these particular English kids were willing, if not bright. Fanny and Danny were brother and sister from a poor family with whom Merlin had stayed three years earlier in the Midlands. They had been with him ever since, grateful for their keep and their interesting jobs (they might well have been in a factory or down a mine). They were good, amiable little things, but Fanny was nervous and Danny slow to learn new tricks. Merlin sometimes wished he could manage without them, but his was too kind a nature to turn them off, and he could often use them with striking effect, as when he appeared to lift Fanny bodily from the floor by one hair of her head, or suspend Danny horizontally in the air, unsupported except by a single upright pole.

More worrying than the children was his girl assistant, Emerald. That was not her name, of course. She was Emmeline by baptism, but

131

it didn't look well on the billings. She had been a pretty creature when he had taken her on, a discharged panto fairy trailing miserably away from the stage door of Drury Lane Theatre, crying because she was now out of work and her father would beat her, even though it wasn't her fault. Merlin had stopped her, given her a sixpence, and gone home with her to the wretched court where she lived. There he persuaded her pale, sickly mother, already great with another child, that he was a man of the utmost respectability, who would provide her daughter with work and a living wage and see that she came to no moral harm.

The mother listlessly agreed. He seemed a nice man, she was only too glad to get Em'line off her hands, and if he *did* turn out to be in the meat-market business Em would be no worse off. Who cared anything about morals, on the fringes of St Giles's.

She had been so pretty then, young Emmeline, with an elfin face, fine straight fair hair the colour of primroses, and a frail-boned figure. Who could have guessed that good living and the absence of fear would fill out her face and form until she could have passed for a farmer's daughter? If her brain-power had increased with feeding all would have been well, but contentment made for sloth in her case, and for a most deplorable lack of ambition. Merlin had often caught her languorous blue eyes roving round their audiences for the faces of likely lads. There had been nods and winks exchanged, and a certain youth in an aggressive billycock had turned up at stage-doors too often for it to be coincidence.

Merlin tenderly placed one of his trained doves in a box, cooed to it, shut the lid and made passes over the box, uttering mystic-sounding words. A dramatic chord sounded from the harmonium, he re-opened the box and showed it to the audience, empty. Smiling, he beckoned to Emerald, who was posing at the opposite side of the stage with a similar box. The incantation was repeated, Mrs Seymore struck another chord, and Emerald opened the box. It was empty.

Reading her master's expression, she peered down and said, 'Ow dear.' Merlin thought furiously. No time to tell off the young perisher now. He caressed his audience with a dazzling smile.

'Ladies and gentlemen, my dear young friends, you have just

132

witnessed a miracle. My Magic Dove has dissolved into air – vanished into space, my friends, before your very eyes. The birdie has flown, in fact, ha ha! Now isn't that a remarkable thing?' With any luck they'd be too dense to notice that there ought to have been a dove in the other box.

They were. A ripple of applause and some faint cheers rewarded him. He sighed with relief.

The next trick, he realised with a sinking heart, was the one called Second Sight. Nearly all magicians practised it, since it had been started twenty years before by a Scotsman calling himself the Wizard of the North, with whom Merlin had worked as a boy. For this deception Emerald would sit blindfolded, looking as blankfaced as she could (which was very blank indeed) and identify objects which he would obtain from members of the audience as he went amongst them. The secret was a word-code: one ordinary-sounding word slipped into the question meant 'watch', another 'ring', another 'coin', another 'handkerchief', and so on. In long hours of practice he had hammered the key-words into Emerald's brain, and the performance always drew gasps of surprise.

How fervently he hoped she would not let him down now, as she drifted on stage in a long green robe and sat meekly to have her eyes bandaged. Perhaps the episode of the missing dove had not upset her nerve, as it had his.

But, regrettably, it had. Down among the front rows of stalls he realised that there would be precious few watches or rings – he had been a fool to keep the illusion in his particular matinée. He would have to cut it short and keep it simple.

'Now, Emerald,' he called up to her, loudly and brightly, 'can you tell me what I am holding in my hand?' (With the tips of my fingers, he might have added.)

'A handkerchief.'

'Quite right, my dear. Now, can you tell me if it belongs to a young gentleman or a young lady?'

A long pause. 'A young – lidy.'

'Garn, that ain't right,' said the owner of the handkerchief indignantly. 'I ain't no young lidy.'

Merlin hissed at him, 'Shut up and I'll give you a penny.' Moving on hastily he removed a gaudily beribboned hat from the head of a child whose particular treasure it was, having been bought special for her off a stall in Petticoat Lane. She set up a fearful wailing, causing Merlin to replace it hurriedly, as he asked Emerald to identify it in a question laden with the letter H.

She got it wrong again, as she had known she would. Among the audience there were murmurs of complaint, and the word 'fake' began to be heard, from one child, then another, joined by a catcall which was soon a chorus.

Merlin hurried back to the stage. He wished the floor would open and swallow the lot of them, including himself, but such miracles were not at his command. The show must go on. He muttered to Emerald, 'Get off, I'll talk to you later.'

'Ow, I'm ever so sorry, Magus, I don't know what ... '

'Get off, will you?' From a table he snatched up a pack of cards and fanned them out spectacularly. Nothing safer than cards, and they didn't require any assistance from that stupid young mare. Question was, should he give them Double Trouble or the Divining Dagger? Better keep it nice and simple for this lot. What about Foresight?

He riffled the cards again. 'I shall now,' he said, 'astonish you by a demonstration that even before I arrived in these halls today I knew which card a member of my audience would choose from the pack. 'Pon my honour, I did, friends. Now, may I have a lady or gentleman up on the stage to assist me in this amazing exhibition of Powerful Prestidigitation?'

He looked invitingly round the theatre. Silence, punctuated by a few giggles. 'Well? Nobody coming forward?'

'We're scared, mister,' piped up a voice from the front row.

Merlin suppressed an exasperated sigh. Suddenly his practised eye, roving about, spotted a young woman standing in the side-aisle, leaning against the wall. Her expression, which he could see clearly, was of intent interest, the sort of expression he liked to see on faces. He addressed himself to her.

'I see a very charming young lady whom the management has most inconsiderately not provided with a seat. Yes, you, madam.'

Nell was startled out of her trance of fascination. She had been glad of the chance to leave her seat and give it to a crippled child with a crutch, who had hobbled in late. And now he was – what, reproving her for standing, distracting his attention?

'If you'd be so kind, so very kind, as to step up here, my dear?'

Eagerly Nell complied. He noted how gracefully she walked, and how she bounded up the short steps to the stage. '"I never lov'd a dear gazelle to glad me with its soft brown eye"' he reflected in the words of a popular song, 'but it would turn out to be as stupid as twenty half-witted owls. Well, we'll see.'

'My dear child,' he said, 'my dear young lady. What a happy day. Won't you tell me your name?'

'Nell, sir.'

'Nell. Little Nell. Not so very little, either.'

They surveyed each other. At close quarters, she could see the greasepaint, the powder settled in the wrinkles, the artificial black lines and shadows round the eyes. But the wrinkles were lines of laughter, not of age, and the long white beard was false. How extraordinarily bright his eyes were in their deceptive surroundings, how merry and shapely his mouth among the artificial whiskers. She extended her hand to be shaken. Instead he kissed it, and she blushed beautifully.

'My dear Miss Nell,' he said, again fanning out the pack of cards, 'won't you select a card? Here you see them before you – study their faces carefully, and then point one out – quickly. Any one.'

She obeyed. 'Eight of hearts,' he announced. The complicated trick (in fact one of his easiest) proceeded as it should predictably enough, as he worked with a rough-smooth deck, the backs of some cards coated with a roughening solution made from gum arabic and the faces of others with a soapy powder which made them slippery. Triumphantly he produced a duplicate of the card Nell had chosen from a sealed envelope. 'You see, ladies and gentlemen? Miss Nell's chosen card.' Applause greeted the only trick to go right.

Nell was sent back in time, weeks, or was it months ago, watching the stage at the Oxford Music Hall being prepared for a magic act. That was when she had felt this strange sensation before, of being in

135

her rightful place. She came to herself to hear Merlin asking her to take a seat, to stay with him until the end of the performance. And there she sat, on a chair from which innumerable ladies had vanished, magicked away behind a white sheet, watching as this marvellous person passed solid metal rings one through another, though no opening could be seen in them, and finally produced from a top hat bouquet after bouquet of brilliant paper flowers.

The performance was over. The young audience, casting awed looks over their shoulders, began to shuffle out, and still Nell sat there, watching the red curtain come down, stagehands shifting furniture, fascinated by the sights and sounds and smells of this exotic environment.

Suddenly she remembered Harry. She ran to the curtain's edge and looked round it. He was there, standing forlornly in the aisle, gazing towards the stage. 'My young brother,' she said to Merlin, 'may I fetch him?'

'What? Brother? Certainly. Any brother of yours welcome.' He was collecting props and on his way to the wings. 'Be with you in two shakes of a bat's tail.'

Harry stood on stage, blinking, dazed. 'What did that man call you for? Do you know him? Why are we here?'

'He wanted me to help him, dear. Do you like it? Isn't it wonderful?'

Harry was staring about him. 'When we went to the pantomime it wasn't like this. There were lots of people, and music playing, and Uncle Gil bought us ices. It's – not real, is it.'

Nell was unsure herself what was real and what was not real, and in no position to answer searching questions. Eagerly she waited for Merlin to come back.

In the tiny, stuffy dressing-room he was confronting Emerald. She had changed from her stage costume into her day clothes, and was in a sullen, unrepentant mood.

'You let me down,' he told her. 'You let the whole act down. Didn't you get the cues? And what became of the dove – where's my Beauty?'

She pointed up to where, in a corner of the room, a white shape cowered on the top of a tall cupboard. 'I couldn't catch the silly thing. She's been there ever since. And I never thought, when I went on stage ... '

'You scared her. How'd she get up there with her wings clipped? You scared her out of her five wits, that's what you did.'

'I never. I never touched 'er. And I don't 'alf like the way you speaks to me, Magus.' She stood with her hands on her hips like a fishwife. 'I ain't used to such manners from the gentlemen with what I mixes with.'

'Meaning the young masher in the billycock, I s'pose?'

'Mr Frederick Bumpstead to you, if you please.'

Merlin bowed sardonically. 'And something tells me Mr Frederick Bumpstead isn't too far away, at this present moment.'

'At the stage door same as usual.'

'Then kindly put on your hat and join him.' He fished in the jacket pocket under his robe and produced a guinea. 'Wages in lieu of notice, as they say in the servants' hall. I'm finished with you, my girl, and you can be thankful to get your money.'

'Ho! Thank you for nothing.' But she pocketed it swiftly. 'Can't say I'm sorry to get out o' this lot. Loony sort of way to earn yer bread, ask me. And yer welcome to *that* rotten tat.' She kicked the green stage robe across the floor towards him and slammed out.

Merlin picked it up, mechanically folding it. He had paid for it; it was not hers to reject. He had paid for every stitch she had on, since the day when he had taken her from her wretched home, and had asked nothing of her but her professional assistance, such as it was. All she had and was she owed to him.

The dressing-room's small window was directly above the stage door. He looked down, and saw Emerald talking animatedly to Mr Frederick Bumpstead, who was ogling her, his hat at a cheeky angle. Then she nodded emphatically, took his arm, and was marched off towards – what? The altar, and the title of Mrs Bumpstead? Or, ultimately, the Haymarket meat parade and a convenient little room where gentlemen customers were allowed and no questions asked?

It was no concern of his. And yet he felt responsibility, anxiety for the young creature he had all but brought up, who had rewarded him by all but ruining his act. He sighed deeply, more sad than relieved that she was gone.

Fanny peeped in. 'There's a loidy on the stoige. Where's Emerald?'

'Not coming back, Fanny. Feed the doves, will you, and get 'em fresh water. I'll bring Beauty.' The frightened dove on the cupboard came to his call, fluttering down on to his shoulder and giving him an affectionate peck on the cheek. He had never hurt or frightened any creature used in his tricks, unlike some conjurors who would torture a bird to make it perform and wring its neck when it had been 'vanished'.

So it was that Nell saw him, in his own likeness rather than Merlin's, a tall man, even without the stilt heels, slim and graceful. His age was impossible to guess, for his hair was silver in contrast to the youthful look of his face. The grease used in stage make-up was a valuable preservative of complexions. His skin was pale, his mouth mobile and sensitive, his nose high-bridged and long, and even without the contrasting dark shadows the eyes were brilliant, sherry-brown in colour, and alive with expression. It was not, Nell decided, a handsome face, exactly, but a very attractive one. She judged the attractiveness of a man by whether one could bear to kiss him – even enjoy kissing him. Now that she saw Merlin as he was, the answer in his case was yes, she thought she would enjoy it. But he was old, of course, compared with Barnaby. And Barnaby's was the face in her dreams, when she dreamed of kisses.

'Thank you for stepping in, Miss Nell,' he said. 'I hope it didn't put you out at all.'

'Not in the least. I was glad to do it. Indeed, I was quite fascinated.'

Merlin was startled. The voice and manner were a young lady's, yet here she was at a charity matinée, escorting what was supposed to be a Poor Child, though the boy bore none of the signs of dirt and raggedness exhibited by most of the audience. He felt greatly curious about the pair. Now that he looked at her, she was dressed in good clothes grown shabby with wear; her skirt was marked and stained with dust from the pavements which a girl in good circumstances would have had removed by her maid, and she had a general look of

138

not having been cared for lately, any more than her clothes had. Curiosity overcame him.

'If you'd fancy it, I'd be most honoured if you'd let me take you' – he had nearly said treat you – 'for a – a cup of something. Er, tea or coffee, and a bite to eat. I always have something myself between shows.'

To his astonishment, her eyes visibly lit up, and the boy smiled for the first time.

'We'd be glad of that, sir. Wouldn't we, Harry? It's most kind of you.'

'Least I can do, having made use of your services in the show. Let's get out before we're swept off.' For stage-hands were sweeping up all round them, clouds of dust flying up from the boards. Merlin hurried them out of the empty theatre and into the Strand. It would not be proper to take this superior young person into a public-house, though plenty offered non-alcoholic drinks nowadays. Instead he led the way to a cocoa-room, one of the establishments opened some years before by a religious and charitable body, to provide an alternative to strong drink for working people. It was a cheerless little place in a side street, its dark green walls hung with texts and sacred pictures, and the female behind the counter was elderly and plain enough to offer no temptation to the most lascivious cocoa-drinker.

Merlin saw the eyes of his guests go straight to the plates of cakes, pies and sandwich-rolls displayed under glass domes. He ordered the removal of the domes, and invited them to help themselves. Personally he would not have touched the food, which resembled the notorious fare offered to railway travellers. But to Nell and Harry the stale, hard pastry was manna, and the cheap cocoa nectar. Merlin watched them eat with fascinated interest, particularly the girl's polite effort not to seem ravenous. He waited until she had finished the last crumb on her plate before asking cautiously, 'Will you have far to travel home, Miss Nell?'

Harry answered. 'We haven't a home now. We live in lodgings in Bouverie Street and I don't like it.'

Nell darted an annoyed glance at him. 'I'm sure Mr Merlin doesn't want to know about that, Harry.'

'Oh yes I do,' Merlin said. 'To be quite frank, and you'll excuse me if I seem to pry, I'm anxious about a young lady like yourself and a lad like this being out alone in the London streets. Funny things can happen, you know.'

'I do know.' Nell met his eyes squarely. It would not do to reveal too much to a stranger. It had been such a near thing with Mrs le Bel. But she liked and trusted this man, with no sound reason for doing so – stage glamour was something different – and she was growing desperate about their situation. Choosing her words very carefully, she gave him a heavily censored version of their recent adventures, leading him to conclude that she had come under some unjust suspicion while employed as a governess, and that her late employers were trying to find her, which would not be at all desirable. The occasional stern glances she threw at Harry warned him not to interrupt, however far she went from the truth. She was relieved when she had reached the end of what might have been an unconvincing story.

Merlin's mind-reading act owed nothing to the supernatural, but long practice with innocent subjects drawn from his audiences had given him some skill in picking up clues. He could read from the clear eyes holding apparently nothing but sincerity, and interpret the voice that paused every now and then for the speaker to arrange her next words. She was telling fibs, or at any rate not the whole truth. It made him no less concerned for her, and he was conscious of a strange but strong desire to protect her and the child who was so like her.

He was a quick thinker. A plan was forming in his mind; it would not do to overwhelm her with with it, or seem to be laying a trap for her. He arranged the objects on the table – cups, saucers, plates, cutlery – in a neat row, watched suspiciously by the steel-spectacled eyes behind the counter. It helped his concentration to lay out objects as he would for a trick.

'I needn't ask you, Miss Nell, whether you've ever done any stage work – unless it might be home theatricals?'

'Not even those,' Nell answered, smiling.

'Ah, I thought not. But, if I may say so and you won't be offended, you have a very nice graceful way of moving, and a ... a pleasant

140

appearance.' There – he had alarmed her, he was sure. She would rise and sweep out, insulted by such personal remarks. But she was still smiling.

'No woman could be offended by being told she had a pleasant appearance, sir.'

His face cleared. 'Then that's all right, and I can say what I set out to. My assistant's left me – very suddenly, this afternoon. Can't say I'm altogether sorry, after a few things happened. But I don't know how I shall go on, now she's gone. The two kids, Fanny and Danny – they come in tremendously useful for some acts. But it's not the same as a proper female assistant, someone to hand me things and ... look pretty,' he finished lamely. He was so obviously deeply embarrassed that Nell almost reached out her hand to clasp his reassuringly.

'I understand,' she said. 'Do you mean that you think I might replace her?'

He stared. 'How did you – I mean, I hardly thought you'd ... I thought you'd be above it.'

'Do I look above anything? Anything respectable, that is? I need to earn a living, Mr Merlin.'

'Respectable it would be, above all else,' he said earnestly. 'And if I were to offer you living accommodation that would be respectable too, though I hardly expect you to credit it, for I'm not a married man and you might well think I'm out to – to ... ' He gazed at her helplessly.

'I don't think you're out to anything. And do go on, please. About living accommodation.'

'Well. I've got a substantial place of my own. Just outside London. In fact, it's in Kent – I'm proud of that. Never did think of myself as a Cockney, which I'm not, even if I sound like one. Pair of houses, it is, which my grandma left me, not that she held with me going back to the theatrical business. I live in one, so does Mrs Seymore. Mrs Whitty's in the other, with Fanny and Danny, and George, that's her chap – husband. He's my stage carpenter, very important job, that is, and Mrs W. keeps an eye on the kids. So you see, you'd be properly chaperoned. I'm not one of your Bad Barons if you know what I mean.' She did.

'And Harry — would there be room for him?' she asked.

'Plenty, plenty. And we'll find a school for him to go to.'

'A boarding-school?' Harry asked nervously.

'No, we don't go in for them much, down our way.'

'Then that's all right.' Harry heaved a relieved sigh.

Nell's emotions were a mixture of joy and thankfulness that she was being shown a way out of the tangle she had got herself and Harry into, and grateful liking for this honest, tongue-tied man whom she trusted thoroughly. He radiated goodness, and at the same time a curious glamour which had come with him from the stage, the lights, the indefinable something which had caught her imagination at the Oxford on that memorable evening: the lure of illusion, that beckons on and will not be resisted.

'It's all right,' she told him comfortingly. 'I believe you, and I'm not quite a fool, though you might think so. If we may go back with you tonight I'll tell Mrs Parkins and settle up what we owe. Will that suit you?'

'That'll suit me, Miss Nell.' He put out his hand and she shook it ceremoniously, noticing how long and supple and altogether elegant it was. From St Bride's church near by a sudden peal of bells began, the Sunday ringers at their practice.

'I,' Harry announced, 'should like another sausage.'

'Have one, me boy. Or two or three. As many as you like.'

While Harry ate, and the bells rang, the magician and his new assistant gazed at each other, and wondered, and smiled.

XI

Edith and Ethel

'It's a long way,' Merlin apologised as they took their seats in the ten o'clock train at the London Bridge terminus of the South-Eastern Railway, North Kent Line. 'Seventeen miles, and a shocking crawl on a foggy night. But I like it. Gets you out of the smoke. I always feel sleeping in London's like having a dirty feather bed on top of you. Are you quite comfortable, Miss Nell?'

Nell said that she was. More, she was oddly content. The small second-class compartment was full of people she knew; it was like being in a family going on an outing. Merlin, still a theatrical figure with a cloak lined with dark blue silk swathed about him, sat by her side, having given her the window seat facing the engine, such as a lady liked to occupy. Harry sat on her other side rapt with interest at the sights and sounds of the busy terminus, the billowing white smoke smelling of sulphur, the passengers hurrying to take their places on this, the last train of the evening.

Opposite them sat George Whitty, a sturdy four-square man with a face surprisingly brown for one of his profession. His arms encircled Fanny and Danny, one child on each side, leaning against him, the only father they knew. Traces of make-up were still on their faces, and Fanny's frock was by rights one that ought to have been in the property basket in the guard's van, along with the non-basketable props which had filled a whole cab on their way to the station, while they travelled in another. But she was too tired to care. It was understood that the children always slept for the entire railway journey, and were removed from the train, still sleeping, to be put to bed.

George Whitty eyed Nell unfavourably. She was a stranger, come

143

to upset the little family, he had no doubt. How could she be trusted not to chatter in public and give away the secrets of the profession? She looked flighty enough, worse than that fat Emerald, and she'd been bad enough, good riddance to her. He hoped that the Magus was not going to become soft about young women, after all these years of staying free of them. His stare at Nell became a glower.

In the opposite corner Mrs Seymore sat, bolt upright, gazing at the carriage window. The swinging gas-lamp gave out just enough illumination to prevent her seeing anything outside beyond the pin-point lights of houses, a glimpse of masts as the train ran close to the river, the massive bulk of Woolwich Arsenal. She was not aware of these things, for only music occupied her mind, tune following tune, each heard in its completeness, whether a piece for orchestra or a solo for piano. She had perfect recall of tune and harmony, and the words of songs.

Her father had taught music, she had grown up surrounded by it. Then she too had taught, but always with the knowledge that one day she would play, in public a recognised and admired professional musician, an ornament to the concert stage. She practised far more than did her pupils, sometimes far into the night, until the tenant of the second floor front beat frantically upon his floor for her to stop.

When she was nineteen her girl's fancy had been caught by the flowing whiskers and saucy glances of a second violin in the orchestra of the Olympic Theatre. A popular ballad of the time, 'The Gipsy's Warning', held a stern caution – 'Do not trust him, gentle maiden'. But Adelaide was too infatuated to care about such things. Within two years she had been abandoned, robbed, and deserted by the faithless Seymore, who had skipped overnight to prey on someone else and play his violin in another orchestra, where with luck she would never find him.

It was not easy to concentrate on music when one was heartbroken: Adelaide's ambitions faltered and seemed to expire. For years she lived, not very prosperously, by teaching children and looking after her ageing, sickly mother. Then her mother had died, and she had met Merlin: she barely remembered how or where, for she had been unhappy enough to want to forget everything.

He was not a true practitioner of magic, Adelaide knew that. But he had some sort of magic about him, in his warm persuasive voice, in his keen lively glance, that made her instantly feel better. She could never love again, of course, after Adolphus – it was not like that at all. But when he asked her, deferentially, to take up the post of travelling musician to his magic show, she agreed without pausing to think. And somehow, as she sat at her neat folding harmonium raising spirits and devils and angels and fairies with her clever fingers, all the old dreams of a musical career crept back and filled her thoughts, though now she was not restless but content. For was she not a public performer, admired and recognised and influential, making people shudder or swoon or sigh at her pleasure?

She hardly noticed that Nell had joined them.

Nell, too, stared out into the unknown countryside, unseeing. Dark shapes and bright lights sped past, but her mind's eye was filled with scenes from the past week. The hopeless days of walking in the threatening streets. The girl who had thrown her to the ground in the Middlesex saloon, the man who had attacked her outside it. The barber, eyeing her hair. The small wrinkled face of the landlady in Bouverie Street, thanking Nell, between coughs, for the week's money paid up in full. Nell had not understood her gratitude; but to Mrs Parkins a lodger who would do such a thing was a rare bird indeed. Most would have flitted with half a week's rent owing.

But it had cost Nell literally her last penny. If Harry had not seen Merlin's poster outside the theatre of varieties, where would they have been now, and with what hopes? She knew all about the painted girls who strolled up and down the Haymarket or lounged in doorways and under lamp-posts. Now she knew why they did it. There was nothing else for them, no other way of making a living. Perhaps she would have come to that, too, and before long. Nell shivered. But at least she would have known something beforehand about that awful mystery, sex: Indian temple carvings were very explicit, and her mother had been nervously frank. What dangers, what horrors she and Harry had escaped, in the sinister house by the Cemetery, in the streets, in the seeming safety of Uncle Gil's rooms ...

145

She thought of her mother, worrying with no news of her children. And of Barnaby, her friend, who had tried so hard to help them – what would Barnaby think of their disappearance, without even a scribbled line of gratitude? She remembered his voice, his anxious face, his kind manner to Harry when the child was distressed. When they reached wherever they were going, she would write to him and to her mother ...

The rhythmic tune of the train's wheels faded into a blur of dream-voices, and Nell slept.

'Where are they?' Mr Channer repeated.

'I don't know, sir.'

'Of course you know, boy. You were in it with them, don't tell me otherwise. How could that girl have got away with a sick child, and not left a trace? The truth, now. My patience is wearing thin, I warn you.'

That statement was very true. Mr Channer had been visited by Eudora and Minerva, and browbeaten within an inch of his life. They could just comprehend his reason for parting with their nephew when the child was ill with an infection they would not have wanted under their own roof, but that he had taken no steps to trace Harry irked them sorely.

'My sister and I have done all we can.' Eudora banged the ferrule of her umbrella repeatedly on the floor, and Minerva nodded rapidly. 'We have told the police all we know of the girl's haunts in London, where we allowed her to wander too freely.'

'Much too freely,' agreed Minerva.

'The vicar whose confirmation classes she attended is under instructions to let us know if she approaches him – not that there's much likelihood of her doing anything of the kind. A watch has been set on our brother's lodgings, in case she should visit him, as I feel convinced she will.'

'Birds of a feather,' Minerva said.

'You do realise, Mr Channer, that the girl, *our* niece, is wanted on a criminal charge?'

'But,' Channer said, 'how can I possibly help, madam? I hardly knew your niece.'

'That boy,' Minerva put in. 'That impudent boy who rode up to our house to see her. I always thought something doubtful was going on there. "Man is fire and woman is tow", the saying goes. He knows, mark me.'

'Quite, quite. Barnaby Lyon. I will ask him, of course, though I doubt ... '

Barnaby was interrogated in the grim little study where as a boy he had often been beaten. Yes, he had met Miss Carey when she was living at Highgate. Yes, he had taken her brother to see her without asking permission. He had not seen either of them since he had escorted the boy to Mr Pye's house, on instructions. No, he had not had a letter from Miss Carey. He knew where they were no more than Mr Channer himself did. (But he had wondered so often, had agonised for the sick little boy and the loving sister who had carried the news off so cheerfully and bravely. Perhaps she too had caught the infection. Perhaps they were lying now in some fever hospital; perhaps one was dead, perhaps both. Nell had brought life and beauty into the dreary round of his days at Yew House, and he could hardly bear the thought that he might never see her again.)

When Channer asked him once more where the missing pair were, he burst out, 'I wish to God I knew, sir, and that's the truth if you want it!'

At last the headmaster believed him. The boy genuinely did not know, but he could be made to find out. Quite clearly he was sweet on the girl and could be used as an instrument to trace her; but only if he failed to realise that he was being manipulated. He would want to find her on his own account, not to hand her over to justice. How to make him set out on her trail? Channer, dismissing him, meditated.

That night, returning to the house from the stables, Barnaby was jumped on from behind and thrown to the ground. Before he could defend himself he was assailed with brutal kicks to his head and body until he lay helpless, all one fire of pain, bleeding from mouth and eyelid, sobbing and gasping. Then his assailants were satisfied. They had been told to half-kill him, not finish him off, and they considered their duty done. The two senior boys, one of them Nugent, who had

147

been chief tormentor of Harry, the Young Nabob, stole away to their dormitory, richer by a shilling each bestowed by their headmaster.

Half-conscious, Barnaby watched the dawn spread over the skies. As the first sounds of life told him the servants were about in the house he slowly struggled to his feet, groaning, barely able to move for pain and stiffness. At the back door, the one that led into the general kitchen-yard, he stopped and knocked. A face, the kitchen-maid's, peered out. Seeing him, she yelped and banged the door shut.

A side door used by staff remained closed until he had banged on the knocker repeatedly. Then, cautiously, it opened. A boy who was half-pupil, half-servant, stood there, night-shirted and sleepy-eyed.

'We're not to let you in,' he said.

'But why? Look at me ... '

'Head's orders. Can't help it.' The door slammed and a bolt went into place.

Barnaby stumbled away, across the yard, into the gardens, back towards the stables. He crept into Tennyson's stall, where the brown horse stood dreaming. It whickered as he entered, advancing a nose to be stroked. Barnaby touched it gently.

'I'm done for, Tennyson, I think. Let me in, there's a good fellow.'

The hay was sweet-smelling, warm and soft after the hard ground he had lain on. Tennyson bent his noble head and nudged his friend, sensing distress, then stood still, not venturing a hoof near him. During the hour that passed some kind of sleep visited Barnaby. Awaking to pain, he wondered wryly whether horse-liniment would be any good for the bruises he bore, but doubted it. Outside in the stable yard was a trough used for watering the horses. He doused his head in it. Restored a little by the shock of the cold water, he straightened up and looked about him, at the shut house, the windows from which no face looked.

So the school had finished with him, he was rejected, the problem of what was to be done with a penniless orphan solved by one sharp stroke. He was cast out, he must go. But where? It mattered very little. He found himself at the carriage-entrance of Yew House, the Great North Road stretching ahead of him, north and south.

He chose the south; just as Mr Channer had hoped he would do.

'I trust you'll like them,' Merlin said as they approached the end of the journey. 'Get on with them, as it were.'

'Who?' Nell was too sleepy to pay much attention, but she thought he answered 'Edith and Ethel', and wondered what relation they were to him, and whether they would be at all like her aunts. By the time the travellers had bundled themselves out at little Dartford station, and into a cab, and their props packed into another, she had forgotten everything except the prospect of a bed.

Half a mile or so from the station the cab stopped and they were all bundling out again. Merlin took her arm and led her forwards.

'There they are. 'Like 'em?'

Nell stared. She was looking up at two houses, joined together but detached on each side from their neighbours. Their stuccoed façades were gently classical in style, in a pretty fashion which had gone out with the late King William. On the pediment which capped them Nell read by the light of the street-lamp EDITH VILLA on the left half, ETHEL VILLA on the right.

'They're very comfortable,' Merlin assured her. 'Small, but comfortable. You and Harry can share Ethel with me and Mrs S. There's plenty of room.'

Mrs Seymore had joined them on the pavement. '"Be it never so humble,"' she sang dreamily, '"there's no place like Home."'

'That's right, Mrs S. – nor there is. Now let's get indoors and have a nice warm up.'

The next half-hour was a whirl of activity. Mrs Whitty, a large, plain, wholesome young woman, appeared from some downstairs region like a fairy in a pantomime, greeted her husband, shot a few dubious glances at Nell, scooped up Fanny and Danny and bore them upstairs to be dealt with by unseen hands, and whisked Nell and Harry through a communicating door into Ethel Villa. Nell glimpsed rooms (and the small houses had a surprising number of rooms) full of strange shapes and odd-looking furniture. While they watched, holding the candles which had somehow appeared in their hands, she propped open the door of a back bedroom and with incredible speed removed from it a table carved with satyrs' masks, a stuffed peacock, a cardboard rose-tree in full bloom, a drum and a Japanese screen, all of which she dumped at the foot of the attic stairs. The room was now revealed as a pleasant small bedroom with a half-tester bed, a wash-stand, a comfortable chair and a wardrobe.

'It wasn't like that before,' Harry said wonderingly. 'Is this a magic house, Nell?'

'I shouldn't be surprised if it was.' Mrs Whitty was on her knees at the grate, where in seconds she had changed a pile of twigs and coals into a blazing fire.

'Good thing I kept it laid,' she said. 'Thought I'd better.'

'But you couldn't have known we were coming,' Nell said. 'Mr Merlin wouldn't have had time ... '

'Ah.' Mrs Whitty shook her head inscrutably. 'You get your things off and I'll fetch you a hot brick and a flannel nightie. Come along with me, young man.' Harry was whisked off as Fanny and Danny had been, and Nell, alone, began to undress, shocked at the shabby, dusty look of her clothes in this clean, fresh room.

She was in bed, comforted by a warm drink, a wash in delicious hot water, an all-enveloping red flannel nightgown which was almost certainly Mrs Whitty's own, and a well-wrapped hot brick at her feet. If this was all a dream, she decided, it was such a nice one that she would try hard not to wake up. On which thought she fell suddenly and deeply asleep.

It was a welcome surprise to find herself in the same bed when she awoke. But now the curtains were open and warm sunshine streamed in through the window, lighting up the walls cheerfully patterned with roses and the crimson carpet where whole gardens of nameless flowers bloomed. Hot water was steaming in the ewer, brought by someone who had evidently skimmed into the room and out of it without disturbing its occupant.

Nell washed, dressed, and found her way through the communicating door and downstairs, through a general pleasant waft of cooking and warmth, into the back parlour of Edith. Merlin stood by the fireplace, leaning casually against the grey marble mantel. The parlour was a typical room of comfortable middle-class dwellers,

150

bright, cluttered, hung with cheerful coloured prints and decorative plates. Peacocks' feathers adorned a vase, pink geraniums scented the air on the sunny window-sill.

Merlin alone was not quite the figure to suit the setting. He wore a dressing-robe of shot silk, which changed as he moved from blues to greens and coral-pinks, sinuous as the scales of a snake. A bow of black satin gauze, loosely tied, was at his neck, Persian slippers on his feet. His hair shone silver, almost glittering in the morning light, and years had fallen from him with sleep. Nell wondered if she would ever find out how old he was.

'Miss Nell, good morning,' he said. 'How spruce you look. I hope you slept well?' He sounded not at all like the showman she had met less than twenty-four hours ago, yet the same warm ring was there in his voice, which was not like other voices.

'Beautifully, thank you. Where is Harry, and the others?'

He waved a hand. 'Downstairs. Mrs Whitty looks after us all.'

'But not you?' Nell ventured.

'Sometimes. And sometimes I look after myself, and my guests. Like this.' A Persian slipper moved, and from a flower in the carpet at his feet a pole shot smoothly up and expanded itself like an umbrella before settling down to become a mahogany table-top. Nell, who had uttered a faint shriek, blinked at it and him. He smiled, made a pass in the air, and outside the room a little carillon tinkled, a faint sweet chime fragile as Japanese wind-bells. Almost at once the door opened; a small servant-maid stood smiling and bobbing.

'Ah, Ethelberta. Breakfast, please. What will you take, Miss Nell? Tea, coffee? Buttered eggs, minced ham on fried toast, kippers, a sausage, a grilled chop, mushrooms?' Nell fully expected to see all these items materialise in the air for her inspection, and was not aware of ordering any of them in particular, and yet in no time at all the little maid had reappeared, covered the table with a cloth and brought from the hall a tray laden with savoury dishes and pretty china.

'You see, Miss Nell,' said Merlin, when they were seated before the spread, 'we must eat well if we're to work well, and work is what we must do today, if you're to learn in a week what it took Emerald to

151

learn in four years. Have a sausage, do. I wonder what to begin with –
boxes, fans, rings? The Miraculous Casket or the Vanishing Bird?
The Omelette of Doves? More butter? More coffee?'

'If you please.'

Merlin murmured something that rhymed, and waved a hand over
the coffee-pot. Instantly it leaped to attention, raised its lid in salute,
and slid gracefully across the tablecloth towards Nell. She squealed in
surprise.

'Don't be alarmed,' said Merlin. 'In my house, things learn to
obey.'

XII

Crystals and Doves

Nell could not have guessed that there was so much she herself would have to learn, or that it would take so much learning.

Most fortunately Merlin had a week's break between engagements. He liked to separate them, he said, to give himself time to practise difficult routines and perfect new ones. Up at the top of the villas a long dormered loft ran from one to the other. Round its walls stood tables, screens, chairs, boxes, drapes, every conceivable kind of apparatus, like objects in an exhibition. No sound drifted up from below; even the faint pleasing tinkle of Mrs Seymore's piano-playing could not filter through the heavy well-fitting doors, or the dark green carpet covering the floor boards. In the trim garden below Danny was picking apples from a laden tree, George Whitty digging, and the maid Ethelberta hanging washing on a line.

'We shall work,' Merlin said, 'all day, every day. At meal-times we shall go down and eat with the others, but not too much. A magician mustn't starve nor yet guzzle. Emerald ... ' he sighed. 'She liked her food, that girl. I expect you do, too?'

'Well, we haven't had much in the last week, Harry and I. But it only takes one or two good meals, like that delicious breakfast, and one's all right again.'

'In spite of the coffee-pot?'

'I like the coffee-pot. He has nice manners.'

'He has, he has.' Merlin was putting on his robe of crimson and black, with the gold designs of sun, moon, stars, circles and crosses, Greek letters and Egyptian hieroglyphs. He noticed Nell's look of surprise.

'Wondering why I'm wearing this, when we've no audience? I

need it, that's why – couldn't work without it. I'll show you.'

Flinging it back from his shoulders he revealed the presence of two deep pockets in the back lining, about where coat-tails would have been, their openings, slanting downward from centre to side.

'*Profondes*', he said. 'For concealing articles, or disposing of them. And these are *pochettes* – same purpose, but shallower, easier to get at,' showing two smaller pockets set behind the thighs of the black tights he wore. 'And these.' Under each arm of the robe was a wide pocket opening perpendicularly. Just a nice size for holding a rabbit.'

'Rabbit?'

Merlin pointed down to the garden. 'Three hutches of 'em, all colours. White one vanishes, reappears as a black one. Gentle as lambs. We only work with does, of course, bucks aren't to be trusted – too frisky. Not like you, eh, my pets? Come on, then.' He was gazing round the room, at picture-rail level, whistling softly. Four white shapes fluttered down and perched on his outstretched arm, eight pink jewel-eyes blinked lazily. Nell cried out with pleasure.

'Like them? Beauty, Faith, Hope, Charity.'

'May I ... would one come to me?'

'If I tell her to.' He enclosed one of the doves in his hand. 'Hold out your arm.' The bird made no protest as its master transferred it to Nell, murmuring to it. On its new perch it shuffled for a moment, pecked at its breast-feathers, then began to coo softly to itself, echoed by one of the others.

'It likes me!' Nell cried. 'Oh, it's got pink feet, just like its eyes. What a dear, lovely little bird.'

Merlin regarded girl and dove thoughtfully. The birds had never taken to Emerald, wouldn't have done even if her hair had been full of worms and bird-seed. Once there had been several dove tricks in his repertoire – The Vanishing Bird, The Dove Omelette, The Flying Cage – but one by one they had been dropped, except for the simple trick which Emerald had managed to mess up at what turned out to be her last performance. Perhaps it was something she ate that put them off, and she'd always been afraid she'd catch ticks from them. This girl was different. He studied the angle of her head, bent towards the dove, which had shuffled up to her shoulder: the soft rose

154

of her cheek, the creamy-white of her skin, contrasting with the pure white of the bird's plumage, the glowing lock of hair straying over the soft feathers. Pictures began to form in his mind.

'Nell ... ' he began.

'Yes?'

Merlin was embarrassed. She was too grand a young lady to be addressed in such a free and easy way. 'I mean, Miss Nell,' he said hurriedly, 'your name won't do for stage work. A magician's assistant needs something showy, picturesque, sort of foreign, like as it were a Nymph or a Houri.'

'I don't think I look much like a Nymph or a Houri,' Nell said doubtfully.

'Oh, but you could. It's amazing what costume can do ... costume. Let's see.' He went to a rack of hanging garments and took a few off the rail. 'These were Emerald's – see what you think.'

Nell surveyed them, one by one. There was a green gauzy robe, very low-necked and short in the skirt, a pink tunic-like thing trimmed with fringing of tarnished gilt, a pair of Grecian-type boots which had been cheaply regilded, a little-girl-type frock with a wide lace collar, and a leopard-spotted leotard with a pair of brown cotton tights pinned to it and a bunch of imitation grapes sewn on to one shoulder.

'You can try them on if you like,' Merlin suggested, not hopefully.

'I don't think I'll need to, thank you.' Nell took them over to a long pier-glass and held them up against herself, one after another, the dove seeming to study its reflection with interest. She turned to him, making a comic face. 'Well?'

'They're AWFUL, quite AWFUL,' he said. 'Why didn't I see it before? They seemed to suit Emerald all right, but she was – well, different. Not in your class, if I may say so, not the thing at all. I mean, you're a lady – wouldn't do for you to wear tat like that. We'll have to find something new.'

'Oh dear – I don't want to put you to a lot of expense. I expect I can manage if I alter them a bit, here and there. Except ... she was a bit shorter than me, wasn't she, and – well, plumper.'

'Assistants have got to be short, so as not to draw too much

155

attention, and because sometimes they've got to go into not much room, like in the Bellows Table. You're just about right if you wear low heels. Wait!' He dashed to a cupboard and returned with an armful of bolts of cloth.

'Stuff Mrs Whitty keeps on hand. She's a marvellous dressmaker, that's her machine over there. What about this, now, and this?'

Nell gasped with admiration. Swathes of filmy blue, rose, scarlet and gold ran through his hands like coloured rivers, glittering and flashing, some plain, some woven with intricate raised patterns, others embroidered with silk designs and rosebuds of tulle.

'They're all beautiful! I never saw such stuff – oh, except in India.'

'India? You been in India? Wish I had. They know a lot about magic there. But these … ' he was glancing from the materials to her, and back again. 'No, I don't think any of 'em'll do.' At her face of disappointment he smiled. 'Cheer up – this will.'

It was a bolt of something that at first appeared to be pure white and shining. Then, as Merlin displayed it, Nell saw that it was a net foundation covered with sequins, sewn so closely together that they formed a surface like the scales of a fish. They were studded here and there with a jewel of rock quartz, bright as a diamond. As the full light caught the sequins they shimmered, the pearly lustre breaking up into pinks, blues, lilacs, greens, then twinkling into whiteness again. Nell stared, with infatuated eyes.

'Allow me,' said Merlin. He unrolled a length and held it under her chin, draping a fold over her arm so that the still-perching dove formed part of the gleaming image in the mirror.

'Beads,' he said softly, 'only beads. but an't they a wonder to look at! Real pearls couldn't look better. Real diamonds couldn't shine better.'

'Crystal,' Nell murmured.

'That's it, crystal. Beautiful word, wish I could think of such. That's what you'll be, the Crystal Girl. And Beauty here … ' he laid the material over the back of the dove, which had now gone to sleep with its head under its wing. 'She shall have a bit of sparkle, too. That'll make the Vanishing Bird and the Flying Cage quite a new thing. We could have two doves fancy, or one fancy and one plain, depending how it looked from the front. 'Yes.' He flung out a great swathe and draped it round Nell, so that she stood like a statue made of pearl.

While Mrs Whitty sewed away at the new costume, demanding frequent fittings, Nell spent long hours of application in the rehearsal-loft, sometimes with Merlin alone, sometimes with Fanny or Danny or both, often to the tune of the clacking sewing machine. Merlin was immensely interested in what Nell could remember of the native Indian magic she had seen.

'It's so long ago – and it seems very unreal, now. But Papa thought it was good for English children to know about Indian ways, and he used to take me to see the *fakirs*, though Mamma thought they were horrible. They used to beg for alms in the market-places by doing things that didn't seem possible. One used to lie on a bed of nails without seeming to feel anything, and then, when he was in a trance, they'd put him in a coffin and heap sand on top of him and shut it up. He'd stay there for about twenty minutes and then push the coffin-lid off and sit up, quite all right.'

'Ah,' Merlin nodded. 'So could you and I, if the nails were close enough together, and if we knew how to breathe slow enough.'

'Then what about the ones who tortured themselves, sticking pins into their skin and threading sharp things through it? Now that I didn't enjoy, and even Papa used to look away.'

'Belief, all belief, my dear. When you go on the stage you must believe in magic like the audience does, and never mind that you know it's all tricks, known since you were a little bit of a kid like Danny, working for that chap called himself the Wizard of the North. He told me the same thing: once the belief goes out of you, you're finished. Old and finished.' For a moment the bright look went from his face, changing its aspect. He was Harlequin with the mischief gone, Pierrot watching Columbine dance away with someone else.

Nell touched his hand. 'Don't worry, Magus. That won't happen to you, or if it does I'll work for you and keep you in luxury in your old age.'

'I believe you would; I truly believe you would.' Briefly they shared a dream, a dream of an eternal stage-world in which everything turned into something much more interesting than itself, paper flowers bloomed all the year, an endless supply of drinks poured themselves from an Inexhaustible Bottle, and darkness and cold were unknown. Then the vision was gone and the real world back with them; only half a week left to rehearse.

Because Nell was fascinated by the mystery of appearances and disappearances Merlin took the time to demonstrate an illusion in which she would never figure. He had questioned her keenly about the legendary Indian Rope Trick, in which a boy was said to climb up a rope, to the piping of an enchanter, and disappear into thin air at the top of it, while the rope remained upright, against the nature of ropes.

'I never saw that,' Nell said, 'or I'd have remembered. But I've heard Papa talk about it.'

'Ah, that's the old story. Everyone's heard of it but nobody's seen it. Sometimes I disbelieve it's ever been done.'

'*We* do it,' Danny said.

'That's true, my son, but is it the genuine article, the real Mackay? I have to confess it an't.'

'Don't see why not, Magus. There's the rope, I goes up it and I disappears. Ain't that right?'

Merlin smiled sadly. 'Correction, Daniel. I throw up the rope – it's got a hook on the end which engages on the bar on the fit-up that the audience can't see. You get to the top, a weighted black cloth drops down and hides you, then unrolls itself and hides the rope, while I pick up another coil of rope, which makes 'em think it's the first one. All a matter of timing – quickness of the hand deceives the eye. But it's clumsy stuff, clumsy. Don't I just wish I knew how the real thing's done. Tell you what,' he addressed Nell, brightening, 'We'll do the Indian Basket Trick for you. That's one I can be proud of.'

As Nell watched raptly, he called Fanny forwards to join her brother. 'You'll have to imagine these two are dressed alike,' he said. Then he pulled forward a dress-basket, some five feet long by two

158

deep, and lifted it on to a low stand on wheels. 'You can do that bit when the time comes, if you like' he said, 'it's not heavy. Now watch.' Retreating to a corner, he advanced again with a drawn sword in his right hand and an apparently reluctant Fanny dragged along by the other, while he scolded her alarmingly for some nameless crime and loudly vowed revenge. Screaming realistically, she pulled herself free and ran off, followed by her tormentor. But, once presumably out of the sight of the audience, he took Danny's hand and led him, screaming, back to the basket, leaving Fanny in the wings.

Still protesting, the boy was pushed relentlessly into the basket and the lid shut. Then Merlin proceeded to thrust his sword through the basket, again and again, drawing it out each time with its end bloodstained, while the shrieks coming from the basket grew fainter and fainter. Nell knew it was illusion, yet shivered in spite of herself.

The screams died away; all was still. Merlin stepped forward. Pleasantly smiling, he addressed his imaginary audience. 'Ladies and gentlemen, I fear you imagine I have injured or even slain the young lady who was the subject of this ... experiment. Pray put away such a notion. She had disobeyed me, and I was determined to punish her by giving her a little fright. But that was all. The fact is, she had left the basket some time before I thrust in the sword. Ah, you don't believe me, I see. Allow me to show you, in the first place, that the basket is empty.'

He tilted it on to its side and raised the lid. It was indeed empty. 'The young lady has vanished, you see. Let her come forward and show you for herself that she is safe.' He stretched a hand towards the wings, from which Danny tripped forward, beaming.

Nell clapped. 'Bravo! Now show me how it's done.'

'A pleasure. They're dressed alike, as I said, in something the audience can't mistake. And where's Danny, you ask?' He beckoned Nell forward, lifted what appeared to be the bottom of the basket, and there lay Danny, grinning.

'It's a false flap, you see, fixed at right-angles. When I tilt the basket, down it falls and Danny's concealed, while the audience think they're looking at the real thing. Right: now we'll deal with the Bellows Table. You watch carefully.'

159

It looked a perfectly ordinary little table, such as might be found in any drawing-room – about two and a half feet high, four slender legs, a round top, and a table-cloth of intricate pattern in reds and greens, hanging to within a few inches of the floor. Merlin raised this, showing that the table-top was only about three inches deep.

'Not room for much in there, is there? Up, Fanny.'

Fanny climbed on top of the table and struck a statue pose.

'Time to put the light out,' Merlin said, and taking a large wicker cone shaped like a candle-extinguisher covered Fanny with it. Nell was by now prepared to see the table-top empty when the cone was lifted. As, indeed it was, though only a moment had passed.

Merlin whipped off the cloth, revealing a hollow cylinder below the table and Fanny crouched into a ball inside it. 'You see,' he said, helping the child out, 'it's quite simple really.' He explained that the table-top was made to collapse under the weight of a person standing on it, dropping down inside a tube in which the disappearing person lay crouched until the fall of the curtain, when she could be released. 'That's the snag,' he said. 'You can't show the assistant somewhere else, or let 'em see the inside of the table. It wants working on ... we can do better, I fancy. All right, Fanny, and you too, Danny, run along.'

Nell was examining the table. 'It's wonderful.'

'Think you could do it – curl up small inside that space?'

Nell surveyed herself ruefully. 'I don't know. I think I'm too big.'

'Try it, on the floor first. It all depends how supple you are.'

Nell sat on the floor and, at his direction, curled herself up in a foetus position, her knees up to her chin and her hands on opposite shoulders. It was amazing how little room a full-grown woman could take up, but the hoops of her crinoline stuck out ridiculously, making them both laugh. 'I'll take it off if you like,' she offered.

'Don't trouble, I can tell. Your legs are too long, that's what – ' he stopped, afraid that he had offended her mortally. A man did not refer to a female's legs, or even allow himself to think that she might have any. He was surprised when she did not react; what a strange young woman she was. A real lady, of course, yet as frank as a boy. He had not met any such before.

160

'We'll have to think of something else. There's one illusion ... I haven't got it right yet, but it would suit you down to the ground. Fact is, I want to cut down the kids' acts. Word gets round, even when we're touring, that there are two of 'em, like as two peas, and it spoils the effect. Besides, I want 'em to have some schooling. There's an old dame down by the church – vicar's daughter, I've heard – turned her house into a school and runs it like clockwork, they say.'

'Could Harry go there?' Nell said, suddenly inspired. 'I want him to settle down and have some peace. It's been so terrible for him lately – he's been through so much.'

'I'd thought of that. She takes all ages, kids whose fathers can't afford the big schools.'

'Oh! but ... Of course, there'd be fees. I couldn't afford ... '

'When we start working, you'll be getting a salary. Don't you fret yourself, Miss Nell.'

Nell, still on the floor, sat back on her heels, looking up at him. 'Why are you doing all this for us – for Harry as well as me?'

He found it hard to answer her. Because she was beautiful and strange, honest and good-tempered, sharp-brained and quick to learn, superior in birth and breeding to him, yet never coming the fine lady? Because, with all his retinue around him, he was a curiously lonely man?

He answered her, 'Because you're going to be the best assistant any magician ever had, that's why, Nelda. There! It came to me without thinking. Nelda, that'll be your stage name. Sounds right to you?'

'Exactly right. Nelda – Nelda – Nelda. It's my name. Now tell me yours.'

'Mine? You know it. Merlin.'

'No that's only your stage name, the sort of name magicians call themselves. And Magus only means 'wise man', I know that. I mean your real name.'

'I don't use it.'

'But you'll tell me.'

He had not meant to, preferring to live cocooned in the world of illusion he had created around himself. But he said, 'It's Thorn.'

161

'What else? John Thorn or James Thorn or Albert Thorn?' Her eyes teased.

'Silvester Thorn.'

'Silvester – Thorn. I like that. It's got a romantic sound, a sort of woodland sound, trees and shepherds and poetic things like that.'

He was surprised to find himself volunteering, 'It used to be something else, a longer name, but one of us changed it, hundreds of years ago, I've heard tell, because he was in trouble with the law and didn't want to be traced. He was a conjuror too, my granddad used to say, but nobody remembered what he'd been up to, to get wrong side of the coppers.'

'That's odd. One of my ancestresses was on the stage, according to the family stories, in Queen Elizabeth's time. Only of course there weren't any actresses then, so she must have been something like us ... '

'A trouper.'

'That's it. A trouper. But then she went up in the world and married a knight.' Thinking of the Lady Jacquette, and the old picture, which now hung on the wall of her room in Ethel Villa, she did not notice the shadow which crossed Merlin's face. He said, 'I shouldn't be surprised if you don't.'

'Don't what?'

'Marry a knight. A gentleman, anyway, a swell ... Let's get on, eh, while you're still with us. Now this table's called a Lynn, after the chap who invented it ... '

Harry was glad to hear that he was going to school, a very different school from the last. The worst memories of Yew House had been obliterated by his illness, but scars were left, too tender to probe.

'Shall I be living there – at the school?' he asked anxiously. 'Magus said I shouldn't.'

'No, dear, here with Mrs Whitty looking after you. And she'll rely on you to take Fanny and Danny and look after them.'

'I shall like that ... Nell, do you suppose Mamma knows where we are?'

'Not where, exactly. It wouldn't be safe to let her know that. I just wrote to say we were well and happy, and Merlin got someone to post it in London. You *are* happy, aren't you?'

'Yes. But I'd like to see Barnaby.'

'So would I. Oh, Harry, so would I!'

XIII

Eudora is Floored

The Great North Road seemed endless. Barnaby forced his feet to move along it, though he felt all his muscles screaming in protest. It was better to walk than to sit still and stiffen up. How gladly would he have been riding Tennyson or Dickens; but to have taken either of them would have added a charge of horse-stealing to his troubles. He had not even said goodbye to them. Who would look after them now, and would they miss him?

He knew where he was going. There was very little choice for a young man with no family and no friends. His grandfather, who had brought him up kindly, had died long ago, leaving him to the mercies of the young woman he had married in late life. It was she who had despatched him to Yew House and left him there, unvisited. For a few years a wretched pittance had paid for his board, then even that had ceased. He was as friendless as a ghost.

One thing alone held a promise for him. In his pocket was a slip of paper bearing the address of Nell's Uncle Gil, given to him on the day he had taken Harry to Ashurst Lodge. 'If you ever need help,' she had said, 'or to get in touch with me, if I'm not here, go to him. I wish I could tell you to go to Mamma, but what would be the use, with those two dragons always there?'

Barnaby plodded on. In Highgate he hesitated, wondering whether he dare call at Manfred Pye's house on the off-chance that Nell had returned there. But it might only get her into trouble. He had listened unashamedly at the headmaster's study door when her aunts had called, and gathered how relentless was their pursuit of her. Yet he cut down Swains Lane for the double-edged pleasure of looking up at the house where she had lived. A cheerful-faced nurse

164

was in the garden, patting and tucking in the contents of a perambulator. At the sight of him she wheeled it hastily round a corner towards the rear of the house. Barnaby smiled, painfully, wincing at what the smile did to his split lip. He must look a regular vagabond the morning after a public-house fight. In a way he would rather not find Nell at her uncle's lodgings, looking as he did; but then it was very unlikely that she would be there, with a watch kept on the place.

Kentish Town, Camden Town. Early morning still, people abroad, carts and carriages rattling along past the solitary walker, on his way to an unknown destination, an unknown fate.

Not long before he reached the part of Gower Street where he had visited Nell a hackney-cab had collected a fare from the very same house.

Amy had not slept well. She never did, since her two children had vanished from Highgate. Horrible dreams drove her into wakefulness full of grisly imaginings of what might have happened to them. Sometimes the morning brought renewed hope that they might not, after all, be dead or in a situation almost as bad; sometimes the miasma of horror was still upon her when she went listlessly down to breakfast with her half-sisters.

This morning, her senses sharpened by sleeplessness, she knew as soon as she opened the door that she had interrupted a conversation which concerned her, and closely. The silence she walked into buzzed as with electricity, that new and thrilling element. As though by its light she could read the minds of the two who sat at the table; she said bluntly, 'Good morning. Something has happened. May I know what?'

Two pairs of eyes slid round to exchange a message, then were raised to hers.

'What can you mean, Amy?' Eudora asked.

'What could possibly have happened, at this hour of the morning?' Minerva backed her up. 'Your breakfast is getting cold.'

'I am not hungry. What were you saying before I entered? Something about me, no – about Nell and Harry. What have you heard? Tell me – I must know!'

Eudora stirred her tea vigorously. 'You imagine things. If we had any news you should know it, of course.'

Amy's normally gentle spirit had been rubbed raw with anxiety. 'Liar. Tell me or I'll scream and the servants will come.'

'You're hysterical. Go back to bed.'

'No.'

They were eating, drinking, ignoring her. She watched them carefully, Minerva employing both hands, Eudora's right hand going furtively to her lap. Amy made one pounce. As Eudora screamed her chair went over and the two women were struggling on the floor, one emitting short sharp shrieks of shock and fear, the other as fiercely implacable as a tigress. Minerva was by the fireplace, tugging at the service bell, her hand to her mouth.

The contest was over, Amy on her feet, Eudora scrabbling about in an attempt to get up from the floor. Patty had appeared at the door, where she was standing transfixed. A pool of spilled tea spread over the table-cloth and dripped on the floor.

Amy went to the window and read the crumpled letter.

'Dearest Mamma: I am so very truly sorry for not writing before, and I know how worried and upset you must be. This is to tell you that Harry and I are well and happy and in very good care, and nothing dreadful has happened to us. I cannot say more at present for I know my aunts would find out where we are and try to fetch us back. I will write to Uncle Gil next time so that they won't get hold of the letter, which I wouldn't put beyond them, the cats. TRULY we are quite well and in no danger and send you all our love. Your own

NELL.'

Amy put the letter away in her pocket. 'I suppose you were going to call in the detective police to trace her through this,' she said. 'What was the postmark, by the way?' She moved a step or two towards Minerva, who backed nervously. Eudora, now seated quivering in her righted chair, held out a ball of paper. Amy

166

straightened it. ' "London, Western Central" ,' she read out. 'That should help you a great deal.' With which she left the room and returned to her own, where she began to throw possessions into her one small trunk.

In half an hour she was down, dressed for the street, presenting herself in the little parlour where the sisters were sitting, pretending to share *The Times*. She thought they looked shrunken and small.

'Come in, Amy,' snapped Eudora. 'I hope you are on your way to church to ask for forgiveness for your monstrous behaviour.'

'We thought you had gone mad,' piped up Minerva.

'No,' Amy said calmly, 'I am not mad, though I think I must have been to stay here so long, and I am not going to church, but to our brother Gil, who is man enough to look after me. I advise you not to persecute me there, or try to find my son and daughter. I suppose I ought to thank you for keeping us all this time, but really, I don't believe it cost you very much and I think you quite enjoyed it in your nasty way. I hope I didn't hurt you at breakfast, Eudora, but perhaps it will teach you not to read other people's correspondence. Goodbye.'

They sat in silence, hearing the servants trundling her trunk downstairs; they saw her from the window, being helped gallantly into the cab by the driver.

'Well!' exploded Eudora. 'Of all the wicked, ungrateful hussies – after our charity towards her. Who else would have taken her in? Who else would have put up with her brats?'

'Nobody, sister. And to attack you so brutally! We should have her taken for common assault.'

'Of course. I will drive to the police station before luncheon and inform them.'

But by coincidence, before she could do so a police inspector called upon the sisters. A very polite young man from the Highgate Division brought them an even politer letter from a Superintendent Worels, informing them that since the imprisonment of Manfred Pye in the House of Detention, Clerkenwell, careful and persistent questioning of him had confirmed that Miss Eleanore Carey had been an unwilling and innocent accomplice in the act of desecration he had perpetrated. No further search for the young lady would be made, unless her relatives requested that she be found for her own safety and welfare. That was, if she had not already returned to them.

'No, she has not,' Minerva snapped. 'We neither know nor care where she is. Her mother knocked my sister down this morning.'

A curious expression crossed the inspector's face, as though he were trying to appear shocked and hide a broad grin at the same time. 'Dear me, ma'am' he said, 'dear me.'

'Never mind that.' Suddenly Eudora was anxious not to have the undignified scene at the breakfast-table brought to light. 'We wash our hands of Eleanore, Inspector. And of all her family. Perhaps you'll convey our compliments to Superintendent Worels and say that we wish to hear no more of the matter. Good day.'

Repairing briskly towards Tottenham Court Road police station to invite a colleague to a bit of food at the Feathers, the inspector reflected that Miss Eleanore, whoever she might be, was extremely lucky; and so were her family. If ever he'd seen with his mortal eyes a couple of holy terrors, a brace of proper tartars, they were the ladies he had just called on. Even the servant-gal hadn't been worth a courtesy pinch ...

'Here, here! Now, now, hold up – what's all this?'

Amy was laughing and sobbing in Gil's arms like a creature demented. The tigress of the breakfast-table had reverted in the cab to a frightened kitten escaped from its pursuers. Gil patted her shoulders, mopped her eyes, made soothing noises and finally administered a little shake, for her own good.

'There, that'll do. Come sit down, there's a dear good girl. Have a sup of this. Sticks and stones may break my bones, remember, but hard words never hurt me, isn't that right? Hush, now. What's the matter? Who did it? Was it Them?'

Amy, sipping brandy, choked back a hiccup. 'Yes, them. That is, until ... ' She embarked on the story of the concealed letter and the scene that had followed it, while Gil listened raptly, his bloodshot eyes wide with admiration.

'Oh, well done, tremendous. Wish I'd been there, don't I just!

168

Pity you didn't break the old witch's neck while you were about it. No, no, mustn't say that, she's me own sister. But what a turn-up, eh? And best of all, you got the letter and you know the young ones are all right.'

Amy wiped her eyes. 'Yes, that's worth everything. I haven't slept, Gil, imagining ... you can guess.'

'I can. Done a bit of imagining myself since they went.'

She looked up sharply. 'Went? They've been here?'

'O' course. But then you don't know.'

Amy listened to the story of her children's arrival and sudden departure. 'I might have known they'd come here. But to run away like that – oh, how silly and impetuous Nell can be! And yet she says they're safe. It is true, isn't it Gil – it must be true? Here, read it.'

Gil read the crumpled letter, nodding. 'That's her fist, all right, and I'd know her style anywhere. Depend on it, she's fallen on her feet – thank the Powers.' He poured himself a stiff measure, watched anxiously by Amy.

'You've been drinking a lot.'

'Yes. Sorry, Sis. I knocked it off when they were here, but since ... what with the worry of it, I've had the proper horrors sometimes, thought I was in for the D.T.'s, rats climbing up the bed-curtains, worms in the pepper-pot. *You* know.'

Amy was by now quite collected. 'No, I don't know, Gil, but I'm afraid you'll do yourself a real mischief if you go on drinking to excess. Why do you do it, dear?'

He shrugged. 'How should I know? Habit – and loneliness. Yes, I think that's about it.'

'Then you needn't do it any more, since you won't be lonely. I may stay, mayn't I, Gil?' Her little hands clutched his sleeve, her still-wet eyes searching his.

'May you? What do you think? It'd be like having an angel in the house, with you here. I'll be good, I promise. I'll – I'll even drink cocoa, if you make it, s'welp me Bob, I will.'

'That's a very vulgar expression,' Amy said primly, then laughed. 'All right, I'll make you some now, and you see if it's not nicer than that horrid stuff in the bottle. Where's the tin kept? Oh, what an

169

awful rusty old thing. Never mind, put the kettle on.'

It was into this pleasant domestic scene that Barnaby was ushered by a somewhat confused Mr Vigo, far from sure that he should be allowing this well-spoken but bruised and battered youth into his friend's apartments. Brother and sister stared at their visitor, Amy shrinking back against Gil, for Barnaby was not a reassuring sight. One side of his face was a massive bruise, an ugly gash disfigured his forehead and his lower lip was cut and swollen. His wounds had bled again since he had doused his head in the horse-trough, and he limped after his long walk on legs that had been thoroughly kicked.

'Says he has an errand to you,' Mr Vigo said, and retreated.

Gil advanced, prepared to defend his sister's life with his own.

'Don't think I know yer, young man. Mind telling me your business?'

Barnaby tried to smile, aware that the effort only produced an alarming leer. 'No, sir, you don't know me. But this lady does. You saw me at Yew House, ma'am, very briefly, when Master Carey was taken there, and I've seen him and Miss Nell since – it was I who took him to Mr Pye's when he had the fever. Barnaby Lyon, ma'am.'

Amy's face lit up, 'Barnaby Lyon! Of course, I remember. You were very kind to Nell and Harry, I know. But what *has* happened? Have you been knocked down? The roads are so dangerous now –'

'Knocked down, in a sense, ma'am, though not by a horse and cart. I got into a fight at the school, and – well, you see. I had the worst of it.'

Amy began to bustle. 'You poor thing. Gil, find a bowl and pour some hot water. Where do you keep liniment – and clean cloths?' Gil, murmuring good-humouredly that the place was becoming like one of Miss Nightingale's hospitals, went in search of these things, while Barnaby and Amy exchanged their stories. Barnaby made very light of his battle to defend Harry, but Amy read beyond his words, and was deeply grateful, innocent as she was of the horrible experiences her son had endured. She could not but notice how many times Nell's name came up. It was not hard to divine the boy's fascinated admiration for the girl he had met only a few times, and the impact she had made on him. Her maternal match-making instincts got to work. Clearly the poor lad had no fortune, and Nell would need to marry well, but who could tell what rich uncle or guardian might lurk behind the scenes? Or perhaps he was brilliantly gifted and might turn into a famous lawyer or ... her imagination failed her. He did not look like someone who was going to be a famous lawyer.

'Horses,' Barnaby was saying. 'The only thing I'm any good with. I thought perhaps I might get work at Astley's.' Secretly he was seeing himself working at the famous Equestrian Amphitheatre, appearing in the ring in command of beautiful performing steeds, being seen by Nell, who loved horses too and might be drawn to the new theatrical sensation, *Mazeppa's Ride*, in which the actress Adah Menken shocked and delighted by appearing seemingly naked, strapped to a spirited horse. It was the talk of London – rumours had spread even to Finchley.

Amy's hopes declined. He was so nice in every way, but she could not wish Nell married to a groom, even a theatrical one. Meanwhile, what were they going to do?

'No question of it, you must stay with me,' Gil pronounced. 'Vigo won't mind. Two good rooms going begging upstairs – regard this as Liberty Hall, if you please.'

'But the – the watch that they put on the shop,' Amy said. 'Won't the man see where we go, and perhaps trace Nell through us?'

Gil hooted scornfully. 'Watch? There was a shabby cove keepin' an eye on us for a bit, but he's gone now, floatin' like a feather or something on the soft summer air.'

'"Zephyr", not "feather",' Amy interrupted. '"Floating like a Zephyr".'

'That's right, Zephyr.' Gil played a few bars of the popular song on his flute, reflecting. 'You wouldn't catch my sisters shelling out for a man's wages above a day or two. Depend on it, nobody's watching now, and this police business'll soon blow over. No: you stay here, my dears, and we'll all go and search for Nell, when we like, wherever we like.'

'"Western Central".' Amy sighed. 'Such a wide area. I hardly think it would be worth looking. Oh dear. Piccadilly, Regent Street,

171

the Strand – she might be anywhere. I must say I still worry, even after that letter ... '

'Don't, ma'am,' Barnaby clasped her hand. 'I'll find her; just you see.'

Nell's costume was almost ready. Mrs Whitty, tutting impatiently, crawled on her knees round the back, where the faintest suggestion of a feathery train flowed from the briefs that barely covered the wearer's hips, and were edged with glittering bobble-fringe. The sequinned material appeared even more lovely worn than it had done in the width, accentuating every curve of the body to which it clung, so that when Nell moved the lights in it shifted and changed colour, one iridescent sheen. The high square neck was edged with tiny mother-of-pearl shells in two rows, the sleeves, of a plain material between white and blush-pink, puffed at the shoulders, then narrowed to the wrists. Filmy tights covered Nell's long, beautiful legs, and her slippers were buckled with rhinestones.

For all its conspicuousness, the costume presented not one difficulty to its wearer when she had to curl up into a small space or move quickly. It was the result of careful, expert thought by Merlin, and ingenuity by Mrs Whitty, a dressmaking genius.

'Isn't it wonderful!' Nell looked down at herself and stroked the shining curves. 'Did you ever see anything more gorgeous?'

Mrs Whitty uttered a sound between a cough and a sniff, which might have meant anything. Nell peered at her face; it wore no smile of pride. In the days since she had come to Edith-and-Ethel she had noticed a change coming over the housekeeper's manner towards her. Whitty resented her, that had been obvious from the start. Whether or not he had influenced his wife, she no longer showed the motherliness towards Nell that had been there when they first arrived. She was not effusive even towards Fanny and Danny, but always kindly, and to Harry all that even Nell could have wished. Once again Harry Sahib had an *ayah*, though a white one. But for Nell Mrs Whitty had only cold eyes and a toneless voice.

'You *do* think it's lovely, don't you?' Nell persisted. 'There isn't anything you don't like about it – after you've taken so much trouble?'

A silence. 'Wearing wings don't make a person an angel.'

'I don't think myself an angel.'

'Ho, don't you?'

'No. And I don't understand what I've done to offend you.'

Mrs Whitty made no answer, but ordered Nell to turn round, and with her needle secured a straying loop of the fringe. She would give no satisfaction directly, and Nell would have remained baffled if she had not overheard a conversation between husband and wife, on her way to the kitchens of Edith.

'I told you,' George Whitty was saying.

'And you were right. A proper schemer.'

'I don't think you *are* right,' said Adelaide Seymore's voice. 'I think she's a very good, honest girl with no guile about her. "But a simple peasant maid", I'd say, not at all what you think her.'

Whitty snorted. 'And what about the boy, with his lah-de-dah talk? What do we want with him here?'

'He's all right,' said his wife. 'Seen bad times and been dragged about like no child should be, no thanks to her, for from what I can make out he'd been put to school proper and then taken to a gentleman's house. What,' she demanded, her voice rising, 'does *she* want taking to the magic business, her with no training nor skills — blinking her eyes at the Magus and letting on she's so clever?'

'It was the Magus who got her into it,' pointed out Adelaide. 'I was there and I know. It was a children's matinée, and she was in the audience, and he called her up on stage. I remember it perfectly.'

'You don't remember nothing, only your dratted music. She put the 'fluence on him, that's what she did, you mark me.'

'I never liked it from the first,' added George. 'Her sitting next to him in the railway train, a-drooping her head on his shoulder and a-cooing at him like one of them doves.'

'What is it you hate so about her?' Adelaide demanded, sharply for her. 'You never went on about Emerald like this. What has Nelda done to you?'

Neither answered, for neither could put it into words. They only knew that they were jealous of this young woman, who was better-bred, better-spoken than they, even than the Magus himself, and pretty enough to dazzle him, as the puddingy Emerald had not been. They were jealous for their own position, for the little empire that was Edith-and-Ethel.

Nell, listening, was shaken, troubled and angry. All this over a man who had been civil to her, no more – a man who treated her, as no other had done, like an equal: a man old enough to be her father. Well, she was not going to be put down by a lot of jealous nonsense. Tossing her head and putting on a defiant smile, she advanced into the kitchen. She had donned the costume, and the little sparkling cap which confined her hair and which would be swept off when they took a curtain bow, letting the auburn torrent flow round her shoulders. As she entered, a log rolled from the top of the fire, sending flames roaring up the chimney and lighting up the dim room.

As they illuminated the costume its crystals were turned to rubies and rose-diamonds, the wearer to a figure from legend: Brünnhilde in a ring of fire, Joan armoured before the walls of Orleans. The dove Beauty, perched on her shoulder, shone like no earthly bird, its feathers touched with silver paint, fluttering and preening. Their shadows on the wall loomed gigantic.

The three in the kitchen stared, silenced. Adelaide Seymore, a lapsed Catholic, crossed herself furtively.

'Well,' Nell asked, mocking, 'am I magical enough for your Magus?'

XIV

Mystic Wonders

MYSTERY AND MAGIC!!!
THE MARVELLOUS MERLIN,
ILLUSIONIST EXTRAORDINARY
presents for your Entertainment
and Delight
an Evening of Mystic Wonders
including
The Magic Flight
The Hypnotised Cards
The Dove Trap
The Bottle of Pluto
The Birth of Flowers
Second Sight
The Vanishing Lady
Throughout the Entertainment MERLIN
will be Assisted by the Beautiful
NELDA, THE GIRL WITH THE CRYSTAL DOVE.
Come and See with your own Eyes – but you
WON'T BELIEVE THEM!!!

The crimson-lettered posters shouted their challenge, and the public answered with their sixpences and shillings, their oohs and aahs of admiration and their wild applause. The tour which took Merlin and Nell through the winter began with resounding success at the little Theatre Royal, Rochester, where the good people of that town and of Chatham came to admire in numbers. They were often augmented by the redcoats from the garrison and sailors and workers from the great

175

Dockyard, whose whistles and loud blown kisses embarrassed Nell until she became used to them and blew kisses back.

'You've done it,' said Merlin. 'You've put life into the show. Blow me if I know how I'd the face to put it on before.'

'Oh, come. I only do the things Emerald used to do.'

'But not the way she did 'em! All the difference between a cabbage and a ... camellia.'

'Very good things, cabbages,' said Nell, collecting compliments.

'But they don't get thrown on the stage, do they? Ever seen a bouquet of cabbages? No, I picked a winner when I picked you that day. Come to draw a card out of the hat, and out came ... '

'A dove?'

'That's right. A Crystal Dove. Which reminds me, Beauty don't fancy that silver paint or the stuff we get it off with. We'll have to think of something else.'

'What about sequins, put on with something that won't set too hard – jam? No, too messy – it would get all over my hands.'

'I know the very thing,' said Merlin, scrabbling in his make-up box. 'A bit of silver powder that'll brush out afterwards.'

'Don't you think – this is probably quite wrong – that if we did the same with one of the other birds it would be an even better illusion, when the missing bird reappears?'

'Of course, of course! Faith would be the best, she's a real show-off. Why didn't I think of that? And speaking of birds, I've got to work on the Enchanted Portfolio.'

The work, when it was perfected, produced a trick which was guaranteed to astonish even the know-alls. From an ordinary drawing portfolio, fastened with ribbons, such as young ladies keep their watercolour drawings in for the edification of company, Merlin blandly produced, in order: an engraving of a charming girl, bare-headed, a couple of bonnets for winter and summer, four doves in a cage, and three stewpans. The secret was that everything folded up flat, with the exception of the doves, which were concealed as usual in Merlin's *profondes*. The bonnets, cunningly made by Mrs Whitty, were based on watch-spring skeletons, the cage and stewpans were collapsible.

'There should be another thing,' Merlin said. 'At the end of the trick I say, "Nothing left now", and a voice pipes up, "Yes there is", and up pops a little head. Child in stage-trap, of course, moves up with a lever at the right moment. But there, no child available – we'll have to give that one a miss. One of Robert-Houdin's illusions. The Maestro, he is. He used to bring out a chandelier, too, with all five candles lit ... marvellous man. Still working, too. Wish I could think I'd leave a name behind me. Perhaps I will, now I've got you.'

It seemed, indeed, as though a tide had turned in his fortunes. Everywhere the posters went up they drew full houses. Real theatres were few. In the towns on the Canterbury Circuit legitimate companies usually occupied the playhouses. Only at Margate, in the old Theatre Royal, they enjoyed a week of civilised dressing-rooms and professional atmosphere created by the formidable Thorne family. But the winds bit and the sea was lost in grey mist. In such weather Merlin reluctantly settled for lodgings rather than the long, slow train journey back to Dartford.

He hated lodgings, and Nell shared his hatred. True theatrical digs were unknown in the smaller towns, and such landladies as stooped to take in 'playactors' were in the main deeply suspicious of their characters, morals and honesty. A nice quiet-spoken gentleman Mr Merlin might be, but he was a Londoner and you never know with Londoners, not to mention a Conjuror – and if they can conjure rabbits and things into disappearing, what might they not do with your cruet-stand and your best spoons? That Mr Whitty was all right, an honest working man keeping himself to himself, and so was little Percy Tiler, the small but strong stage-hand. But the red-haired girl, of whose appearance on the stage scandalous things were whispered, they wouldn't have her under their roof, and if Mrs Smith next door was easy-going enough to take her in, well, that was her affair.

It took Nell a very short time to realise that she was feared and disapproved of by women. A few girls among the audience would admire her costume and dream of looking like her, but older women, and especially wives, classed her with the Whore of Babylon and the Scarlet Woman of Rome, about whom they knew a good deal, being mostly Chapel.

She learned the truth bluntly from a cottager in Deal, where she and Merlin had spent the first night of their week in separate lodgings, for he was very careful not to compromise her. The woman entered as she was finishing her breakfast in the kitchen.

'I want you out of here, Miss, and quick. Go on up and get packed.'

'Out? But – is something wrong?'

'Everything's wrong with persons like you.' The woman's mouth was a thin line of censure.

'Like me? I don't understand. What have I done?' Nell rose from the table.

'Done? Shouldn't think you'd need to ask that. Oh, never think I haven't heard about last night, you flaunting yourself up on that stage at the Assembly Rooms, what used to be a respectable place, painted like a Jezebel and showing what didn't ought to be seen only by your husband.'

'But I haven't got a husband.'

Mrs Line sneered. 'Oh no? Then you're no better than you should be, travelling round with that man as Mrs Catt took in.'

Nell gasped. 'But – Mr Merlin and I are partners. We – work together – there's nothing wrong ... '

'Work together? I'll be bound you do, but what at?'

A tide of furious scarlet flooded Nell's face. 'How dare you! And what am I supposed to be showing, may I ask?'

Sharp eyes travelled down her soberly clad figure, dwelling on the area covered by hoops and yards of dark blue serge.

'My legs?'

'Don't you name them words to me, Miss. Ladies an't supposed to have such things, nor yet to speak of them. Where was you brought up?'

'In a good, sensible family, unlike you,' Nell flared. 'Everybody knows that dress is permitted on the stage which couldn't be worn in ordinary life.'

'I don't know nothing about stages, I never been to such, I thank my lucky stars. Go on, get upstairs and be off with you.'

Shedding tears of rage Nell banged on the door of the cottage where Merlin lodged. He answered the door himself and listened silently to her furious outpouring, which left her breathless and scarlet-cheeked. 'I was never so put out in my life – to speak to me as if I was a ... a street-woman! That creature – that slut, for her house is dirty, as dirty as her mind, which is saying something. I never –'

'Nell, Nelda, sit down. My dear child, I'm sorry.'

'What have *you* got to be sorry for?'

'For not seeing it before, that such women would insult you. God help me for a fool, but I never thought ... I ought at least to have insisted on you wearing a skirt. Dammit! (if you'll forgive the language) somebody should have told me, warned me that it wouldn't do.'

Yes, thought Nell, Mrs Whitty should. It was she who made the costume – she must have known perfectly well that it would outrage people. But she hates me so much that she let it go. Thank you, Mrs Whitty.

'We'll have to change it, of course,' Merlin said. 'We'll buy some stuff in the town and have it made up into a skirt, not too long or too full, or it'll hamper you. Could be gauze, or muslin.'

'No,' said Nell. 'I've been thinking while you've been talking. I won't have it changed. If those cats want to yowl at me, let them. It's the men who enjoy looking at me, and if it weren't for them bringing their families we wouldn't have any audience. I've got nice – legs, haven't I?'

'Beautiful legs.'

'And I'd look very strange without them, not to speak of having to sit down all the time, so why pretend I haven't got any – why not show 'em off?' She pulled up her hoops and brazenly displayed one, pointing her toes. 'There, I'm not going to have that covered up, nor the other one. If it won't do for the Queen, tell Her Majesty I shan't accept her next kind invitation to Windsor Castle. Can I have one of those muffins? I hadn't finished my breakfast when that old fishwife started on me. Thanks.'

Merlin watched her demolish the muffin. He marvelled at the nature of woman, variable as the rainbow, going from tears to rage to

179

laughter to calm good sense, all in a few moments. He marvelled at her blazing beauty, at this morning hour when most girls would be pale, languid and yawning. He had taken those magnificent legs for granted, as if they had belonged to a statue, until they had now been gratuitously exhibited for his admiration. He had taken her for granted as his pupil and helpmeet, a substitute for the daughter he might have had and trained up to his profession. Now she had spoken to him frankly, boldly, as woman to man, not apprentice to master, and he saw that she was indeed a grown woman, a woman of power and beauty.

And he, who had pushed his own dreams and emotions out of sight, like disused props, suddenly knew himself as they came to life and reappeared. In that drab cottage kitchen, scented with a recent catch of fish, sitting at a table covered with a tea-stained cloth, he realised as by a blinding flash of light that he was in love: in love with Nelda, the sparkling nymph he had created, with Nell, the shabby girl he had taken from the streets, with Eleanore, the child he had never known. Like the Transformation Scene of a pantomime the cottage became a palace glorious with fairy lights, and something strange and delightful happened to his heart, which had gathered dust over so many years.

His nymph, his princess was not invincible against the world. She needed protection, and there was one shield he could and should offer her: his name. They were both free, he had a comfortable home and income by his grandmother's Will. As his wife she would have total protection and respectability. They would be Merlin and Madame Merlin, touring together as blamelessly as the Robert-Houdins. Perhaps he would not need to adopt any more waifs like Fanny and Danny, for Nell with her fine broad hips would give him children of his own. A daze of happiness filled his thoughts, to be sharply dispersed by reality.

She was eighteen years old, he forty-one. If she accepted him, as after her recent shock she very well might, he would be tying her to a husband more than twice her age, whom she certainly did not love. She had hardly known a young man of her own class (which Merlin was not) or had any social life; and he had dragged her into a world where she could have none. It would be taking gross advantage of her to propose marriage. He would gain perfection by it, and she – a grey-haired dreamer, a grown-up child still playing with a toy theatre and a set of parlour tricks?

Coolly, as though his life had not just changed in the twinkling of an eye, he said, 'We'll have to get you a chaperone. I ought to have seen it before, it's not decent for a young lady to go about as you do. Yes, that's it. Well, we've got one ready-made – Mrs Seymore. There!'

Thinking aloud, Nell said, 'But we've nothing to say to each other. I don't think I've ever had more than a dozen words of conversation with her at one time, and then she starts humming or playing on a keyboard that isn't there.'

'She'd be some protection, another woman, an older one.'

'Listen, if I were set on in the street by ten drunken sailors Mrs Seymore wouldn't notice, she'd think they were part of the audience following us, like Orpheus with his harp or whatever it was.'

Merlin nodded. He knew what she meant, but was prepared to stand firm on the point. Nell reached across the table and laid a hand on his; a fire went through him.

'I know the very thing: Mamma. Oh, please let me send for Mamma! It's not just that I'd like to have her with me, but she's been through so much with my aunts, and Harry, and everything, she deserves some fun and jolliness. And you'd like her, truly, Merlin.'

'If she takes after her daughter.'

'No, not at all. She's small and pretty and sweet – in fact beside her I feel like a great hulking Lifeguardsman – but she's more decided than she looks, and I *know* she'd be the right person. Oh, please say yes.'

There was nothing Merlin would not have granted his new-found love, even though it brought another person between herself and him.

And so it came about. Nell wrote to Uncle Gil, who passed the letter, all smiles, to Amy. Overwhelmed with delight, she kissed him repeatedly, ran about his rooms straightening and patting things in her excitement, brought up Mr Vigo from his shop and made tea

181

for them all, putting sugar in each cup twice so that it would have been quite undrinkable had the two been less gallant. Of course she must go, said Gil, with a slight pang for the loss of his housekeeper. He had not been so comfortable for years, but there, everything had to end. The following morning he took her to the station and put her on the train for Dartford.

The train steamed over the long viaduct which crossed the Darent, and there was the little town on the right, and an island-studded lake and a mill on the left, and the station itself, and at the end of the platform two figures waving, the winter sunshine making blazing haloes of their Tudor-red hair. Amy shot out of the carriage with a haste that quite alarmed her porter, and in a moment became invisible, lost in the arms of her son and daughter.

It had been clever of Merlin to insist that she should be taken to Edith-and-Ethel, rather than meet Nell in some strange place. The little villas immediately made her feel at home. Mrs Whitty, always dutiful, had a good fire roaring up the chimney and a pot of Mocha coffee brewed. Harry had been given the day off from school, Nell wore her best day clothes and carried not a whiff of theatre about her, and Merlin tactfully remained out of sight. Everything about the reunion rejoiced Amy's heart. Harry looking as he had done before that terrible school and his illness, but taller and more manly, and yet still somehow her baby son, clinging to her as fondly as ever; and Nell, so womanly and so beautiful, as calm and merry as though all the misfortunes had never happened. It was like a happy dream, except that Amy would not have to wake up from it.

At Nell's suggestion Harry took himself down to the kitchen, where he had an interest in a pudding that was being prepared, and mother and daughter talked alone.

'And are you *sure*, dear, that this life is right for you? It does seem a strange one – almost like being a – well, dancer. I had never thought of such a thing, I must say, and one does worry a little.'

'Don't. It's as right for me as it could be, and I've known that ever since I went to the Oxford that night with Uncle Gil. I belong in Merlin's world, and nowhere else.'

'But it's so *odd*, dear. I know that plenty of girls want to be actresses, but – a conjuror's assistant ... Nobody in our family has ever done anything of the kind.'

'Yes, one, Mamma. Lady Jacquette.'

'Oh. Those stories. Well, we don't quite know what she did, do we? Except that people were surprised when she married a Brome. I never believed that she could have been a witch, of course.'

Nell was not so sure. She remembered curious things: the appearance of a whole figure, not just the head and shoulders of the portrait, in the half-light of her room – a foreign voice speaking to her – a hand. She said aloud, 'I think she was in the same line as we are, an entertainer, who knew the secrets of some of our tricks. Whatever it was, she did pretty well for herself, and so shall I, you'll see.'

Merlin appeared before luncheon was served and was properly introduced to Amy, Mrs Whitty hovering like a sheepdog in the background. To Amy he was the biggest surprise of all. She was not sure what she had imagined, but certainly someone fantastic, eccentric and very old. Instead she saw a man probably younger than herself, not a gentleman, of course, but a gentle man, which was not the same at all and probably better: tall, graceful and personable. Not exactly handsome, but really a very interesting face, like a knight's effigy on a tomb; in her girlhood they would have called it Gothic, and the silver hair only set off the aquiline features. She saw wisdom in that face, and cleverness, and the sort of innocence some people never lost however long they lived or however much they knew. Such a man would never do anything cruel or mean or vulgar, that was plain to see. His voice was rich and beautiful and his London accent fascinating, and his eyes held a sparkle and brilliance quite new to her, as though a hundred stage lights were caught and mirrored there.

All this Amy saw and knew in a moment. Surely Nell must be fully aware of it after so many weeks in his company; she shot a probing glance at her daughter's face, saw nothing there but a frank friendliness, and was guiltily glad of it.

Winter gave way to spring, and spring to summer. The time had been when stage magic shows went out of season, but that time was past. Merlin's acts began to be known among London managers. An appearance at the Crystal Palace in Sydenham was followed by a number of bookings at halls on the southern fringes of London; by autumn Merlin found himself with no free weeks in prospect until well on in the New Year of 1865.

As business prospered he began to improve the show. Another stage-hand was engaged to assist Percy Tiler. After careful thought, Merlin decided to remove Danny from school and put him back in the company. He would never be a scholar, though at least now he could read, write and add, and under-nourishment in childhood seemed to have retarded his growth permanently, making him a perfect 'page' for certain tricks.

He was needed for these, now. Nell, who had continued to grow and fill out even in her nineteenth year, was unquestionably too buxom now for the disappearing act with the Bellows Table, or for the Indian Basket Trick, while Danny was the perfect size for these, and for the one in which he appeared to be suspended from Merlin's hand by a single hair.

'Now we've got him back, why not do the Rope Trick?' Nell suggested.

Merlin was dubious. 'I don't think anyone quite believed it. And it's difficult, moving the apparatus to a split second.'

'There's Ted now – he's brighter than Percy. You could trust him to get the rope on the hook and drop the cloth on time.'

'Even so, you've got to keep their eyes distracted while the boy's going up the rope – and afterwards. I used to give them a spiel about the Mystery of the Inscrutable Orient, but they were too busy watching to listen. I got caught out that way, once.' He shuddered.

'You know what you just said? "You've got to keep their eyes distracted." Well, I could. You watch this.' She went to the costume-rack and took down a length of muslin veiling, then disappeared behind a screen. When she emerged she had taken off her day-dress and petticoats and was swathed, cocoon-like, in the material. 'Whistle something,' she said.

'Such as what?'

184

'Oh, I don't know, anything, so long as it's slow.'

Merlin obliged with a melodious rendering of 'When You and I were Young, Maggie'. To these inappropriate strains Nelda performed a nautch dance. Long ago she had watched the dancing girls of India wreathe and twine their sinuous bodies in tribute to their gods and for the delight of men, and had copied them at home, in a *sari* borrowed from her *ayah*, watched by admiring servants. She remembered every movement.

Watching her, Merlin was possessed by such a wave of desire that he was forced to turn away and think of something else – anything else. He was grateful when the dance finished and she sank down at his feet. Scrambling up, she asked 'Well? Do you think that will distract them?'

'If it doesn't, they ought to see a doctor.'

'Oh, good. I'm glad you liked it.' Nell said demurely. She had known quite well how he had felt. 'So we can keep it in?'

Merlin doubted very much that they ought, since it would be a severe test of his self-control and that of many of the audience. But it was the answer to the Rope Trick problem.

'Yes, why not. But you can't wear that thing.'

'I don't intend to, silly. Leave it to me.'

'Mrs Whitty might – '

'Mrs Whitty's having nothing to do with this. Mamma and I can work up something really stunning, you'll see.' Amy had become their travelling wardrobe mistress, since Mrs Whitty disliked touring and disliked Nell's company even more. Amy was clever and ingenious with her needle. Unlike Mrs Whitty, she had seen genuine Indian costumes. Using golden tissue patterned with scarlet she fashioned a *sari*, sewing imitation jewels in two circles on the gauze vest beneath it over the breasts, between which hung strings of golden and coloured beads. A short veil of glittering gauze was fastened to Nell's hair, which for the dance was allowed to fall loose, and from her ears swung long gaudy earrings of strung beads.

'I wish they'd been the real thing, with little bells,' Nell said as she painted black outlines round her eyes and added a red caste spot to her forehead. 'There, how does that look?'

'You'll be arrested,' Amy said. 'We shall all be arrested, probably. Are you sure you oughtn't to tone it down?'

'Yes, I am. In for a penny, in for a pound.' She applied herself to painting her toe-nails carmine and sticking imitation rubies to her toes with spirit gum, since such dances must be performed bare-footed. For the stage Amy would help her with the make-up during a long card-trick, which would precede her appearance.

They decided to try the Indian Rope Trick out at a small theatre in the Old Kent Road. It had good stage facilities and a fair audience capacity.

Merlin was nervous. 'We shall get the bird, I know we shall.'

'You stick to your cards and leave that to me,' Nell snapped, herself not unapprehensive. A lot depended on how sober the audience were. Too sober, and someone might send for the police, too lushy, and there might be ugly scenes. Before the curtain she told Merlin, 'Keep your lucky charm where you can touch it, tonight.' He nodded, feeling for the tiny crucifix of old worn silver which had been among his mother's possesions. She had said it had been in the family a long time and shouldn't be sold or thrown out.

The first half of the bill, up to the card sequence, went without a hitch. The Rope Trick was to be the last item on it, to give Nell plenty of time to change and scrub the make-up off during the interval. Merlin rounded off his display with the baffling trick of the Rising Cards, performed to ghostly music played by Mrs Seymore on her new miniature portable piano.

It was over. He bowed, retreated into the wings, and the act-drop came down. Taking a deep breath he walked out in front of it, bowed again, and announced, 'Ladies and Gentlemen, friends. I have the honour to present, for the first time on any London stage, the famous, amazing, sensational Indian Rope Trick. There are those who will tell you that it can't be done. Travellers will tell you that they have heard of it but never seen it; and don't believe it exists. We are here tonight to prove otherwise. Watch carefully, observe, make up your minds. Is the Indian Rope Trick an illusion – a triumph of mass hypnotism – or simply magic, the magic of the Inscrutable East?'

Off-stage a clash of cymbals sounded. It was only Amy with a dinner-gong, but the effect was impressive. The act-drop rose, Merlin stepped on to the stage.

Danny sat there, ankles crossed, in a short white robe and a turban, his skin darkened up. A black curtain draped the back of the stage. From it, apparently out of thin air, glided the Indian apparition, Nelda dusky-painted, glittering from hair to toe-jewels. A gasp went up from the watchers. She struck a graceful attitude and intoned, in Hindi, a passage from the *Gita-Govinda*, the Hindu equivalent of the *Song of Solomon*, while the pianist, off-stage, played a mysterious Eastern-sounding air.

> 'Krishna enchanted women by the pleasures he bestowed on them. The touch of his limbs, soft and dark as a garland of lotus flowers, awakened amorous delight in them ... May those wise spirits who seek ecstasy in Vishnu breathe in from the Song of Govinda the essence of Love!'

Nobody would understand a word, but it sounded well. Then she began to dance, weaving and turning and posturing snake-like, using limbs and body like an instrument, sinuous, lithe, erotic beyond anything the Old Kent Road had ever seen it its life. Merlin, poised to throw up the rope to where Ted was waiting to hook it to a bar out of sight of the audience, was aware of a breathless silence more profound than any he remembered in all his days of showmanship. Knowing that whatever he did would scarcely be noticed, he flung the rope up, saw it caught and attached so that it provided a rigid stem for climbing.

Danny rose, bowed, and shot up the rope. As he reached the top Ted released a heavily weighted black cloth to fall in front of the boy and rope. Nelda swayed gently, letting the lights catch her sparkling ornaments to hold the audience's attention and keep them from noticing that another rope had been released to fall limply on the stage. Merlin picked it up, allowed time for them to take in the utter disappearance of the boy, and bowed ceremoniously. Then, taking Nelda by the hand, he left the stage, empty now but for a coil of rope. From the wings the gong reverberated.

The storm of applause told him that they had succeeded: the Rope Trick had been performed in sight of the British Public. He came forward, leading Nelda by one hand and Danny by the other, to take bow after bow.

The acts that followed after the interval seemed tame indeed after that *tour de force*. Nelda in her crystal costume seemed an entirely different girl from the nautch-dancer, and arguments were going on about it. Couldn't be the same, the other one was a proper Indian, you could tell that; there'd been those pictures in *Punch*, after the Mutiny, of Britannia ordering those murdering natives to be killed, and the Indian women clinging together, all dressed like that girl. What if she did seem to have red hair like the Crystal Girl? You couldn't tell with this artificial light. Anyway, she was a knock-out, a proper stunner, a fancy piece to beat the band, and what a good thing Ma hadn't come with us, it would have shocked the drawers off her.

Amy, folding the delicate *sari*, shook her head. She had a feeling that no good would come of all this. It had brought back cruel memories of her husband's death: and she had seen the look in Merlin's eyes as he watched Nell dance.

At the stage door a crowd of admirers surged, all male. They were not too sure about the young person who emerged, dressed in ordinary clothes, with a demure hat hiding the famous hair, holding the arm of a small older woman. But one man stepped forwards, raising his hat so that the light from the lamp over the door showed his face clearly. Nell cried out joyously, hardly believing.

'Barnaby!'

XV

A Carriage Waits

'But how did you know it was me? I mean, you couldn't have expected to find me doing this sort of thing.'

'I recognised you,' Barnaby said simply.

'What, like that – with all that slap on?'

'Nell, dear,' Amy reproved gently. 'She means stage make-up, Mr Lyon.' She blushed often these days at her daughter's slangy language and the stagy manner she had picked up.

'Yes. You see, I knew there couldn't be two young ladies who looked like you.'

'I'm flattered. Once seen, never forgotten. But were you looking for me? And what are you doing here – have you left that awful school?'

Barnaby looked helplessly at Amy, who answered for him.

'Mr Lyon left Yew House a long time ago, dear. He came to see me when your Uncle Gil and I had temporarily lost sight of you, and kindly said he would try to find you for us.'

'I couldn't, of course,' Barnaby said, 'and I didn't like to go back to Mrs Carey and say so. I had to get work, and I knew I wasn't clever enough to teach – I'd had enough of schools, anyway – so I looked for somewhere I could work with horses, and found a place down this way, a livery stables near the Drovers.'

'I'm glad.' Nell took his hand and held it between her own gloved ones. Amy noted the look of adoration on the boy's face. It was thus that Merlin came upon them, emerging from the stage door.

'Now, now,' he said, sharply for him. It was a rule that artistes did not stop to chatter with admirers. For one thing, it damaged the illusion, and for another they could often be nasty customers.

'It's all right, Merlin. This is a very old friend of mine, who was at school with Harry and so good to him. Barnaby Lyon, Mr Merlin, or should I have introduced you the other way round?'

'Never mind,' Merlin bowed stiffly to the stranger. 'If you'll excuse us we have a train to catch. Come along, Nelda.'

Barnaby saw Paradise slipping out of his grasp. 'Can't I see you again?'

'Oh yes! Come and call at the weekend – we live in Dartford, it's not far. If that's all right, Merlin?'

Merlin said shortly that he supposed it was. He stood impatiently by the waiting cab as Nell gave Barnaby their address, making him repeat it. 'Be sure to come, now – just after church, then you can take luncheon with us. Promise!'

Barnaby promised. He would have promised his soul to the Devil on the same terms.

In the cab, on the way to the station, Nell excitedly told the story of Barnaby's championship of Harry, and the strange coincidence that he should have the same Christian name as Edward VI's whipping-boy, because she had been a sort of whipping-boy herself, when she and Harry were younger. Amy was both grieved and glad to see the set expression on Merlin's face, and hear his unusually curt responses. He was staring out of the window at the dark streets, not seeing the shifting population of idlers and drunks moving in and out of the flaring gaslight. He could only see the bright hope and rapture on the face of the personable young man who had known Nell before he met her, and to whom she owed so much.

On Sunday, Barnaby arrived at Edith-and-Ethel not by the dull agency of the North Kent Railway, but on the back of a splendid black horse. Mrs Seymore, playing her piano by the drawing-room window, saw the rider pull up outside the gates, and paused in her playing to call, 'A visitor! Such a visitor – do come and look, Nelda.' Inspired by the vision, she went into the music of an old song.

'Gaily the Troubadour
Touch'd his guitar,
As he was hastening

190

Home from the war.
Singing "From Palestine
Hither I come.
Lady-love, lady-love,
Welcome me home!"'

Merlin looked down from the window of the props room. He saw the rider dismount from his gallant steed, saw Nell with her going-to-church bonnet hanging picturesquely down her back by its strings and her hair streaming, greeting the rider with outstretched hands. Then Harry was running down the steps, to be caught up and embraced by the rider, Amy following more sedately. Welcome me home, indeed.

That Sunday passed happily for everyone but him. Ethelberta and Editha were charmed by the unusual presence of a young man in the house, since their own followers were strictly supervised by Mrs Whitty. She, in her turn, mellowed in her manner towards Nell for the first time, seeing in the visitor an obvious suitor, who would in time take an obnoxious girl away. Amy was equally pleased. Having known Barnaby before only in unhappy circumstances, she rejoiced in his new maturity, good looks, and handsome appearance in the riding-clothes he wore: she thought, somewhat confusedly, like a Centaur. She hoped Nell's rather free manners would not put him off. He might not be quite what she had hoped for in Nell's husband, but well-spoken and affable as he was, surely he would get on in the world. She began to see rosy pictures of the future.

Harry had only one pleasant memory of Yew House School, which was of Lyon and his kindness. A lot of the rest of it had mercifully faded; but here was Lyon again, god-like, no longer a drudge, in charge of the magnificent horse Black Diamond, whom he was allowed to escort, with Lyon, to the stables round the corner, where Diamond condescended to bend his stately head and graciously accept a carrot.

Little Danny shared in Harry's hero-worship of Barnaby. He knew now that he would never grow more than another inch or two, and would all his life have to be content with Imps and Pages, particularly as he wasn't very bright. Fanny was the bright one, and already half a head taller than he was. Because Merlin thought she deserved a good education and a chance in life she had been put to board at the school with old Miss Birtles, and the effect of that lady's refined company was having a better effect than Merlin could have hoped for.

So Danny, simple and good-natured, admired tall vigorous Barnaby, who held such a charm for the ladies that even Mrs Seymore abandoned her musical reveries and coaxed him over to the piano to sing, though he protested he had no voice. This was not far from the truth, but nobly he struggled through a ballad he happened to know.

> 'Then pretty Jane, my dearest Jane,
> Ah, never look so shy,
> But meet me, meet me in the evening
> When the bloom is on the rye.'

As he sang he eyes were fixed on Nell's face, glowing and lovely over the low-cut bodice of her frock. The naughty girl had changed into it much too early in the day, Amy noticed; and very far from looking shy she was returning Barnaby's gaze with one that could be described as bold and inviting.

Merlin saw it, too. Abruptly, he rose and left the room. Nobody saw him go. Upstairs in the props-attic he took off his jacket and set to work on the mechanism for a new illusion.

'Aerial suspension,' he explained. 'Not new, of course. Robert-Houdin used to do it in his Fantastic Scenes. It was just after they'd discovered ether, and he pretended that as well as putting people to sleep it made 'em lighter than air. Gave his little boy a bottle to sniff and then stretched him out in mid-air with only a walking-stick holding him up. Or that's what it looked like.'

'Oh, thanks,' Nell said. 'So is that what you're going to do to me – make me unconscious and then leave me hanging from nothing?'

'No.' Merlin thought he would not have trusted himself with an unconscious Nell. 'The ether was a fake – they put some on a hot shovel back-stage, so the audience could smell it and think the boy

192

was under the influence.'

'And the walking-stick? Sounds uncomfortable.'

'Not too bad. It's a pole, see? With an iron centre, to take the weight. Fixed in a plank of wood. Like this.'

'But it's got an extra piece at the end.'

'Yes.' He was being unusually terse, and showed impatience at her slowness to grasp the workings of the complex apparatus. The secret of it was that she was to wear under her costume (not the crystal one, but a concealing robe) a sort of iron corset which hooked invisibly on to the supporting pole. The pole was placed under her right arm, and under her left an ordinary, innocent wooden pole. She was to stand on a stool, leaving her suspended between the two rods. Then with mesmeric passes she was apparently put to sleep.

The left pole and the stool removed, she remained seemingly standing on air, supported only by the right-hand pole. Then Merlin raised her feet until she lay at an angle of 90 degrees, horizontal in the air. An arrangement of ratchets, straps and springs allowed her to be moved to any angle. Because the apparatus ended at her knees, she could only keep her legs straight by muscle-power. It was tiring and painful, and she complained.

'You'll have to put up with it.' It was not like him to speak so, and when he adjusted the corset he was not gentle in pulling tight the belt of leather and iron, or the iron crutch between her legs.

'Anybody would think you were buckling me into a chastity belt,' she said, 'before galloping off to the Crusades. What is it? What have I done to annoy you?'

'Nothing. Nothing. I'm in a bad humour, that's all.' If only he could have buckled her into a chastity belt! But he had no right to such thoughts, no right to criticise even to himself her flagrant enticement of Barnaby on his now regular weekend visit.

Taking off the uncomfortable corset behind the screen, after several practice runs, she called out, 'I don't think I like Aërial Suspension. Must we do it?'

'Yes.'

She emerged, fastening her bodice. 'Why?'

'Because of the doves.' Of the old birds Faith, Beauty and Hope had died, within days of each other, leaving only the lonely Charity. The new young birds would take weeks or even months to train, and the most promising of them objected to having its wings silvered. 'We need another spot to feature you.'

'But I can't wear my crystal costume for Aërial Suspension.'

'That doesn't matter. We'll find you something else striking.'

Nell was still unhappy, and hurt by his changed manner to her, for which she could think of no reason.

When, only days after they had perfected Aërial Suspension, Merlin announced that he had a new illusion to teach her, she groaned.

'Not like the last one, I hope and trust?'

'Not a bit. You won't need to move. I know of another man who's working on the same idea – and I want to beat him to it. He's calling his The Cabinet of Proteus, so ours shall be the Priestess of Isis.'

George Whitty's skilled carpentry produced a very passable imitation of an Egyptian mummy-case, and Harry, who showed a considerable turn for drawing and design, was sent up to the British Museum to copy the emblems on such caskets. He came back proudly with pages of drawings.

'Let me paint them too, Magus,' he begged. 'They'd be nothing without the real bright colours and all the gold. I won't make a mess, I promise.'

The first audience to witness the results of all his careful work were enthralled. The great wooden shell blazed with colour: animals, birds, reptiles, flowers and hieroglyphics in gorgeous colours covered it all over, and Harry had been given all the gold paint he wanted. The sarcophagus stood semi-upright, centre stage, Merlin beside it, while Mrs Seymore, invisible, played a solemn, mysterious melody.

Then Merlin turned and addressed the awed watchers.

'Friends, you are about to see a miracle. The beautiful Sesheta lived in the land of Egypt more than three thousand years ago. She served the goddess Isis as her priestess, and was famous for her great wisdom and miraculous powers. She died young, and her body was entombed as splendidly as if she had been royal. In our own lifetime it was

194

discovered by an English professor, who brought it back to England with him. It is by his kind permission that I am permitted to exhibit it to you now.

'Sesheta has kept her wonderful powers even in death. She has preserved her beauty intact. Even more wonderfully, she can cause her body to disappear from your sight, only her spirit remaining within the mummy-case. When she returns to it she may appear for a moment to be alive, before sinking back into the peaceful sleep of death.'

He paused to allow the information to sink in. It had been a long and difficult spiel to learn, and he had had to leave out the word 'archaeologist' because it tripped him up every time. There was a commotion at the back of the hall, as someone who did not wish to see a dead body left hurriedly. When all was quiet again Merlin tapped the case, which slowly opened down the middle.

Inside it, utterly still, arms crossed over her breasts, lay a female figure in a robe of dazzling white linen. Her face seemed like porcelain, being painted a uniform colour, the hue of a white rose with the faintest blush of pink, the full lips a deeper shade, just as artificial. The eyes, which appeared to be open, were dark and unmoving, surrounded by heavy black eye-liner. A straight black wig brushed the shoulders and lay across the brow in a square fringe; the thin gold coronet round it bore in front the *uraeus*, the sacred asp of Egyptian royalty, a figure like a snake poised to strike.

Harry clutched Barnaby's arm. 'It doesn't look like Nell. It can't be!'

'Shush!'

Merlin, after allowing long enough for the vision to be studied by all, again tapped the case, which closed as slowly as it had opened. So it remained for all of a minute. When it opened once more, it was empty. Merlin invited two persons from the front row to step up on the stage, walk round the mummy-case, and assure the rest of the spectators that there was no aperture by which the body could have escaped. Casting timid glances at the dull gold of the interior, they obeyed, then went back to their separate places.

'Now,' said Merlin, 'again I close the coffin. I make no promise of what we shall see when it reopens. Has Sesheta returned forever to her native gods, or will she again present herself before our eyes?'

She was there. As still as though carved in wood she lay as she had lain before. But with a difference: the sightless eyes were alive, dark and sparkling, moving and blinking, and the sensuous painted mouth curved upwards in a faint smile.

As the coffin closed for the last time a crash of applause and a surging movement towards the stage warned Merlin to make a sign for the two stage-hands to remove the mummy-case on its wheeled base. There were those present who were less sober than they should be, and others inquisitive enough to lay hands on coffin and priestess.

In the dressing-room Harry, Amy and Barnaby watched the late Sesheta take off her wig and start to remove the thick layer of paint.

Harry said, 'I can see you've got artificial eyes painted on your eyelids, so that would account for the way your eyes came alive. But how is it done – the disappearing?'

'Shan't tell,' Nell's voice was muffled behind a towel.

'But you've always told before.'

'This time it's a secret because of Mr Pepper and his patent. If you think the Magus will tell you, ask him – but he won't.'

In after years, when Harry, a grown man, took his children to see the now famous illusion, they in turn asked him how it was done. He would only answer, 'I was told they do it with mirrors.'

That was the night when Barnaby, seeing the party off on their train from London Bridge, drew Nell into the shadows behind the platform goods hoist and kissed her for the first time. She responded with an ardour that surprised, even slightly shocked him. The kiss was a long one. Yet, when their lips parted and he looked into her face, he knew quite well, without a shadow of doubt, that she did not care deeply for him, and first love, which had burnt so bright in him, flickered and died.

Nell knew it too. When he had first come back into her life her memories of him as a figure of chivalrous romance had come back too. She had flirted and coquetted, taken pains to dazzle him, and had found out very soon that the charm he had once held for her had been born of gratitude and the peril of her Highgate days. Since then she had lived almost completely in theatrical company, and somehow it made ordinary company seem dull. Barnaby was a nice, worthy young man with whom it was pleasant to flirt, since he obviously adored her, and she had enjoyed his kiss, though she guessed that kisses could be a good deal more exciting.

She longed to experience such kisses and whatever went with them. The admiration of men had left her in no doubt that she was beautiful, love-worthy, clever – clever enough to go on the legitimate stage and cause a sensation like Miss Ellen and Miss Kate Terry. I could learn to act, or dance or sing, she told herself, or marry a duke if I chose. And now I want a lover. It was not enough to know that Merlin was bewitched by her, though gratifying to her vanity. If she could conquer him, why not others, more powerful, more highly-placed? Her beauty might be the key to any kingdom she chose.

The fame of the Priestess of Isis spread. Within a week or two of her appearance Merlin was offered a booking at the Egyptian Hall in Piccadilly.

What, after all, could be a more suitable showing-off place for her than the old building in the style of a Pharaoh's palace, adorned with statues of Isis and Osiris: and it had been London's Home of Magic for many years. At last Merlin's ingenuity would have fitting audiences, impeccably respectable families, no drunks or rowdies from the docks and markets, private boxes and seats up to £2. The little company polished and re-polished the acts, Mrs Whitty sewed some new astrological decorations on Merlin's robe, and Nell's scanty costumes were overhauled. Amy hoped they would not prove too scanty for the susceptibilities of parents.

She need not have worried. Those who brought boys and girls with morals to guard took the usual comfortable English view that if they're foreigners it doesn't count, and these exotic creatures must be foreign, apart from Merlin himself, whose accent never strayed far from the south bank of the Thames. Cheers and prolonged applause saluted a programme carefully composed of popular acts leading up to the cream of the bill. These prosperous theatre-going Londoners had seen plenty of wonders at the Egyptian Hall in the days of Henri Robin, the French conjuror, and they were on the whole not inclined to take the vanishing and return of Sesheta too literally; but it was a brilliant trick and they loved it.

Besides, it was an entirely new thing for a magician's assistant or accomplice to be beautiful and alluring. The tradition was for them to run to small size and costumes which ended well below the knee. One, billed as The Mysterious Lady, had only favoured audiences with her back view, which closely resembled that of Queen Victoria. Miss Nelda, in all her sparkle and bloom, burst upon them like a radiant heathen goddess. The boys fell in love with her and the girls envied her and resolved to practise the same effect at home.

Nelda was changing from her Sesheta costume after the last matinée of the week, helped by Amy, when Danny's head appeared round the door.

'Loidy to see you,' it said.

The woman behind him was immensely elegant. She wore a walking-costume of deep violet, its spreading mantle trimmed at the hem with a deep black lace flounce, and the same lace fell gracefully from the long full sleeves. A charming bonnet, whose brim encircled a cap of artificial flowers of mauve and white, framed a thin sharp-featured face which Nell recognised at once – the face of Claudia Pye. The girl by her side had grown and improved in looks, and the slightly open mouth and prominent teeth lent her an appealing air of helplessness. The toddler whom Claudia held by the hand was unmistakably the baby whose arrival had shaken the household. His coat of pale blue velvet set off his ebony complexion, as his kilt of Royal Stuart tartan did his chubby knees. He smiled dazzlingly at Nell.

'Mrs Pye! How delightful to see you!'

Claudia swam forward and kissed Nell affectionately. She smelt of something delicious. 'My dear Nell, I couldn't resist coming to see you. I knew from the posters that it could be no one else – the likeness is really very good.' Nell brought forward a chair, which completely disappeared under the spread of Claudia's flowing garments. The children leaned against her on either side, making a group which would have enraptured a fashionable photographer.

'You remember your pupil, Caroline – isn't she grown a great girl? Her nasty colds have quite gone, thanks to you and your fresh air prescription. And this is her brother Alexander, whom I don't suppose you remember.' (Who could forget? Nell wondered.) 'Make your bow to Miss Nelda, Alexander.'

The infant made a neat and courtly bow, flashed another ivory smile, and lisped that he was very pleased to see her. He spoke beautifully. Nell guessed that his name would never be shortened to Alex, and that he would one day make his mark in the world.

Nell introduced Claudia to Amy, who looked perfectly dumb-founded by the three visitors, but took to Claudia after their first exchange of greetings. They began to chatter about Nell, regardless of her presence, while she showed the awed Caroline the mock jewels she wore as Sesheta, the costume on its hanger, and the pots of make-up.

'You looked very beautiful,' Caroline said. 'I thought it was all real.'

'Far from it, Caroline – all unreal. Nobody would give me a second glance without it. I hope you won't think for a moment of going into the magic business.'

'Oh, no, Miss Carey. I'm to be presented when I'm old enough, Mamma says. No, Alexander, you are not to touch.' The little boy had picked up a gold ornament and was playing with it. Nell saw Claudia shoot a sharp disapproving glance, then take the trinket from him and replace it on the dressing-table. She knew, without telling, that Alexander was not to be allowed anything that looked barbaric, even as a toy. He was, after all, an English gentleman.

'Nell, have you – ' Merlin stood in the doorway, draped in his rainbow-shimmering dressing-gown. He had taken off his make-up but traces of colour still remained on his eyelids and cheeks. Nell performed introductions, knowing that Merlin would realise the connection with the earlier magician in her life. Claudia broke in quickly.

'But I'm not Mrs Pye of Highgate now, my dear. I had really had quite enough of that house and the Cemetery and pretty well

199

everything else there. We live in Kensington now, so much pleasanter, the children love the gardens and the Palace.'

And Alexander's been firmly removed from everyone who'd gossip about him, Nell reflected. She will carry it all off beautifully in Kensington, people will whisper that he's an African prince she adopted at birth. When Merlin had gone she asked Claudia impulsively, 'Are you happy, Mrs Pye? Because you look it.' Impossible to ask openly about her husband.

'Very, my dear. *Felix est qui sorte suâ contentu vivit*, and I'm extremely content with *my* lot. And delighted to be quite free.' Her fine eyes flashed a significant glance at Nell. Could it be that the wretched Pye was no more? It was to be hoped so. Claudia hastened past the possibility that such a question might be asked.

'And you, Nell – I can see that you are more than happy. What an enchanting man your Mr Merlin is – I don't mean to joke, he really is quite seductive when one sees him at close quarters and without all that beard. I hope you're madly in love with him, if he's not married, that is?'

Eyes less keen than hers would have noticed that both mother and daughter blushed. How interesting: could it be for the same reason, or different reasons? She extended a cordial invitation to both to take tea with her in Holland Street. Then she could find out all she wanted to know: and the Careys could see Alexander at home in all his glory.

The booking was extended by a week. After a tenth performance a hot-house bouquet was delivered to Nell's dressing-room, a heavily-perfumed florist's arrangement of early spring flowers and others out of season, roses, lilies, iris, stephanotis, wrapped in silver foil and tied with satin ribbon. Nell stared at it, spellbound. A bunch of cottage blooms had been the most she had ever received before. Amy looked at it with suspicion, Merlin with suspicion mixed with pride.

'Well, unwrap them.'

A note in a silver-edged envelope, like wedding stationery, was attached to the ribbon. Nell very much wanted to read it when she was alone, but several pairs of eyes were fixed on her. Pretending carelessness, she ripped open the envelope. The writing was elegant and dashing.

'Miss Nelda: will you do me the supreme honour of taking supper with me one evening after your performance? It would give me the greatest delight. Rather than entertain you publicly, I would suggest my rooms above the Orpheus Theatre, where I have the pleasure of receiving friends in comfort and privacy. May I hope for your charming company on Wednesday or Thursday this week? A carriage will be sent for you. Your most devoted admirer,
AYTON FORRESTER.'

'Well!' Amy exclaimed. 'The great actor-manager. Who'd have thought *he* would have come to see us?'

'Whatever he came for he seems to have liked it.' Nell's tone was casual, but her heart beat rapidly.

'You won't think of accepting, of course,' Merlin said. Nell rounded on him.

'What on earth do you mean? Why shouldn't I? The first proper invitation I've had, and from such a grand person. Certainly I shall accept. I'm very flattered.'

Amy shook her head. 'Flattery! I hope I have not brought you up to trust flatterers.'

Nell brushed her hair violently, wound it into a coil and stuck pins into it. 'That's as may be, Mamma, but I've been asked and I shall go.'

'Not if your Mamma forbids you,' Merlin put in. 'You're not of age yet, in case you'd forgotten.'

'Thanks for the reminder, but I hope I'm old enough to decide such things for myself, and what's it to do with you, in any case?'

'A lot, considering I employ you.'

'Mustn't I have any time to myself, then? Even an apprentice-boy gets let out to play now and then.' The argument was threatening to turn into a vulgar verbal brawl. It continued in the cab to the station and on the train journey, Danny listening with wide eyes and George Whitty pretending to sleep through it. They had almost reached Dartford when George's patience gave out. 'Oh, shut it. Let her go to the Devil her own way.'

Merlin and Amy were silenced. Both realised that he had probably given them the answer. The Nell they had both known had been transformed into Nelda, a wilful beauty with a high temper and a turned head; if she were thwarted there was no saying what she might do.

After she had stormed up to bed that night Merlin and Amy were left to thrash it out, Adelaide Seymore having drifted tactfully away from something that promised to be troublesome. George Whitty, by the kitchen fire, fulminated to his wife on the folly of the Magus in taking in such a light-minded flibbertigibbet of a rampageous chit. 'I always knew she'd let the Magus down, but he *would* set his heart on her.'

'So has somebody else got their heart set.'

'Who's that? Oh, young Lyon.'

'No, Whitty. I declare, men see nothing. Mrs Carey's as sweet on the Magus as he is on that Nelda.'

'I don't believe it! How do you make that out?'

'You've only to use your eyes. Well, I must say, if anyone catches him I'd as soon it was her. A mousy little thing, she is, but modest and seemly. *And* she'd leave the running of the place to me.' She sewed placidly.

'You're deep, Mag, deep. Maybe you're right, at that.'

The man and woman who also sat by a fire on the floor above were not talking. Amy sensed Merlin's wretchedness as though it were her own, and was a little guilty because she could not share it. Alarm for her child, yes, she felt that. But Nell was headstrong enough and enterprising enough to get herself out of any corner; and if she were to move into the world of the theatre under such a patronage as Forrester's she would be outside Merlin's sphere, safely out of his reach. Amy longed to go over to him, where he sat gazing into space. He looked older tonight, his fine features sharpened, as he would look when he was dead ...

Unable to restrain herself she left her chair and knelt beside him, touching his hand.

'Don't worry. There's nothing to worry about. She shall go to this

202

supper-party, and I can chaperone her.'

A smile touched his lips. 'Of course, love. That's the answer. She won't come to any harm then.' He pressed her hand, sending a wave of joy through her. He had called her Love, he cared a little for her, so much more suitable to him in years and temperament than her daughter. She was glad she was wearing the little diamond earrings, her husband's gift, treasured through so many years. Moving her head, she knew that they swung and twinkled in the firelight, and willed them to catch his eye so that he would see her smiling, love-filled face.

Nell disposed of their comfortable decision in a few brisk words. 'I don't need a chaperone, Mamma. Don't you see how ridiculous it would make me look? Besides, there's not the slightest need – Mr Forrester is sure to have many other lady guests. Do you suppose they'll all bring chaperones? No, I won't have it and you can't make me.'

Amy shrugged. 'Do as you like, if you have no regard for the conventions. But I should at least like to know how you propose to get home.'

'I shall stay in Buckingham Street, of course.' Merlin kept a room in a respectable lodging-house off the Strand for occasional London use. 'Do you suppose Mr Forrester would let any harm come to a guest of his, a distinguished actor like him? He's appeared before the Queen, you know, at private performances, and all sorts of Society people receive him. Besides, he's been married for donkey's years – his wife will probably be there. Now can I be dressed, please?'

The carriage was prompt, arriving exactly twenty minutes after curtain-fall. It was also private, Ayton Forrester's own. Nell stepped into it gracefully and grandly, like one used to riding in State, but her hands trembled, clasped tight in each other, as the carriage progressed along Piccadilly, through the Regent Circus, into Soho. The streets and roadways were thronged with traffic and pedestrians, the theatre frontages still lit: London went to bed late.

They were at the Orpheus, the pretty playhouse with a Moorish façade built some twenty years earlier, now Ayton Forrester's own property and little kingdom. Nell knew it well from the outside.

Now, escorted by the driver, she was being led to the stage door.

A manservant in livery awaited her, bowing. 'If Madam will kindly follow me.' He preceded her through a door leading to a staircase carpeted in rich crimson obviously not used by the public, the walls hung with theatrical prints. At the top a door stood open, a savoury waft that was part perfume and part cookery coming from it. Nell sniffed: whatever they were having for supper, it was not tripe and onions.

In the corridor they entered a neat-capped, black-clad maid smoothly replaced the manservant, taking Nell's pardessus, the plain over-mantle which was the nearest thing she owned to an evening cloak. 'If Madam wishes – ' the maid was indicating a large wall-mirror, framed in enamel cupids and roses. Self-consciously Nell straightened her hair, which after much thought she had parted in the middle and bundled into a gilt snood. It made her look older and more dignified. Her dress of peacock-green tarlatan was cut low enough to show the full expanse of shoulder, the fichu caught at the bosom with a paste ornament. In the expensive surroundings of the small drawing-room into which the maid showed her she felt shabby, under-dressed, and very reluctant to face the toilettes of the other, wealthier guests.

She turned back in the direction of the mirror. But a door had opened at the other side of the room, and Ayton Forrester stood framed in it.

He was the most impressive figure Nell had ever set eyes on. A perfect command of stage technique had made him London's expert at magnifying his own image. He was not young, yet the spring in his step, his straight shoulders and upright bearing, suggested youth and immense vitality. He was not much above the middle height, but managed to look imposingly tall. His beaked nose and ruddy complexion bore witness to good living, his naturally portly figure had been disciplined to elegance. Above all he exuded a bountiful charm which few could resist. Nell did not even try.

'My dear Miss Nelda ... You'll hardly believe it, but I never even ascertained your surname. How could I have been so careless, and will you forgive me?' Advancing, he raised her hand and kissed it with a gallantry seldom seen off the stage.

Nell murmured that her name was Carey, but he seemed hardly to hear, so intently was he gazing into her eyes while registering admiration, humble submission to her charms, and delight in her company.

'Most honoured, most honoured. That so talented – and may I say so hard-working a young lady should spare me the time, after an exacting performance ... '

'Not really exacting, sir, at least not tonight. We didn't do Aërial Suspension, which is trying because I – ' she stopped hastily, turning crimson, aware that she had been about to confide a secret of her trade to one outside it.

He seemed unaware, though he was not. 'Quite. Such a light, fairy-like effect, yet the ingenuity, the concentration, the detail, all unimaginable to the ignorant viewer.' He had closed the door through which he had entered; Nell imagined that the other guests were in the room beyond, and that he had come alone to reassure her before introducing her to the company. He moved, steering her lightly by the arm, to a side table which bore an array of bottles and decanters.

'A little refreshment? Sherry? You prefer Manzanilla, Amontillado, or perhaps a mellow old Solero?'

Nell preferred none of these, since sherry to her was simply sherry, but murmured that she thought the Solero sounded pleasant. He poured into a narrow, dainty engraved glass a good measure which Nell drank off in two gulps. Her colour rose and her voice strengthened as she politely admired the room, opulently furnished with a touch of the Oriental in its décor. In no time she was telling him about India, her childhood, her transition to England, while he watched her eyes and mouth, smiling. As she talked, and drank rather more slowly the second glassful, she thought idly how odd it was that it should have been sherry she drank that night long ago at the Oxford, when the excitement of the magical business had first seized her.

'You must be famished, Miss Carey,' Forrester was saying. 'I thought a cold collation – something light but appetising – would be acceptable?'

Nell came to herself with a start. 'Oh! Yes, thank you, I *am* hungry. We're usually home by this time, and we never eat before the show. I don't expect you do, either?'

He was showing her into the room beyond. Soft lamplight showed the glow of satins and velvets, fine old furniture from the last century, a life-size portrait over the fireplace that was recognisably Forrester in Georgian costume, snowy lace and a white curled wig. He followed her gaze.

'Myself as Sir Peter Teazle. I admit I was loth to face the fact that my years had compelled me to abandon Charles and take on Sir Peter – *eheu, fugaces!*' Nell had not the least idea what he was talking about, but shook her head sympathetically in response to his tone. She was wondering why the table in the centre of the room was only set for two people, though most elaborately laid with silver cutlery twinkling under a five-branched candelabrum.

'The others,' she said. 'I thought you said some friends of yours would be coming, sir.'

'Did I? Well, perhaps I did. But then it seemed to me unkind to subject you to the trials of unknown company, at our first meeting?' (He said this to all his *ingénues*.) 'This is my home, my little domain, my plot of Theatreland, and I like to be comfortable and quiet here after the – ah, stresses of professional life. Isn't it pleasant, now? Just the two of us.'

Three, in fact, for the liveried footman was gliding in and out, placing dishes under silver covers on a sideboard, silently cutting bread, testing the temperature of butter in a dish floated in iced water, and finally bringing to the table a three-legged stand containing a silver bucket and more ice, on which sat a foil-topped bottle. At a nod from Forrester he uncorked it with the most discreet of pops, and as discreetly vanished.

'A little of the Great Wine of France – the spirit of laughter and levity?' The host poured a discreet measure of champagne into Nell's glass.

And another, and another, to go with the iced consommé, lobster in aspic, the salmi of wild duck, forced asparagus, *petites crémes de jambon en gelée* and Pudding *Surprise à la Louise*. But long before the pudding course was reached Nell was too overcome with champagne to notice what she was eating. She chattered, she laughed, she told one or two stories which had circulated in her hearing back-stage, and laughed heartily at them, to Forrester's intense amusement, for he was sure she failed to understand all their implications. If there had been a dish of grapes to hand this Bacchante would have twined them in her hair.

They looked at each other across the table. Forrester had removed the candelabrum and set it aside. Nell's face was soft, plum-bloomed, velvety in the dimmed light from the wall-lamps, Forrester's nobly handsome, something between Mark Antony in the Banquet Scene and the late Duke of Wellington. He used his fine eyes under their thick eyebrows to make his intentions absolutely clear.

But it was needless. The girl was not a fool, though she had been, so far, one of his easiest conquests after a routine seduction technique which he always enjoyed, even when it ended disappointingly. He did not think the lovely Nelda was going to be disappointing. She gave no signs of being about to be sick or have a premature attack of alcoholic remorse.

Ayton Forrester was a selfish man, or he would not have reached his present eminence. He saw to it that he played all the best parts in the Orpheus's repertoire, showing off his versatility by alternating high tragedy and comedy – Hamlet this week, Falstaff the next. If a play, however suited to his actors, proved a poor vehicle for him it was booted out. Any actor who had the nerve to upstage him would receive a friendly, veiled warning in rehearsal, and if he proved incorrigibly successful would find himself handed the key of the street, as the saying went.

Critics liked him, because he offered them courtesy and hospitality. The British Public liked him because he had the gift of projecting a warm affection for them across the footlights, even when he did not particularly feel any. In maintaining his own high standards of amiability and unrelenting self-publicity, he denied himself tantrums and temperamental outbursts.

Thus he got what he wanted, when he wanted it, publicly, and privately as well. It was quite true that he gave large supper-parties in the rooms above the theatre – the dining-room could be extended to twice its size by the opening of the folding doors – but when the fancy took him he also gave very small supper-parties, like this one, and paid his servants so well that nobody tattled about them. His once beautiful wife, still stately and handsome, preferred life at their country house in Buckinghamshire, and took very little interest in what her distinguished husband did, though she graciously attended all first nights and any Society functions at which it suited him to have a lady on his arm. He was a favourite son of Fortune, and knew it.

Rising, he moved behind Nell's chair, neatly detached the snood and helped her hair to fall about her shoulders. 'Danäe in a shower of gold,' he murmured. A voice as mellifluous as his could have made a list of the omnibus routes of London sound seductive: Nell leaned her head languorously back against his shoulder, smiling sleepily. Not too sleepily, he hoped, as with an arm about her waist he led her towards heavy embroidered curtains through which lay a small, luxurious bedroom containing a wide, crimson-upholstered half-tester bed and a number of most unusual and curious prints.

He removed the paste brooch, unpinned the fichu and deftly pushed down the scanty bodice.

'You were about to tell me of your professional secrets before supper, I believe,' he said softly, into her ear. 'Won't you let me into some that are – less professional?'

XVI

Welcome me Home

'I am – I confess it – just a little surprised. Pleasantly, of course.' Forrester gracefully stifled a yawn.

'Surprised – why?'

'Well, how shall I put it delicately – to find so lovely a young woman inexperienced. Er, in these matters.'

Nell sat up, shaking her hair back from her bare shoulders. 'Was I very awkward?'

'Oh, my sweet child, no, quite the reverse. So young and yet such a talent, such a charming gift for love. When I said inexperienced I meant that you had not had ... '

'A lover before? How did you know?'

'I – er, guessed. That being so, where did you learn to be so voluptuous – so deliciously wanton? Hardly the sort of lesson a young lady learns at school.'

'Well, I think it must have been India. It would be difficult to grow up there and not know about such things. The temple carvings and the paintings. I've never forgotten them. I always thought I would like all that – I do, Ayton.'

'You know, you are a most original creature. I doubt if anybody calls me by my Christian name who had not known me at least twenty-five years.'

'Oh, is it wrong? I'm sorry. I'm so used to calling Merlin Merlin, you see. But Mr Forrester sounds dreadfully starchy, in the circumstances. Do turn the lamp up.'

'Willingly.'

'Now I can see you. Oh, I do long to see you on the stage, in costume. How noble you must look, and how proud I shall be, to think you belong to me. Kiss me.'

It was a long kiss, for lovemaking was not the only thing to occupy Forrester's mind, and he needed time to find the right phrases.

'My dear, charming Nelda, you will be discreet, won't you? I would very much rather you didn't talk about me – about this – to your friends and colleagues. It really wouldn't do. The theatre is a very small world, these things get about.'

Nell's eyes rounded in disappointment. 'But I'm your mistress now. Mistress! People will have to know that, surely.'

'Just do as I say, there's a dear girl. And now get up and dance your nautch dance for me.'

'But I haven't my costume with me.'

'All the better.'

The night paced on towards dawn, bringing Nell more pleasure than she had ever thought possible. Now she was a woman, fulfilled and enraptured with new knowledge, mistress to a famous man who would transform her life. Of course she would be discreet at first, if he wanted that, though it sounded silly. But in time she would come out of the shadows to share the power and the glory that surrounded him.

The power and the glory.

When she woke Ayton had gone, leaving no signs of his presence in the room. The maid she had seen before was there, wearing the most inexpressive face and the widest skirts Nell had ever seen on a domestic. She laid a tray of coffee and toast on a small table at the bedside.

'Good morning, madam. I took the liberty of pressing your dress.'

'Oh. Thank you.' When the maid had rustled out Nell contemplated her clothes, neatly laid out over the back of a chair. The low-cut dress would look very odd, worn by day, but perhaps Ayton would have something more suitable put by, perhaps from the theatre wardrobe. Eating heartily, though aware of a throbbing headache from the previous night's mixture of wines, she wondered what they would be doing that day. A drive in one of the parks, perhaps, as the sun was shining. Yes, that would be nice. Her head was aching quite badly, and the air would do her good.

She was washed, dressed, and sitting by the open window, watching the street, when a tap at the door announced Ayton. Nell flew to him and embraced him. 'I thought you'd deserted me. How are you? Did you sleep well, in the end? Do you feel as happy as I do?'

He disengaged her gently but firmly. 'Good morning, my dear. Had your breakfast? Good. Now someone is going to call a cab for you, and you must tell the man to take you wherever you want to go – at my expense, of course, you're not to pay him.'

'But – Ayton. I thought we were going to be together?'

He laughed, his light social Charles Surface laugh. 'Today? Hardly. I have a rehearsal called for ten o'clock and a performance tonight. No, you run along and don't forget the cab is at my expense. Thank you for a very charming, surprising and memorable night.' He kissed her lightly, meaninglessly. 'Now don't look so disappointed. What did you expect?'

Her lover looked very different in formal morning dress from the flushed lascivious Antony of the night before. It was not possible to say the things she wanted to say to anyone looking like that: where shall I go, what shall I do? I thought I was yours now, at your disposal, and you at mine. Things aren't the same, can't you see? This is me, I mean I, your Cleopatra, your Sesheta, your Parvati.

All she managed to say was, 'But I shall see you again?'

'Of course, silly child. I'll send for you.'

He watched her leave in the hansom, wanting to make sure that she had really gone and would not be found lurking about the theatre. Delightful, astonishing creature, so naïve, too innocent to know that she was a natural whore. He had not met anything quite like her in all the roll-call of nubile young women he had taken up and dropped. He had summoned her only on an impulse and meant to make her the pleasure of a single night, but she merited more than that; he would certainly send for her.

Nell told the cabbie to drive to Buckingham Street. There might be something there, since the rooms served as a London base for anyone who needed it as a resting-place, Dartford being such a distance away.

211

In the big wardrobe there was a shabby old dress she had almost forgotten owning. She was glad to change into it out of the finery of the night before. She lay on the bed until her headache had subsided, helped by a pot of tea made by the landlady in the basement, then went out and wandered the streets, quite in the manner of the time she and Harry were refugees. If the police were still looking for her, they showed no signs of it. She wandered into the National Gallery, the Portrait Gallery in Great George Street, Westminster, the Geological Museum in Jermyn Street, the Abbey and two or three churches. The glowing splendour of the night had been damped, but not extinguished, by Ayton's cool treatment. Still she could dream and smile and blush at what had been, reading everything by its light, seeing it in the experienced eyes of women in paintings, the stone forms of women on tombs. Now I am one of them, she thought, now truly myself because I belong to him.

Footsore with walking, she rested at Buckingham Street before going to the Egyptian Hall at the usual time. Percy Tiler and Ted Neaps, moving props, on the stage, greeted her. Both lived in London and were not aware that she had not gone back to Dartford the previous night.

In the dressing-room Amy was mending a robe. She looked up as Nell entered, went pale, then red, and looked down again at her work, not speaking.

'Well, Mamma?'

'You had a pleasant supper?' Amy was still not meeting her eyes.

'Yes, delightful.'

'And where have you been since?'

'At Buckingham Street.'

'Liar.' It might have been one of Amy's half-sisters speaking.

'But I have.'

'All night? Keep your lies. We called in there on our way to the theatre. Mrs Goodall told us you'd returned there at half-past ten this morning.'

'Yes. But ... ' As she approached Amy swung round, turning her back. Dismayed, Nell went to look for Merlin, who was in his own dressing-room laying out a card deck. A glance at his face told her

212

that he had been one of the callers at Buckingham Street.

'So I'm a *paraiyan*, am I, a social outcast, because I didn't sleep at Buckingham Street? I've seen Mamma and she told me how you went there prying after me. Who else went – Adelaide Seymore, Danny? What an interest you all take in me – I'm flattered.' She stood, hands on hips, challenging him to look at her, to see how new and alluring she was. But he only glanced, saying, 'It's nothing to do with me. Go and get ready. The programme's the same as last night.'

Defeated, Nell went back to her dressing-room, and tried to draw Amy into conversation with small talk. 'How are Pretty and Bonny coming on? Do you think they'll ever match up to the old doves? I do miss having a dove in the act, I must say. Oh look, one of these crystals has come off – sew it on for me, there's a dear.'

Amy's mouth remained obstinately set. Only when Danny put his head round to say that the house was full and the curtain would go up in five minutes did she lift her head and look Nell in the face.

'I'm glad your father died when he did, Eleanore. I wish I had died with him, rather than live to see our daughter behave like a trollop.'

'Mamma!'

'What else would you like me to call it?'

'I can explain ... if you only understood ... '

'I've no wish to hear. Don't talk to me.'

Adelaide Seymore knew, too. She was not going to enter into uncomfortable discussions but her spectacled eyes held reproach, and she shook her head when Nell asked, 'Not you as well?' Only Danny behaved as usual, since nobody had thought him old enough to be told.

That night Nell's concentration failed. In the Aërial Suspension illusion she lost control of her legs, held stiffly in mid-air unsupported. As they slipped downwards Merlin stepped in front of her, masking her from the audience, and with a deft adjustment of the levers in the apparatus moved her to an easier position. Nobody seemed to notice, but she was badly shaken.

Merlin said nothing about the slip, and seemed not to hear her apologise afterwards. As she dressed after the curtain Amy said: 'We think it will be best if you come back to Dartford tonight to collect your clothes. After that you may stay in Buckingham Street – when you need to.'

'Oh, Mamma! Don't be so cold to me – please listen!'

But it seemed that the old Amy was gone, and that neither she nor anybody else would listen. At the station Nell defiantly got into a carriage with other passengers, leaving the rest of the party. None of them offered to accompany her, though Danny looked after her, troubled.

It was lonely in Buckingham Street in the impersonal room littered with spare belongings. Wandering about London all day was tiring, in the hot close weather. Nelda took to staying in, reading books from a lending library, eating without appetite the dull meals which were all the landlady knew how to prepare, and staring out of the window. There was not much to see. At the end of the street workmen were building the new Embankment, almost obscuring the view of the river and its boats. Irregular roofs and twisted chimneys were the haunt of blackened sparrows and shrieking gulls, under flat grey skies. It was a relief when the time came to go to the Egyptian Hall. Nell walked there and back for exercise, by roundabout ways, conscious that she was putting on weight.

The dullness of the days was not so bad as the unpleasantness of the evenings, when her mother's disapproval made itself so sharply felt. Amy thought she would never get over Nell's shame and disgrace, especially as it brought Merlin no nearer to her. He seemed to have withdrawn into himself off the stage, though on it he was as professional and efficient as ever. Amy listened unashamedly one night, seeing him enter Nell's dressing room after the performance.

'He won't send tonight,' he was saying. 'It's past the time now.'

'I know.'

'Well, then. Why don't you drop it all and come home with us?'

'Because you don't want me, any of you!' Nell flashed back. 'You can't forgive me for the first thing I've done wrong – in your eyes, that is, for *I* don't think it's wrong to want to better myself and go up in the world.'

214

'I'm not preaching at you, Nelda, but if you ask me, you're going down in the world, making yourself cheap to a man who doesn't care a button for you.'

'He does, he does!'

'So how does he show it, then – introduce you to his famous friends, does he? Take you about with him? Promise you marriage when he's got his divorce – which he won't? I've been asking around –'

'Spying.'

'Call it what you like. Neither of 'em's going to let go of the other in a hurry, now there's a rumour that the Queen's thinking of knighting him some time. And when that comes, Nelda, if it does, you won't even be his fancy girl – he'll have had a dozen others meanwhile. I know about Ayton Forrester – there's plenty like him. Even if the rest of it were ironed out, he's far too old for you.'

'*You* can hardly talk! You're old enough to be my father.' It was deliberate cruelty, and she saw him wince.

'I could give Forrester fifteen years. Or more.'

'You don't understand. Ayton is the first love of my life, and I'd go through anything for him, fire and water if need be.'

'Don't talk such a lot of rubbish. And if I were your father, I'd put you across my knee and spank some sense into you.'

Nell burst into tears. Amy retreated; she had heard enough. On their way back to the station she told him: 'My position is unendurable, as things are here. At the end of the week I shall go and live with my brother.'

Merlin knew and liked Gil, who had many times been to see his niece and met the others. He suspected that if anyone could soften Amy's heart towards her erring daughter it would be he.

'Yes, do that,' he said, cheerfully, to her disappointment. 'He's a lonely man and needs you –'

'More than you do!' she flared.

A light broke on Merlin. He had been too absorbed in anxiety for Nell to realise that her mother cared for him.

'Yes,' he answered gently. 'Much more. It's best that you should go, Amy – best for all of us.'

215

Nell was in sparkling spirits next time Forrester's carriage called for her. She had defied everyone, made her stand for independence and soon they'd see how right she had been. As though in proof, Forrester behaved to her at supper more charmingly than he had ever done over their many suppers. The meal was even more sumptuous than usual, his manner was courtesy itself as he waited on her. She had learned now not to drink too much wine, only enough to heighten her pleasure. They drank to each other, to the play he was about to open in, to the Queen, to the end of the Civil War in America. Finally Nell raised the last glass and looked across the table at him, gaily challenging.

'To the Future!'

Forrester's face did not change, but he only murmured an echo of the toast. Suddenly he pushed back his chair, rose and drew her with him to the walnut escritoire.

'I have a little object here which I think you'll treasure, my dear.'

'Oh, a present!' It would be the first he had given her.

Opening the drawer, he took out a small, silk-wrapped parcel. Nell unwrapped it and exclaimed with delight at what it contained: a silver link bracelet, broad and ornate, with a central enamel plaque representing the head and shoulders of a florid gentleman wearing a white wig. Looking closer, the engraved decoration proved to be a circle of tiny lions and unicorns holding a crown between them.

Forrester smiled at the wonder in her face. 'Yes, a Royal jewel. It was given by the Duke of Gloucester who became William the Fourth to Dolly Jordan. Superb comedienne, charming. She bore him ten children or so, the present Fitzwilliam clan.'

'It's so beautiful. And really for me? Oh, you are so kind, Ayton.' She kissed him and held out her wrist for him to adjust the bracelet. As he did so he said, 'So you will always remember me when you wear it.'

'Remember you? But why should I have to? You'll be there – with me.'

His smile grew a shade more mechanical. 'Not after tonight, my dear. All good things must come to an end, and this is the end for us.'

He had discarded her a little sooner than usual. She was fresh and

216

warm and willing, but her boundless energy tired him, and he had become bored with her naïveté.

The strength went out of her legs; she dropped into a chair.

'It isn't true. We were going to be ... You said I was the most beautiful girl you'd ever known. You said ... you loved me.'

'Naturally. It's usual.'

'But it wasn't true – you were just using me for pleasure?'

'You can't deny that both of us had plenty of that.'

'No, but – it was so much more. You said – all those beautiful things, Shakespeare ... '

His fingers were tapping impatiently. 'I believe I generally do, in the circumstances. However, the Bard has a word for everything. Recall what Duke Orsino said about music? "Give me excess of it, that, surfeiting, the appetite may sicken and so die." That is the fate of appetites of all kinds. Now don't cry, for heaven's sake, I can't endure scenes. There really is nothing more to say, Nelda. I've entertained you royally, taught you a great deal, and you have taught me something, so I think the scores are even, eh?'

Nell could not speak for the constriction in her throat, but by an effort she managed to stop the tears from spilling over. For the first time she looked at Ayton Forrester as he was, the veil of high romance stripped away, and saw a man nearing old age, his face lined and puffy with self-indulgence, the jowls sagging. Already the eyes were beginning to lose their splendour under lids drooping at the corners, but that was nothing, one didn't love people less because they were growing older. It was the mouth, so finely-cut, that gave its owner away: sensual, fleshy-lipped, yet unmistakably cruel and petulant.

There were no stars in Nell's eyes now, only tears, and those she blinked away. She looked down at the bracelet clasped on her arm. 'I remember about Dolly Jordan. William sent her out to work for him and gave her all those children and then turned her away when he had the chance to marry a princess. It's a very appropriate gift, very well-chosen. Goodbye, Ayton. Don't ring, I'll see myself out. I know the way pretty well by now.'

A night of wild, abandoned weeping left her drained and calm. You fool, she said to her ravaged face in the mirror. You stupid, vain, thick-headed, blind idiot, not to see what he was. All that passion, wasted on a cold lecher, virginity squandered, reputation ruined, the name of Love taken in vain, and for what? Dismissal, like a servant, but without reference, and a bracelet which had belonged to another discarded woman.

She was scornful of Ayton, sick at the thought of him; but her real fury was against herself. Her punishment was beginning, the punishment of having to live with what she had been, what she was.

The river ran so near. A jump from one of the bridges would end all troubles, all self-reproach, all memory. The Embankment workings lay between, but there were ways through. It would be a classic, dramatic end, fitting for the romantic heroine she had so recently thought herself.

But the filthy waters of the stinking Thames would very probably poison before they drowned, and it was impossible not to remember a very bawdy song of the music-halls.

'See her on the bridge at midnight
Crying "Farewell, blighted Love!"
There's a scream – a splash – good 'Eavens,
Wot is she a-doin of?'

It seemed not so funny now, with the Thames itself so temptingly near and herself already drowning in a black swamp of misery. All day she sat in the cheerless room, deliberately making herself suffer by neither asking for a fire or food. Time dragged past. A clock somewhere struck six. With a shock she realised that she should be at the Egyptian Hall. A glance at her swollen face in the mirror told her that she could certainly not appear like that. And it was unthinkable to face them, in her present state of self-disgust, to crawl back, humiliated.

Merlin would have to do without her. It was unprofessional, unforgivable, but if she had chosen the river he would have had to do without her permamently.

By the next morning, Saturday, she was weak and languid with lack of food and sleep, for horrid reminders of what had happened had kept waking her every few minutes through the night. All that day she lay on the bed, covered with a counterpane, alternately brooding and dozing. Guilt gnawed at her for the missed performances, yet she failed to rouse herself to get up and go to the hall.

Quite suddenly, in the middle of Saturday evening, she flung off the counterpane and went down to the kitchens to ask for supper. On the verge of an actual illness she had pulled herself back into common sense. In the morning she would go home to Dartford.

'Ho, so you're back.' Mrs Whitty sniffed expressively.

'Yes. Could you give me a hand with my bag?'

'No, that I couldn't.'

'Thank you. What a charming welcome.'

'Welcome is as welcome deserves.' The woman turned a broad back on Nell and retreated towards the kitchen.

The parlour in Ethel was chilly, as chilly as Nell felt after her exhausting night. She knelt to light the fire. As she sat back, watching the sticks and paper ignite, the door opened.

'Oh – Nelda!'

A young woman stood on the threshold. She was not tall, and so slight that her waist seemed almost impossibly tiny in contrast to the full billowing skirts of her blue dress and the bishop sleeves which ended at her fragile wrists. Her face, with its coronet of brown curls, had a delicate elfin beauty, and her voice was a lady's, yet there was something in it Nell recognised.

'I didn't know you were back – they said you were living in London.'

'*Fanny*! Can it really be you? My goodness, how you've changed!'

Fanny blushed prettily. 'Yes, I know. Miss Birtles is very strict about deportment and speaking and things. Oh dear, I shouldn't talk about "things", Miss Birtles says it's meaningless. How nice to see you again, Nelda.'

'How nice to see you, Fanny.' And how difficult to believe that this fairy-like young lady was the same imp who had hidden in the Indian Basket and the Bellows Table, and spoken with the ugly twang of the south Midlands. As they talked, Nell learned that Fanny now played the piano, sang, and studied French and the guitar. She came home to Edith-and-Ethel only occasionally, for Miss Birtles wished to keep her under surveillance as much as possible.

'And I suppose you're quite a socialite in Dartford, Fanny?'

'Well, I'm allowed to go to a ball now and then – Miss Birtles chaperones me, of course. I do love ices, don't you? There, I've used the verb "to love" about an article of food, which is *quite* wrong – it should only be applied to a human object.'

'I would doubt that,' Nell said bitterly. 'There are plenty of worthier ones.'

Fanny looked puzzled. 'What an odd thing to say, Nelda. What were we talking about? Oh yes, dancing. And I ride as well. Barnaby's giving me lessons. He comes down every weekend.' The blush was deeper than the earlier one, a rich rosy pink. Her hands flew to her cheeks.

'He's here now,' she said. Her ears had caught footsteps Nell had missed.

Barnaby was surprised, startled, to see Nell. But not overwhelmed with joy.

'Nell! I thought you'd left. That is, Mrs Whitty said … '

'No, I haven't left.' Nell gave him a bright social smile. 'How are you, Barnaby?' Did he know of her disgrace and blame her as the others must, or was there feeling enough left in him to accept her and what she had done?

'Very well, thanks. Er, Harry's getting on well with his pony.'

'I'm glad.' His eyes strayed past her, lingering on Fanny. There was an unmistakable look in them, a look that had once been for her, Nell, but now it was protective as well as adoring. 'Do you want me to go to Miss Birtles' and fetch Strawberry, Fanny, as it's so fine today?'

Fanny bent her graceful head and fluttered her lashes. 'No, I rode her over myself. I did just as you told me and she behaved beautifully.'

A silence fell in the room, the unmistakable silence generated by two lovers who wish ardently to be alone together.

With that realisation a hope, which had been hiding at the back of her mind, dissolved into nothingness. Barnaby, who had worshipped her once, might have been her refuge from the disgrace she had brought upon herself. Well, it had been an unworthy hope and was better banished. Barnaby deserved more than to be saddled with somebody else's leavings. Besides, she didn't love him: for her, love and its disguises were over.

Talking with pretty, quaint Fanny had cheered her, but now the gloom edged back. Leaving Fanny and Barnaby, she wandered restlessly in and out of the rooms of Ethel. The house seemed to be deserted. But from the props-attic came a faint sound of hammering. It would be better to go up and face whoever was there, since they must all be faced some time or other.

Two staircases led up to the attic, at opposite ends, one from Ethel, one from Edith. When Nell entered, the hammering stopped. Merlin and George Whitty were there, Merlin surrounded by paper flowers, George working on a small table. Both men looked up, Merlin's face impassive after the first wince of shock.

George Whitty said nothing. Disgust written all over him, he laid down his hammer, dusted his hands together as though removing something unpleasant from them, and left the attic by the door to Edith.

'I'm back,' Nell said.

'So I see.' Merlin ran the flat folded blooms through his fingers, then laid them out in a pattern of assorted colours.

'I'm sorry I missed those performances, I don't suppose you can forgive me, and why should you? I let you all down – the performance, and everything.'

'We managed,' Merlin said. 'It's all over – no hard feelings. I knew it was something you couldn't help.' He let none of his immense relief show.

Nell advanced into the room as firmly as she could, trying not to let her nervous reluctance show.

'Don't you want to know what happened?' she asked.

'If you want to tell me. Did you lock that cupboard at Buckingham Street, by the by? I've a notion Mrs Whatsit helps herself to the brandy.'

'Yes, of course I did. Never mind the cupboard and the brandy. I do want to tell you, and I must.' She stood in front of him like a schoolgirl before a teacher, hands clenched at her sides.

Merlin sighed. 'Fire away.'

'Well, you were right. He didn't care a button for me. I've remembered what you said, and it was all true. After a month he'd had enough of me. He gave me my marching orders.'

Merlin studied a flower critically. 'Well, you're a soldier's daughter – you can take marching orders.'

'Yes … But it wasn't like that. It made me feel terrible, disgraced, loathsome. You don't know what I'd … you don't know what I've been –'

'No, I don't know, but I can guess. I've knocked about the world a bit, Nelda, and I'm not shocked, in case you think I am. It don't signify what you've done or what you've been, and kindly don't mention it again. I'm not going to say I told you so, because nobody ought to say that. If you want a lecture I'm sure Ma Whitty will give you one – just don't ask me to do it. Don't mind George, he'll come round. It'll all blow over in a little while, and worse things happen at sea. And speaking of worse things, you're not –'

'No, I'm not. Mr Forrester is far too clever for that,' Nell said bitterly.

'Then there's no harm done.' He brushed the flowers into a neat pile and stacked them in a bowl. 'Did I tell you George is making a Decapitated Head?'

'A *what*?'

'A talking head – new illusion. Various coves have been playing about with it – I hear Colonel Stodare's got one he calls The Sphinx, but we won't call ours that, with an Egyptian act in the programme already. Let's race him to it, like we did Pepper. Don't know if Danny could do the voice, though … George has started on the pedestal for it, see. I bring in the box, with the head in it – or that's what it looks like from the front – and drop it over the hole on top of the pedestal. What do you think the Head ought to be, Arab sage in a turban, Roman in a laurel wreath?'

222

Nell listened to him talking, trying to put her at her ease, gently bringing the atmosphere down to normal. So long as he and she behaved as though nothing unusual had happened the others would accept, and gradually forget – even her mother, though it hurt that she had not stayed to see Nell through her trouble. Uncle Gil would bring her round in time.

Merlin was drawing sketches of the Talking Head, adorning it with a wreath, aware in every nerve of Nell's eyes on him. He dared not hope that the Ayton Forrester business had changed her or could change her towards him.

Yet it had, and she was beginning to realise the extent of the change. Ayton had led her down a false path into a valley of humiliation. He had also awakened her senses and shown her to herself as a woman, not a selfish ambitious child. She could see Merlin now as a man. Why had she ever been cruel enough or blind enough to compare him to Ayton Forrester? He was younger by many years, still in his prime, a man of delicate silver, his flesh unspoilt by grossness, his eyes full of clear light, his mouth sensitive and beautiful. When she stopped aching from rejection she knew that she would desire him – perhaps desired him already, but was too ashamed to admit it.

He had desired her, and she had treated him with contempt. Might it even be that he loved her? She had come to him for punishment, and he had given her instant absolution. Love suffereth long and is kind …

But it was too much to hope for, and too soon to hope. She sat watching him, feeling she could be content to watch him for ever under this new enchantment. Merlin and Magus to others, Silvester Thorn to me … Quite suddenly Lady Jacquette came into her mind, and the conviction that the long-dead girl of the portrait had felt like this, for just such a man. But it was only the edge of a memory, slipped from her grasp like a half-recalled dream.

Silvester Thorn, who would never be Merlin again to his chosen love, looked up and met her eyes. What he saw in them contented him deeply. He smiled; to Nell it was like the sun coming out after the worst of winter.

The young dove, which had been preening its feathers on top of a cupboard, suddenly fluttered down and settled on Nell's shoulder.